PRAISE FOR |

'Explosive' —*Sunday Wor*

'*Love/Hate* meets *Ulysses*'—*Irish Times*

'Gaffney has created a smart and irreverant voice.'
—*Irish Times*

'I loved this debut, for its intelligent authenticity.'
—Sue Leonard, *Irish Examiner*

'*Dublin Seven* reads like one long, crazy high. An
extremely strong debut.' —*Dublin Inquirer*

'If you want a realistic . . . portrayal of cocaine
drug-dealing gangland life in the 2000s – this is the
real deal. It's *the* most authentic cultural portrayal
I've read.' —Karl Parkinson, RTÉ's 'Arena'

'Unnerving, page-turning suspense . . . an evocative,
fast-paced journey through Dublin's underworld.'
—Dr Michael Pierse, author of *Writing Ireland's
Working-class: Dublin After O'Casey*

'An incredibly accurate portrayal of the realities
attached to Dublin city life . . . will have you reading
from cover to cover.'—*OTwo*

'A razor-sharp vision of gangland existence, inter-
woven with intricate relationships, and reflections
on a life under threat.'—*Tn2*

Frankie Gaffney came of age in Dublin's North Inner City. His father spent time in prison, and he was himself immersed in the city's underworld. In his mid-twenties he left this behind and went to Trinity College Dublin, where he studied English Literature. He has since been awarded the Ussher Fellowship to conduct literary research there. *Dublin Seven* is informed both by the milieu in which he grew up, and his formal study of great literature.

First published in 2015 by
Liberties Press
140 Terenure Road North | Terenure | Dublin 6W
T: +353 (1) 905-6072 | W: libertiespress.com | E: info@libertiespress.com

Trade enquiries to Gill & Macmillan Distribution
Hume Avenue | Park West | Dublin 12
T: +353 (1) 500 9534 | F: +353 (1) 500 9595 | E: sales@gillmacmillan.ie

Distributed in the United Kingdom by
Turnaround Publisher Services
Unit 3 | Olympia Trading Estate | Coburg Road | London N22 6TZ
T: +44 (0) 20 8829 3000 | E: orders@turnaround-uk.com

Distributed in the United States by
Casemate-IPM | 1950 Lawrence Road, Havertown, PA 19083
T: +1 (610) 853-9131 | E: casemate@casematepublishers.com

ISBN: 978-1-910742-11-2
2 4 6 8 10 9 7 5 3

A CIP record for this title is available from the British Library.

Cover images © Caroline Brady and Freepik
Cover design by Liberties Press
Internal design by Liberties Press

DUBLIN SEVEN

Frankie Gaffney

Acknowledgements

The first person I must thank is Sue Booth-Forbes, whose wonderful writer's retreat on the Beara Peninsula, Anam Cara, provided the nourishment (intellectual, spiritual and culinary) necessary to realise this project. If it weren't for the incredible creative space provided by Sue, you wouldn't be holding this book. I'm in her debt also for an introduction: to author Cauvery Madhavan, who gave crucial and timely encouragement, not to mention an unwavering belief in my ability as a writer, based on the flimsiest of evidence.

The entire team at Liberties Press have been outstanding in their commitment and enthusiasm from the moment they received the manuscript, and very tolerant of my whimsical demands throughout the publishing process. I thank them for making a brave choice in pulling this rude novel from the ever-growing pile that clogs their offices.

There are others who contributed to this book in various ways who I won't name – but you know who you are, and I thank you. Just as some crimes go unpunished, some bills remain outstanding.

The dedication expresses a debt I could never hope to repay.

For Ma,
who else?

And one man in his time plays many parts,
His acts being **SEVEN** ages. At first the infant,
Mewling and puking in the nurse's arms.
And then the whining schoolboy, with his satchel
And shining morning face, creeping like snail
Unwillingly to school. And then the lover,
Sighing like a furnace, with a woeful ballad
Made to his mistress's eyebrow. Then a soldier,
Full of strange oaths and bearded like the pard,
Jealous in honour, sudden and quick in quarrel,
Seeking the bubble reputation
Even in the cannon's mouth. And then the justice,
In fair round belly with good capon lined,
With eyes severe and beard of formal cut,
Full of wise saws and modern instances;
And so he plays his part. The sixth age shifts
Into the lean and slipper'd pantaloon,
With spectacles on nose and pouch on side,
His youthful hose, well saved, a world too wide
For his shrunk shank; and his big manly voice,
Turning again toward childish treble, pipes
And whistles in his sound. Last scene of all,
That ends this strange eventful history,
Is second childishness and mere oblivion . . .

—Shakespeare, *As You Like It*
London, England 1599

DUBLIN, IRELAND, 2005

1

The sun blinded Shane as he stepped into the morning light. After closing the door of his da's gaff behind him quietly, he toddled down the path, squinting. Unsteady on his feet, he pulled on his da's jacket, which he'd taken from the banister post. He huddled his shoulders against the chill. Then, in the pocket, he grasped a small, lumpy bundle, unexpected.

When he pulled it out, his dull curiosity turned to surprise. It was a plastic bag, like the ten-penny bag of sweets he used to buy from the local shop. White, but see-through at the same time. Also familiar was the texture, because tightly wrapped inside was a cluster of pills. The bag was tied at the top – full enough to be stretched, revealing the shape and colour of the tablets.

Shane looked back at the house before stopping. Somewhere between drunk and hung-over, he was muddled. It was his da's jacket. Why would his da have a bag of pills? He'd always been anti drugs. The lads even slagged Shane because they knew his oulfella had been involved with the 'Concerned Parents' groups. They joked that he was a 'vidjo' – a vigilante. Only the night just gone, his da, suspicious of his lethargy, had warned Shane against smoking hash. If he'd known that Shane's prolonged retreats to bed were ecstasy comedowns, he'd have gone ballistic.

A doorman in town, Shane's da had taken him to the club where he worked for a drink – and a lecture on the dangers of drugs. They'd even stayed back after hours, drinking until dawn near. But the anti-drug sermons had clashed with the effects of the ecstasy Shane had swallowed when his da was too drunk to notice. When they'd gotten home, his da had fallen into bed, and sleep, snoring brazenly. Dwindling amphetamines had assured Shane's insomnia, and he'd decided to head back to his ma's.

Now different explanations for the bag of pills in his da's pocket flickered through his addled mind. The only scenario that made any sense was that his da had confiscated the bag off a dealer in the club. Why take it home though?

Shane used the tip of his key to release the knot. He swayed as he unfurled it, before taking a tablet out with the tips of his fingers. They were neat little parallelograms, cleaner-looking than the crumbly mottled pills Shane was used to. They had a waxy sheen, and each side had a different motto emblazoned in clean lines. One read: 'VGR 100'. The other: 'Pfizer'.

In his befuddled state, it was some moments before he realised what he was holding. Viagra! The shock woke him up, and he pondered what to do. Taking one himself even crossed his mind. But he replaced the pill and retied the knot. He reset the bundle in the pocket and walked back to his da's, opening the door gently and putting the jacket back where he'd found it.

More disturbed than amused – though both emotions jostled for position through his drunkenness – Shane again started the journey home. He wanted to get back to his ma's, back to his own bed. Curl up in a ball and nap. Drink some milk, settle his stomach. His ma was off work, she'd feed him when he woke up. Nurse him through his hangover.

But finding the Viagra forced upon him the alarming thought of his oulfella with a raging erection. Then, even worse, his da impaling his ma. Hung-over comedown trembles turned to shudders as he tried to steer his mind away from his own conception. Gorgeous girls from the night before intruded on his thoughts. They'd looked more glamorous than the young ones around the area where he lived. Well dressed and spoken, they had shimmered under the disco lights as they danced. The oulfella was confident when he was working there too – having the craic with the crowd as he screened them through the door, joking and bantering with the other staff. Shane had made sure to sear the girls' images in his memory. Something for the wankbank. Now his oulfella romped all over the pictures. What felt like the start of an erection mingled with disgust, turning to nausea.

He felt a hum vibrate against his leg, wakening him from these unsummoned dirty dreams. This was followed by the muffled theme tune of the mobile-phone company ringing out from his jeans' pocket. The screen flashed urgently:

Chops . . .

Chops . . .

Chops . . .

Shane pressed the green button.

—What's the story Chops? he mumbled, finding it hard to make his mouth form the words.

Everyone used Chops's nickname, to the extent that they'd forgotten his proper name was Derek. Even his ma and da called him Chops – ever since he was a little kid and every time they'd ask him what he wanted for dinner he'd always just enthusiastically blurted 'Chops!'

—Howye man, what's the craic wit ye?

—I'm just after leavin me da's gaff. In bits so I am. Was back at a lock-in in town all night, Shane said proudly. — Wha has ye up at this hour?

—We're all goin down the earlyhouse, are ye buzzin? Chops asked.

—Ah I dunno man. I'm bleedin bollixed.

—Come on down . . .

Chops switched to a whisper.

—We've a bag of charlie here and all man.

—Ah, I'm knackered, replied Shane.

—C'mon . . . Chops stumbled, struggling to come up with an argument. —It's the first Monday of the week!

Shane laughed. He still had most of the money his da had given him the previous day.

—C'mon down, it'll be a good bit of craic, said Chops, pressing the point with drunken repetition. —Sure it's the summer, c'mon.

There was a pause as Shane thought.

—Ah, fuck it, go on so, he said. —I'll hop in a joer now. See yis in there.

Chops laughed as he hung up.

★

It was Shane's first time in the earlyhouse, on the quays just past the Four Courts. A foreign doorman gave him the hardman stare as he walked in. Shane didn't get the sense he actually cared who entered the place though. This was borne out by what he encountered inside. It was just after half seven on a Monday morning, and the place was buzzing. Everyone was pissed. Most were out of it on something else too. A row of wizened oulfellas sat lined up along the bar, supping pints with relish. Down the back were groups of young people – some talking, others dancing and stumbling. Electronic music from the jukebox clashed with the worn wooden furniture. Shouts and laughter completed the soundtrack. The chaotic atmosphere and misshapen customers reminded Shane of nothing more than the bar scene from *Star Wars*.

Even though it was a small pub, it took some effort for him to find his bearings and spot the lads. Sunlight poured in through the clear tops of the stained-glass windows, dazzling him. The shine off Chops's shaven head provided a beacon through the glare, and Shane smiled as he walked toward his best mate. He was over in a corner with the rest of the lads. They were in high spirits, sitting at a low table, pint glasses crowded in front of them. Two older fellas were on the bench with them – big tanned fellas. One had a pint, the other was dividing a can of Red Bull among three vodkas, pouring the sticky fluorescent liquid over crackly ice.

—Yeeeeeoooooow! Chops roared as he stood up, arms outstretched to welcome Shane.

—What's the craic.

—Ah look who'ris! one of the lads shouted.

—Howyis.

—Here. Here. Ye know Griffo don't ye – and this is Lynchey, said Chops, introducing Shane to the two older fellas at the table.

Shane had never met Griffo properly, but he recognised the arm entwined with tattoos that shook his hand. They were from the same area, but Griffo was in his thirties and none of Shane's group had hit their twenties yet. Shane copped Griffo for a gangster straight away. He had the image. Flash car, designer clothes, muscles, tan. The other man with Griffo – the fairheaded, taut-featured Lynchey – Shane had never seen him before.

—What's yer name? Shane is it? Griffo asked.

—Yeah.

—Get yerself a pint and sit down there.

—Are yis alrigh for a gargle lads? Shane asked the table hesitantly.

It was the done thing to ask, he thought.

—You're graaaand man, you go on your own there, Griffo answered for everybody.

Shane probably wouldn't even have had enough for a full round anyway.

Clutching a score in his hand, he stood at the bar. Trying to get served quicker, he held the note out to catch the barman's eye. He ordered himself a pint of Bulmers. The sugary acid of apples tasted nicer to him than gassy beer. His mates were engrossed in giddy conversation when

Shane returned to the table – except for Chops, who was swaying at the jukebox, focussing harder on sorting through the change in his hand than on choosing songs. Shane took a sup of his pint. The first taste was sharp, but as soon as he swallowed it he wanted another. Drawing on its dull sweetness, he joined in with the banter.

After a while, Shane's bladder pressed at him and he reluctantly left the craic. In the gents, Griffo was standing, halfway out of a cubicle, hunched over in conversation with the foreign doorman. They both stopped talking and looked up when Shane walked in.

—He's alrigh, he's alrigh, said Griffo, looking back down at his hands.

He held a ripped piece of blue plastic, torn from a super-market bag. There was a clean, chunky white powder inside. He scooped up a little pile on the end of a brass front-door key and held it for the doorman, who leaned over, placing one nostril against the key tip. Covering the other nostril with his finger, he snorted. Shane pissed in the dirty steel urinal trough.

Griffo dipped the key again, and the doorman repeated the gesture, with the other nostril this time. He nodded to Griffo and walked out past Shane. Finished pissing, Shane nodded at Griffo too, then turned toward the door as he zipped up.

—Here youngfella . . . Shane is it? Go on there.

Griffo gestured toward the bag. First he used the key to dose himself a snort, then he offered Shane the same.

—Eh . . . cheers man, said Shane.

He bent over the key and snorted hard, ingesting the lump of white powder. He could taste it through his nose –

a powerful chemical flavour, sharp and clean. An invigorating numbness seeped across his face.

—Nice one man.

—No bother.

—D'ye want a pint? Shane asked Griffo.

—No you're grand youngfella.

Shane's wariness had been shaken off. The coke woke him up, but it also gave his underlying drunkenness free rein. He pressed the point.

—Go on man, wha're ye drinkin?

—Yer graaaaand, don't be stupeh. It's only a sniff.

Shane blocked Griffo, speaking earnestly.

—No seriously, wha're ye havin?

Griffo chuckled at Shane's seriousness. He humoured the drunk teenager, putting his muscular hand firmly on Shane's shoulder.

—It's no bother kid, c'mon we go back in. You're grand honest to God. Sure you're doin me a favour takin a bit off me for fuck sake, I'd do it all meself otherwise!

Griffo laughed and sniffled, rubbing his nose.

—Alrigh, are ye sure?

—Yeah no bother. C'mon in here and sit down till we hear wha these eejits are on abou.

—Sound man. Nice one.

Shane felt good comin out of the jacks with Griffo. Confident. Taller even. The buzz coursed through him. It felt good to tense his muscles. He imitated Griffo's bodybuilder walk as they made their way back to the table. Griffo slapped him gently on the shoulder as they sat down.

—Let us in there will ye, Griffo said.

His mate Lynchey moved lazily.

The next pint went down quickly for Shane, and he bought another – then another, enjoying the banter. Griffo had insinuated himself into the company easily. The younger lads deferred to him. For his part, he playfully treated them like equals, cracking jokes and laughing at theirs. Lynchey lay back in the seat, aloof.

A few girls joined them. Griffo chatted away with ease, taking one of them into the ladies to give her a line. The rest of Shane's mates had their own bag among them. It was tiny in comparison to Griffo's, and it soon ran out. But Griffo doled out more coke as the morning wore on.

—Jaysis, that's lovely stuff, Shane told him.

Shane had done coke before – back at a party if someone was putting out lines. He'd only bought it once, going halves with Chops one night they were going into town.

—C'mere. D'ye know where I'd get a bit of tha stuff? he asked Griffo. —It's deadly so it is.

He knew Griffo was a drug dealer, but didn't want to say it straight out.

—Yeah no bother kid, it's always there if ye want it, anytime. Here I'll give ye one of the lads' numbers. Just tell him I put ye onto him if yer ringin. 086 . . .

Shane keyed the number into his phone.

—We do just get a bit between us now and again, me and the lads. A oner bag or somethin if we're goin ou like, said Shane.

—No bother. But if yis ever want weight it's there as well. Twelve hundreh fer an ounce of tha stuff. Yeh'll get at least twenty oner bags ou a that. Throw a mix in on top of it, yeh'd probably get another six or seven bags ou of it. I'll give it to ye straight off the rock if you're buyin the ounce, I don't throw anythin on top of it meself. Yeh'll get away with puttin at least another quarter of mix in . . . an d'ye know wha? It'll still be nicer than the shite bein sold around Dublin these days.

Shane had only ever thought about getting a bit for personal use. Realistically, he was unlikely to buy coke at all. Es were only a fiver. You could buy twenty Es for the price a single bag of coke.

—I'll have a think abou it man.

—No bother kid. Just give tha number a ring if ye want anything. And if ye want weight he'll put ye on to me. On tick if ye want, you're from around our area aren't ye?

'On tick' meant Griffo would allow Shane to pay him for the coke after Shane had sold it on.

—Just up at Cairn Road there.

—Sound.

Sitting back down again, Shane thought about the offer. He was locked, but he felt strong. Beside Griffo he felt safe. He wanted to be a part of this buzz, the fella with the bag. He wanted to have the lads defer to him, the girls chase him for a change. His whole life he'd felt scared, felt like he was nobody. Nothing. Now suddenly he felt alive. Content, just like that.

Shane had come down to the earlyhouse in the hope of getting his hole, but the frenetic drink- and drug-fuelled conversation with Griffo totally distracted him. Griffo was only delighted to have an ear for his coked-up macho prattling. Shane's sincerity led Griffo to confide in him. Once the floodgates opened up, a barrage of narcissism was let flow. The cokehead's prerogative. Especially when they're dishing it out for free.

—Ninety percent of the cunts sellin bag are dancin on it. You can wash that stuff up I have, and I'm tellin ye it's fuckin ninety percent pure. The fuckin shite most people would buy and they don't even know the fuckin difference. Yeh could be givin half the cunts novocaine and they wouldn't know for fuck sake.

—Yeah, Shane agreed, looking Griffo in the eye and nodding earnestly.

He hadn't a clue what novocaine was, or why Griffo was going on about doing the washing up. But the swagger engendered a sort of reverence in Shane.

—Them bleedin poshos as well, you have to watch sellin them bag. They get caught with it they'll bleedin rat ye out straigh away, guaranteed. You'd wanna have eyes in the back of yer head with them cunts . . .

Then Griffo tensed up.

—Them youngfellas from town after comin in kid, are ye wide? he hissed at Shane. —Don't look over.

Griffo was looking forward neutrally.

—Bogey cunts.

Shane saw a pack of youngfellas around his own age settling into the far corner. One fella caught his eye, snapping him out of his happy stupor. He was a couple of years older than the rest of the gang. Dark and medium-height, with a savage stockiness. His hair was cropped neat but somehow still managed to look scruffy. Ill-matched designer clothes couldn't mask his roughness. They covered an angular frame, hard and stiff. His square lower jaw protruded from an otherwise expressionless face. He looked unaffected by drink or drugs and scanned the room, reminding Shane of Arnie's Terminator. His eyes stopped at Griffo for a moment, before he moved on to examine Shane unabashedly.

Shane squirmed under his gaze, sobering up. He looked away, but he could still feel the stare on him. Unmoving, gauging him. Unsure how to act under this spotlight, in that moment he supposed the fella felt no moral obligation, no social pressure whatsoever. No fear. He could feel the stare penetrate him. Griffo had clammed up for the first time in hours.

Eventually, from the corner of his eye, Shane saw the fella sit down and start talking to his own mates. The removal of those gaping eyes produced in Shane a relief that rushed to giddy elation.

—Here, Griffo demanded of the whole table. —Lads. C'mon we go on to the next spot. This place is fuckin shite, there's another deadly little place up the road. Open now and all, he said checking his oversized watch. —Does be great craic. Drink up them pints there and we'll head up. Decks and all goin they do have.

—Decks goin at this hour? asked one of the lads, struggling.

—Yeeeah! Fuckin place will be hoppin in a while, said Griffo.

—What's the name of it?

—The Pink Pound. The gay bar up the road there.

One of the lads sniggered in disbelief.

—A fuckin *gay* bar! he scoffed

Shane and the rest of their group looked shocked. Only Chops wasn't paying attention. He was singing along to 'Wonderwall' on the jukebox, staring off into the distance with a melancholic look. Griffo slammed back his last drink, another short.

—Fuckin deadly so it is. Do what ye want in the place! he gesticulated. —Do charlie off the bar an all if ye want.

—I'm not going to a fuckin gay bar. The *Pink* fuckin *Pound*! one of the lads objected.

Griffo wasn't fazed in the slightest by the opposition.

—Up to yourself. Have a good one drinkin here on your own with the oul dipsos.

The youngfella looked around the bar. The numbers had depleted. When you took away their group and the few girls, you were left with a handful of oulfellas, a portion of whom looked homeless. And the bogey youngfellas from town.

—Is it full of queers? the youngfella asked, wavering.

—It's a fuckin gay bar, wha d'you think? Griffo laughed.

—Ah I dunno abou goin there man.

—Grow up will ye, Griffo squinted. —They're fuckin graaaand. Not a bother ou a them. Great craic so they are. Love their drugs and their dance music. Plenty of birds around them and no competition. Would ye rather sit around here and catch bleedin TB off one of them things?

Griffo gestured at the drunken oulfellas staggering around. The place was starting to look like a poorly run old folk's home, where deteriorating geriatric patients had been left to wander around in confusion while the staff were between shifts.

—If anyone's gonna fiddle with ye it will be one of them aul cunts quicker than the queers.

The rest of the boys were coming round to the idea. If Griffo suggested going to the gay bar it must be all right. He was a hardman with a solid reputation around the area. Nobody would mess with him, and he always had plenty of birds. They trusted his judgement. Not one of them would ever have suggested it himself though. They wouldn't have dreamt of it.

They roused themselves and left the earlyhouse messily, a raggle-taggle group, even the new girls gathering up their handbags and jackets to come along. Shane pulled his phone out as they walked. He had four missed calls from his da, two from his ma. Feeling rebellious, he put the phone back in his pocket. He knew his ma was probably worried, and his da was probably angry, but he was enjoying the company and the craic. The phone started to vibrate again. He ignored it.

—See tha fella tha came in? The fella with the townies, bleedin starin everyone ou of it? said Griffo.

Shane could tell Griffo was preparing to offer some lengthy intimation again. Still enjoying his patronage, he suppressed the thought that Griffo loved the sound of his own voice.

—Yeah, yer man with the jaw? Shane asked.

—Yeah tha fuckin scumbag. That's Paddy Lawless. Dangerous, are ye wide? He was in the papers there a few months ago. I'm tellin ye, the likes of him'd stab ye withou thinkin twice. Dirty bastard so he is. No reasonin with them cunts. They'd bring ye down off your buzz as well, makin everyone paro starin them ou of it. Playin mind games. Yer better off just stayin away from them are ye wide? Doesn't matter how much backup ye have – get in a row with one of them cunts, even if ye win they'd stab ye someday when yer walkin down the road. It might be years later. Not worth it kid, are ye wide?

Shane had felt it too – their eyes on him. It didn't make sense that Griffo was nervous of those little shitebags though. He was twice their size.

—I'm tellin ye he's a fuckin scumbag tha fella. People say we're bad, but they haven't a clue. I'm not afeart of anyone, but ye don't wanna get mixed up with cunts like tha – it's not worth it even bein around the likes of him.

Shane thought there must be more to the story.

Following Griffo into the gloom of the Pink Pound, he felt glad to be out of the sun. Inside, he met with a scene similar to that in the earlyhouse, minus the scaldy oulfellas. There were mixed groups of partygoers. More women than there had been in the earlyhouse. House music played from a CD behind the bar.

Pills went around then. Shane lost himself in the music, talking, dancing, hugging the lads. He rang their mate Chalkie – ostensibly to persuade him to come down and join them, but really Shane was just showing off.

—Here listen to this man! he said, raising the phone in the air so Chalkie could hear the music.

He'd put it back to his ear and was talking for a few seconds before he realised the battery was dead. Even though he hadn't been answering his ma's and da's calls, Shane felt uncomfortable without access to his cordless umbilical. He asked the barman if he had a charger.

—I'll stick my wire in your socket any day, came the reply.

A few older gay fellas at the bar laughed, but not unkindly. Shane smiled too. Their attention was more affectionate than sleazy; he sort of enjoyed it. The interest drawn by his boyish blush was a contrast to the stare he'd gotten from Paddy Lawless in the earlyhouse.

—Here.

The barman drew a thin black lead across the bar and let

Shane connect the phone. Soon as it switched back on, he sent a text telling Chalkie where they were. Then he gave the phone to the barman, who left it charging on a shelf beside a bottle of absinthe.

Overstimulation fed overenthusiasm. Shane swallowed a sambuca Griffo had bought him, then poured cider down on top of it, enjoying the sweet sharpness after the sticky kick of alcohol. He was wobbly, even tripping a bit from the ecstasy now. His conversations had deteriorated to repeated greetings and assertions.

—Alrigh man.

—Bleedin deadly isnit?

And so on and so on it went, faces blurring into shapes and words into sounds.

★

He found himself kissing a fat townie bird in a cubicle in the girls' toilets. She was chunky but sexy. Dressed up and made up. Huge tits.

Shane tugged on her breasts and she moaned as they churned their tongues together wetly. She smelt beautiful – light and flowery. He pulled her top down and freed one of her heavy breasts, hungrily kneading the cold flesh. He lowered his head and put his mouth on her nipple. After licking it, he put his lips around her teat and sucked as it stiffened. He sunk himself into her warm comfortable arms. She held him there, suckling. He felt her heart beating as he half surrendered to sleep, leaning against her in the cubicle.

A gnawing queasiness built gradually, wakening him from his pleasant daze. Trying to convince himself it would pass, Shane focussed on the sensation of the girl's breast in his mouth and the weight of her form pressed against him. But still the swirling seasickness mounted.

Suddenly it overwhelmed him. A wave of dizziness and intense nausea crashed over him. His extremities felt weak and his gut burned. He could taste the cider sick before he even began to vomit. He jumped away from her, toward the toilet bowl.

—Jaysis! the girl exclaimed, as Shane boaked up a gigantic slop of cidery puke.

He retched three or four times, huge spills of pink-orange liquid flecked with mucus and brown bits from his depths, expelling themselves into the bowl. He clutched the wet porcelain, not caring about hygiene.

—Ooh Jaysis! Are ye alrigh? she said sweetly, placing her hand on his back.

—Sorry . . . Aw sorry, Shane rasped, a second wave of puke fumes coming from his depths as he spoke.

—Ah yer grand love. Jaysis are ye OK?

Her concern touched him. She seemed not to care about the disgusting mess he was in, just that he was all right. He felt embarrassed puking in front of her.

—Ah ye poor thing. I hate when tha happens. Ye'll be alrigh in a few minutes, just try and relax, she reassured sweetly.

Her presence comforted Shane, and he calmed as she mammied him a bit.

—Sorry . . .

—Yer grand love, don't worry about it.

His body pulsed with another spasm. As he expelled more puke he let a large involuntary fart with a long ripping sound. She stared at him for a second.

—Ah here good luck! said the girl.

She legged it out of the jacks, heels clopping and earrings jangling.

—Sorry . . . sorry, Shane called, gasping for breath.

He locked the door after her, undid his belt and fly, lowered his trousers and sat on the bare bowl, feeling the cold wetness of the toilet against his naked skin. He peered through a chink in the door to check if there were any girls in the jacks doing their makeup or whatever. Nobody. He allowed his bowels to ease themselves noisily, but was racked with another spasm and had to lean forward and puke again at the same time. A smelly snake of shit trumpeted out of his arse. There he sat, expelling slop from both ends. It didn't relieve the nausea. Closing his eyes, he submitted to the swirling sensation. He slept.

—Up. C'mon.

Shane felt a limp, heavy hand slapping his face persistently. He awoke feeling nauseous and faint.

—Get up, c'mon. Up. Now.

He opened his eyes and looked into someone else's – someone staring wide into his being, interrogating his consciousness. Blaring orbs shot with red. It was his da, leaning close over him.

The white dizziness oozed over Shane again and he retched, nothing coming up this time. A silk thread of spit slipped from his lips, leaving a snail's trail of slime across his chin. His da reached under his arms, pulling him upright. Shane became conscious of having his trousers down – he felt the air on his balls and dick. He realised he was still in the cubicle in the girls' toilets. When he'd seen his da, he'd thought he was at home. The realisation he was not was very unwelcome.

Shane wobbled, his da's support keeping him upright.

—Ah fer fuck sake, said his da.

Shane mumbled, not fully conscious, retching again half-heartedly.

—The fuckin state of ye.

His da was talking to himself, Shane was beyond responding. Propping him up against the cubicle wall, his da unfurled a load of tissue from the spool with one hand. Twisting him around roughly, he used the big bundle to wipe Shane's arse.

Shane groaned. The indignity.

—Pull up yer own trousers will ye at least fer fuck sake! his da tutted. —Jaysis.

Shane moaned and pulled up his jeans.

Wish I was in bed, he thought, *in me ma's. Ah me arse isn't properly wiped, pullin up me boxers! Fuck it. This is a load of bollix.*

Absolutely parched, he craved the sugar of cold Lucozade, but didn't think he'd be able to hold down water even.

Bollix . . . have to walk out through this place now. Aw this is fuckin mortifyin!

—Righ c'mon, said his da, jostling him out of the jacks.

The throb of music still pumped as the pair made their way through the little hall. Only the bass was audible until his da opened the door to the main part. It was late evening. The place was still busy. Shane stared straight ahead as his da marched him out through the bar. He noticed a few of his mates in the corner but tried not to catch anyone's eye. His da glared at Shane as they stepped outside, steering him over to his dark red Toyota Camry. It was parked in the bus lane, hazards flashing. His da opened the passenger door, then helped Shane into the seat like a guard would, but a bit more gently.

His da got into the driver's seat.

—Seatbelt.

Shane pulled the belt over himself, but it slipped out of his weak grasp twice. His da leaned over him and inserted the clasp roughly into the buckle.

—Fuckin baby!

He took hold of the wheel, then indicated and pulled out into the traffic. Bracing himself for the onslaught, Shane tried to regain some composure. He felt panicked, dehydrated, nauseous, embarrassed. He noticed his da was wearing the same jacket the Viagra had been in. His attention was drawn back to thoughts of his da, naked, muscular and powerful. Another wave of sickness swept over him and he held down the button to lower the passenger window.

—In a fuckin gay bar! his da said. —Takin God knows what! Wha were ye takin?

Shane tried not to slur.

—I was oney drinkin.

—Bollix.

—I was oney drinkin Da! I swear to Jaysis.

—Me fuckin bollix ye were only drinkin, the state of the cunts in tha place, they were all off their heads. You're forgettin I work in town son, I know wha goes on. Yer mother was worried sick about ye. Didn't know where ye were or wha the fuck happened ye . . . A fuckin . . . *gay bar*!

—It's not.

—It fuckin is! The name on the place sure. Are ye gay now? Is tha it?

—No!

There was a pause and his da sighed.

—How did ye know where I was anyway? Shane asked.

—Don't fuckin get me started on tha!

Shane wondered how he could have found out. He didn't want to aggravate his da further though. He didn't have the energy anyway. He was close to praying his da would let things drop.

—Wha the fuck were ye doin in there?

—Just drinkin Da, all the lads were in there.

—I know, I was fuckin talkin to them. They hadn't a clue where ye were either, all off their heads. In the ladies fuckin jacks I find ye! Are ye a fuckin transvestite or somethin now as well as gay?

—We only went in there chasin birds for fuck sake! There were loads of mots in there!

This gave his da pause for thought. The oulfella knew a few lads who worked on the door of gay clubs in town. He'd join in with the other bouncers slagging them, but they always maintained they got loads of women out of it. No competition, that was the key.

—I dunno, he muttered as they drove.

★

—Thank God, said Shane's ma from the doorway as he got out of the car.

—Don't be thankin anyone too quickly the bleedin state this youngfella is in.

There had been no question of his da taking him back to his own house – he wouldn't want the hassle of dealing with his son. Shane wouldn't have wanted to go back to his da's spartan house anyway. He was rattled, and wanted to be alone with his ma. He felt anxious and ashamed. There were memory gaps. He couldn't remember if he'd embarrassed himself. Rather, he thought he'd definitely embarrassed himself, but couldn't remember how. Instinct directed him toward his bed, but he was ushered into the kitchen.

—A fuckin gay bar, said his da. —Me own flesh and blood drinkin in a fuckin gay bar.

—I dunno, said his ma, looking puzzled and slightly worried.

—Why didn't ye tell me ye were leavin this mornin? his da asked.

—I didn't want to wake yeh, Shane protested.

This was only half true. Shane had revelled a bit in not telling either his ma or da he was going off, rejecting their authority.

—Yeh could of left a bleedin note on the fridge or somethin. Or—

—It's not my fault ye were locked, interrupted Shane.

Shane's da gave him a short hard box into the side of the head, sending him stumbling. The force of it shocked him.

—*Ma!* he ejaculated involuntarily, fearing another blow.

—*Don't!* his ma shouted.

Shane put his hand to his head and looked up at his da, who glared, unrepentant.

—Don't be hittin him! How d'ye think that's goin to help? his ma said.

—Someone has to put fuckin manners on him.

—What's that supposed to mean?

Shane's ma had her hands on her hips, standing between himself and his da.

—Me bleedin head! Shane accused.

His head was throbbing. Numb rather than sore. The power of the sudden movement had frightened him though. He knew his da hadn't even pulled back to punch properly, only thumped him.

—Aw! Tuckens! his da jeered.

Shane felt his lip tremble and tears begin to form – at the humiliation. The injustice. He caught his ma's eyes as a line of salt water escaped from his own to run down his cheek.

—Go on out. Out, go on, said his ma turning to his da.

She pointed to the door. It was a matronly gesture, an adult intervening between two children. His da acquiesced, aware that he could have provoked a harsher reaction. His ma went out too, and Shane heard mumbled arguing in the porch.

She returned businesslike and got him a glass of milk from the fridge.

—That'll settle yer stomach.

—Thanks, he managed, taking baby sups of the milk.

She shook her head as they stood in the neat kitchen. Shane felt pacified, calmer. Exhaustion swept over him.

—I was worried bloody sick so I was. Didn't know what happened yeh. And that eejit's no better. Bringin yeh out drinkin all night, that's what started it.

His ma had tears in her eyes now too.

The milk wouldn't stay down, and Shane belched it into the sink, acrid fumes from his depths choking him as he retched. His ma tutted and fussed. He was glad of her soft hand on his back. More tears filled his eyes as vomit caught in his nose. Trembling, he rinsed his mouth and blew his nostrils clear of the puke and snot. A rash itched his hand,

and as he turned off the tap he noticed a patch of boils between his thumb and index finger. He stood dizzy over the sink, breathing heavily.

After he caught his breath, his ma guided him away from his position bent over the sink, up the stairs and into his bedroom. She put on the lamp as he kicked off his shoes. He got under the duvet fully clothed. Something poked into him, the book he had been reading. *Boy*, by Roald Dahl. He tossed it aside and moved himself into the foetal position, twisting the duvet. His ma pulled the covers back up around him and felt his forehead, lingering for a moment.

—I'll leave the door open here, all right?

—Alrigh Ma. Thanks.

—OK, she said sadly, walking softly back down the carpeted stairs.

The world swam as Shane tried to calm himself and ease his drifting. His face stung from the punch. The pain pulsed with his heartbeat, which had slowed since he'd vomited again, but was still too fast. He tried to avert his mind from the embarrassments that plagued him. His da pulling him out of the place. Puking and farting in front of the girl. Whatever he might have been saying to Griffo. Black spaces where memories should have been gave him further cause for anxiety. Hours missing. His only plan was to remain in bed.

Blurred faces swam up through the darkness and taunted him though. Murky images of the day. Half dreams, half memories, which wouldn't allow him to escape the vulnerability of not remembering. Into this scary world he plunged, his consciousness unwelcome. Flotsam on a sea of images, voices speaking unformed words. Shapes became faces, noises became speech. Surrendering himself to the consequences of the substances he had consumed, he submitted to the sweeping sensations that invaded his head.

Eventually, gratefully, he became immersed. As sleep finally came, he was removed from the unruly collage of information. No longer subject to the torments of apprehension, he forgot even who he was: Shane Laochra.

A PHONE CALL

Brrreeeep beep . . . Brrreeeep beep . . . Brrreeeep beep . . .
Brrreeeep beep . . . Brrreeeep beep . . . Brrreeeep beep . . .

—Hello? the barman asks.

—Shane? Shane's da asks.

—No.

—Who's this?

—Who d'you want it to be?

—Put Shane on to me will ye?

—Now who's Shane? Oh, is that the good-lookin boy?

—Who's this?

—Ah, don't get jealous sweetheart.

—Listen pal, I'm not in the humour of messin. Put Shane
on to me will ye?

—Ooooh, you're very bossy . . . that's sexy.

—Wha? Who the fuck is this?

—Listen chicken, I'm just the barman. He left his phone
charging here. I don't know where he is.

—Barman where?

—The Pink Pound.

—*The Pink Pound!*

—So good they named it twice.

—Tha gay bar in town?

—The very place chicken.

Clickzzzz.

2

From his experience in the earlyhouse and the gay bar, Shane learned that the degree of the hangover is in direct proportion to the duration of the session.

The comedown proper had lasted until that Thursday – but even going out with the lads on the Friday night, he'd still felt out of sorts. He hadn't been able to eat until the Wednesday. All week, his sleep was wracked with doom-laden dreams in which the sea turned to blood. He was a bit scarlet going in to collect his phone from the Pink Pound, but the barman assured him that he'd been no worse than anyone else in the place. A large portion of his concern had just been drug-induced paranoia.

For the rest of the summer, Shane restrained his drinking, staying away from spirits and sticking to cider. But he kept on taking E. He realised that letting his ma know when he'd be home was a minor annoyance in comparison to the towering hazard posed by incurring the wrath of his da. A sunny September came a little too quickly. He'd been given an ultimatum: take up a course or find a job.

University wasn't an option, his Leaving Cert was dire. He was under pressure to get something through FÁS or one of the PLCs. He tried to postpone it for as long as possible though. When asked, he'd invent some waffle about sorting a job through a mate, or a course he was thinking of signing up for. Neither of his parents understood the third-level system. They were easily placated by bewildering talk of 'points', 'application forms' and 'the CAO'.

Only his sister knew he had no plans. A couple of years older than him, Lydia was conscientious in comparison. She'd done a course straight after school, and gotten a steady job in childcare. She didn't like to see Shane idle. Instead of lecturing him against wasting his life, she was clever enough to urge him on conspiratorially, telling him to get something sorted so he could keep enjoying himself without badgering from their ma and da.

—It doesn't matter if ye don't know what ye wanna do, just do somethin! she advised.

—Ah I dunno. The hassle. I wanna just enjoy this year, I'm sick of school.

—It's not like school Shane, it's easy! You'll only be in for about seven hours a week! Sure that's nearly the same as *one day* in school.

—But the assignments an' all.

Lydia leaned in and changed her voice to a whisper.

—Sure ye can just copy them.

—Serious?

—Yeeeah! That's what most people do. Get them off someone who did the course last year. Or the Internet.

—Eh . . . ah, bollix it, I can't be arsed applyin an all tha.

It was harder work trying to convince him than she expected. She thought for a moment, and then tried a fresh tactic.

—Ye get a grant, she said.

—How much?

—Three grand.

—*Three grand?*

—Yeah.

—Jaysis . . .

Shane had never seen even €1,000 before. It seemed impossible he'd get that much. He couldn't see it as real.

—Is tha wha you got?

—Yeah.

—Yeh never fuckin told me about it at the time! Yeh could at least of given me a few quid. Stingy!

—I had things to get out of it Shane!

—Like wha?

—I paid me car insurance . . .

Her da had bought her a cheap little car for her birthday after the Leaving Cert results. Shane didn't get anything for failing his. They never would have been able to afford the insurance premium for young males anyway.

— . . . paid for petrol, bought a laptop. I'd to pay for me meals in college and tha as well, she continued.

—Yeah, it looks like ye ate well alrigh. Three grand's worth around yer waist there.

—Fuck off you!

The prospect of €3,000 was enough of a carrot for Shane,

and he turned things over in his head. Curiosity aroused, a slew of questions followed.

—Wha course would I do?

—It doesn't matter Shane, do anthin!

—Wha though?

—Look at Chops – what's he doin? Film and media production is it?

—Yeah that's in proper college though.

—Wha? Are ye sayin I didn't go to proper college?

—Ah ye know wha I mean. University.

—It's only an IT. Out in Dún Laoghaire.

—Ah whatever. It's better than bleedin Ballyer or wherever you went.

—Least I done *something*, not like you. Ye big dunce! Ye can do anything in them places just the same. The PLCs do all sorts of courses. Coláiste Samhna'd let ye in, she told him.

—But I done shite in me Leavin.

—Just make up some waffle tha it wasn't your fault, they migh let ye in. Would ye not like to do sound engineerin with the music? Or film or somethin like Chops's doin?

—Nah. Chops has the brains for tha. I don't. Maybe I could do business or somethin. Make a few quid.

—Business then.

His sister rang the college and got him an interview. She even managed to convince them to bend the entry requirements. Even though he hadn't studied, he'd done OK in some of the Leaving Cert subjects. He'd got a decent pass in ordinary maths, a pass in geography. Scraped an honour in history. He'd failed French and Irish. English he'd barely passed. He liked English though – the poems and all. The novels were fuckin shite. What did they have to study Jane Austen for? She had nothing to do with anything. Until he saw the film on the telly, Shane had thought *Pride and Prejudice* was about an attack on a gay rights march.

They'd been made to study *Emma* too:

EMMA WOODHOUSE, handsome, clever, and rich, with a comfortable home and happy disposition, appeared to unite some of the best blessings of existence, and had lived nearly twenty-one years in the world with very little to distress or vex her . . .

What a fuckin geebag.

★

—There's Bill Cullen, said his ma when Shane came down for breakfast on the first day of college.

—Yeah, the big businessman! Lydia teased.

—Shut up you, Shane whined.

—Have ye any penny apples?

—Fuck off.

—*Language*, said his ma, vainly.

She sat down to her cup of tea, then got up again just as soon.

—Oh I forgot, she said.

She hustled out into the hall and came back with an Easons bag, emptying out pens and copies onto the table.

—I didn't know what to get, so I just got a selection, she said.

—Thanks Ma.

—Do ye want me to write yer name on the copies?

Frankie Gaffney

They were the same copies he'd used in primary school.

—No yer alrigh.

His sister suppressed a laugh, catching his eye. She was slaggin him surreptitiously, he knew, but he couldn't say anything cause he'd upset his ma. Lydia went upstairs and got him one of her foolscap pads on the sly. His ma gave him bus fare there and back in change, then a twenty-quid note on top of it.

—Eh thanks Ma. Nice one.

—It only seems like yesterday ye were born, said his ma, getting misty-eyed. —1988 . . . Jaysis it doesn't seem tha long ago. Dublin was a kip back then. But the week you were born, they'd big celebrations on for Dublin's millennium. They made these . . . special 50p pieces, cause Dublin was a thousand years old or somethin, and when we were bringin ye back from the Rotunda they had a big huge giant floatin in the Liffey! Somethin to do with yer man Gullible's travels it was! I don't know wha a Disney film has to do with Dublin but anyway there was great craic around the place that week and I knew ye were something special. And now lookit! Off you're goin to college!

—It's hardly college, it's oney a course, moaned Shane.

—Listen I might be thick, but I know 'coláiste' is the Irish for 'college'! If the place yer goin is called a college it's a college righ! snapped his ma.

Lydia and Shane snickered but acquiesced, allowing their ma to have her proud moment. They knew she'd be on the phone, bragging to one of her friends soon as they were out of earshot.

—Do ye not have a satchel? his ma asked as Shane was leaving.

44

Shane had his stuff in the Easons plastic bag.

—What's a satchel? he asked.

Lydia couldn't hold back any longer and she doubled over with laughter beside her ma at the front door.

—What? their ma asked, looking confused. —What's so funny?

—Yeh don't say 'satchel' anymore Ma. It's just a 'bag', Lydia managed through her laughter.

Their ma was bemused, but the slagging didn't puncture her good humour.

—Well in *my* day it was always a satchel.

—I wouldn't wear a manbag anyway, said Shane as he walked out of the garden. —See yis after.

—Goodbye now, said his ma, smiling and waving.

—See ye, his sister laughed.

Fuck sake, thought Shane.

Out of sight of the house, he traipsed forward unwillingly, snail-like. He was nervous going in the first day, not knowin anyone on his course. Apprehension fluttered lightly in his stomach. Unaccustomed to the morning air, he felt cold and anxious as he stood at the bus stop. He dragged his feet and swung his bag, restless. He wasn't used to waiting. Eventually the bus veered into view and quaked to a stop.

—Howye Shane.

The bus driver was one of his da's mates.

—Howye Leo, €1.35 please.

—Go on yer alrigh, said Leo quietly.

—Nice one Leo, cheers.

—Say nothin, Leo winked.

—How's Gemma? asked Shane.

She was Leo's eldest daughter, Shane's sister's best friend.

—Ah she's grand. Out in Maynooth. Studyin computers the past few year so she is. Costin me a fortune. But she's nearly finished.

—Is Ashling in college as well?

Ashling was Leo's youngest. Shane fancied her.

—Oh she's in Cathal Brugha Street now, doin cookery. Brings lovely fresh bread and all home. Gorgeous so it does be. Ye'd wanna taste it! Even the smell of it . . . The other one that's doin computers brings home nothin from college. Only her brain.

Shane laughed as he moved down the back to sit down. He was raging he'd no music to listen to. He stared out the window as he passed row after row of white pebble-dashed houses. Streets with dishevelled edging. Dirty kerbs and uncut grass.

At the college, the bustle of registration was well under way. Without someone taking charge, Shane was unsure how to proceed. He was awkward, worried he'd betray himself somehow. But he followed the crowd to the hall and found the queue for the registration forms. More concerned with the grant form, he asked a woman at the desk.

—Here you go, she said, handing it to him. —It'll take you a while to fill in! You might be eligible for VTOS as well. That's over there.

He didn't know what that was, but sensed it might translate into more money so he joined yet another queue. He felt a tap on the shoulder and turned to see his mate Chalkie. He was relieved to meet someone he knew. Instantly, his anxiety dissipated.

—Ah Jaysis, howye pal!

—What's the story buddy?

—Some mots in here aren't there? Shane whispered.

—Will ye stop! Chalkie replied. —Unreal amount of birds. I'm tellin ye buddy, we'll be doin some ridin ou here so we will!

Chalkie moved about excitedly even as he stood, glancing around the place, taking everything in. The glaring white-and-green Lacoste tracksuit he wore added to this sense of bustling energy. Shane's own tracksuit was dull and scruffy in comparison.

—Wha course are you doin again? Shane asked.

—Theatre, said Chalkie.

—*Are ye?*

—Yeah. I've been workin on me *Hamlet* over the summer. I've tha 'soliloquy' thing nearly perfect an all.

—Really?

—No ye mad yoke. I'm not gay. I'm doin a radio course. Was thinkin I migh get a few gigs ou of it or somethin.

—Ah yeah, said Shane.

Chalkie DJ'ed on a local pirate radio station, talking at ninety miles a minute over tracks.

—Goin ou for all the lads in Coultry in the Opel Vectra tear it up lads this is Sunscreem, 'Perfect Motion'. Rex FM DJ Chalkie . . . all over Ireland . . .

The station barely covered Santry and Coolock, but he finished every sentence with this catchphrase he'd stolen from some other DJ.

Shane filled out the grant form as they chatted. Chalkie wasn't queuing for the VTOS, but he did have a copy of the VEC grant form in his hands.

—Are ye not fillin tha ou now man? asked Shane.

—Ah I'll do it later.

—Three grand ye get man.

—I know yeah. I fuckin hate fillin these things ou though.

—Jaysis it'll be worth it, said Shane.

—I suppose. Ah I'll do it later buddy, me head's up me hole this mornin. Doin yokes all weekend so I was. Them "sharks". Loopy they are. Gettin tha sleep paralysis and all.

—Ye got bit by a shark, said Shane.

—Ha ha, tha's righ buddy – a shark bit me alrigh. Bit me bad. Took a few sleepers an everything, an I still couldn't come down. Stickin to the charlie from now on I am.

Chalkie rolled up the form and put it under his arm. The two of them hung around for an hour or so, checking out the girls that were registering.

—Tha hairdressin, tha has the best birds. All rides so they are, said Shane.

—Ehhhhhhhh . . . I'm not so sure buddy. There's a few nice mots doin the hairdressin alrigh, but they're all done up to the nines. I'm tellin ye man, ye wanna be lookin ou for the birds withou make-up on. If they're nice-lookin without all tha muck on their faces, they're definitely nice for real. Ye have to watch when yer with one of them birds tha have the makeup caked on – ye think she's a ride but when ye wake up the next mornin yer bedsheets are left like the Shroud of Turin an she's in bits.

Shane laughed, but he wasn't so sure. He thought the hairdressin types were unbelievably sexy. Chalkie was adamant though.

—Look at her for example

Mentoring his younger friend, Chalkie pointed at a nerdy girl in jeans and battered trainers.

—Now yeh probly wouldn't put a pass on her in a night-club, but she's nicer lookin than all them birds with the fuckin bleach blonde and the fake tan. With their neckline like a tub of curry.

Shane looked at the girl's face and had to admit she was pretty.

—It's the same with her figure, watch. Now she has a nice hole in them jeans doesn't she?

—Yeah.

—But tha other girl in the hairdressin queue has a nice hole as well. Now which arse is nicer?

—They're both around the same I'd say, Shane ventured.

—Wrong – the geek over there has a way nicer hole on her. The hairdresser one is wearin heels. Tha makes their arses look better than they are. Pushes them up. Firms them.

—Righ . . .

—The geekazoid is wearin flats, look. Pair of Converse. No heels at all in them. Whatever shape her arse is there it'll be the same shape when ye get her ou of the clothes.

— Never thought of tha, Shane acknowledged, seeing Chalkie's logic.

Trying to understand the theory, Shane stared around the room. He started to think he could spot the natural beauties. He no longer took the made-up girls in boots or stilettos at face value. Or arse value.

—Wha abou tits? Shane asked.

—Just forget about tits. So much shit goes on there, ye never know until ye get yer hands on them.

There were no classes that day, just form filling. Then they were given their timetables. The day was divided into hour-long periods. *Could they not just call them classes?*

thought Shane. *It's my first period. How does that sound?* They only had around seven hours in college each week. And the whole day off on Fridays. Shane was delighted.

He still had to drag himself out of bed the next day though, and ended up being late for his first class. He was relieved to see that no teacher was in the room when he arrived, there were just fifteen or so students sitting around. He sort of wished he hadn't spent the whole day before talking to Chalkie, and had met some of the people from his course instead.

He sat down on a dented chair at a table criss-crossed with scratches and ancient graffiti. The words were etched in straight lines, rune-like on the desk. Dublin ogham:

SNITCHES GET STITCHES

SKINS

HORSEY LOVES GEMMA

26 + 6 = 1

BOHS SOCCER CASUALS

FUCK BOHS RATS

TIOCFAIGH AR LA

IRA DUBLIN BRIGADE

ANTO FARRELL DOES THE SUNBEDS

Shane smelt the disinfectant. Schools, health centres, Garda stations – the same smell. The same cold draft as well. Nervous tension brought back memories. Tears on the first day of primary school. Fear on the first day of secondary school.

Thinking about the contrast between the timid child he

was then and the rough teenager he was now relaxed him a bit. He looked around the class. Fifty-fifty, boys to girls. Dubs and culchies. Older ones too – an oulfella with specs, and a large black woman about forty-odd. Shane folded his arms on the table and rested his head in the nest of his elbows, closing his eyes.

A gush of memories surged up: primary-school Irish, when the teacher said, '*Téigh a chodladh*.' Go to sleep. You rested your arms on the desk, nestled your head into them and shut your eyes. The teacher was like a dog trainer or a stage hypnotist with only the one trick. If the principal came in, if one of the mammies came in, if the priest came in, if she wanted to talk to another teacher, if she was correcting class work. If she had a pain her bollix. She'd just say, '*Téigh a chodladh*', and everyone bowed their heads and shut their eyes and their mouths. The main lesson to learn was thoughtless obedience.

Then there was the ones you had learnt off by rote.

—*An bhfuil cead agam dul go dtí an leithreas?* Is there permission for me to go to the toilet?

Pronounced with a plodding rhythm, each syllable remembered separately. And the prayers in Irish too.

—*In ainm an Athar, agus an Mhic, agus an Spioraid, Naoimh, Amen.* In the name of the father, and the son, and the spirit, Christ, Amen.

Gaelic incantations for an anglophone nation. Empty gestures, nothing more. The Hail Mary more often than the Our Father. Beyond a vague sense, Shane had never known what the words meant, he only remembered the sounds. Not the spellings even. Fadas were the trickiest. Never knew where to put them. He was in fifth year in secondary school before he realised they only went on vowels.

Into the room bustled a large man, talking. Shane snapped out of his stupor, lifted his head and withdrew his arms from the table.

—The first thing to remember about technology, said the man, —is that it is not always the most effective systems which come to predominate.

Slowly, the students stopped chattering amongst themselves as they realised the man wasn't addressing some unseen companion. Fiddling with the overhead projector in the centre of the class, he continued his speech, ignoring the students. He then put a bunch of papers on the table and began cleaning the whiteboard.

—This is true in every technological field. Examples range from BETA and VHS, to Apple Mac and Microsoft Windows. Not forgetting the ill-fated Neanderthal man . . . and of course *Homo sapiens* himself. The species to which most of you appear to belong.

He tapped away at a keyboard on the desk and a computer display was projected onto the whiteboard.

—Now, let us take, as an example, a typical institutional website. In this case it is the college's own. Now . . . this tab here will grant you permission to print an application form for full-time courses in the college, this one part-time. None of you need that, you are all fully registered, fully aware, fully developed, full-time students, am I correct? Wonderful. Now, on the right side of the screen – past the picture of the very attractive young lady which is a ubiquitous feature on the websites of third-level education institutes, but not to be found in reality no matter how often you scour the cafeteria – you will see a 'Contact Us' option. This is standard on all websites of any repute. If you click on this you will be supplied with the proper title and address of the institution. Very useful if for any reason you wish to issue a writ – but you'll learn more of that in your business law class. I am here to teach you business technology, which is what I intend to do! Now, moving back up on the left you will see a tab for our careers advisory service – judging by the vacant expressions I see around me, some of you may need this sooner than others . . .

Shane's mind automatically re-entered his default school setting: daydream mode. The thoughts that followed were like screensavers, occupying the conscious part of his brain while he endured the barrage of information he was unable to process. This was no decision. The response was as automatic as digestion.

He teased himself with visions of the geeky Converse girl helping him study in his bedroom. Bending over to pick up a sheaf of papers that fell off the edge of the bed. Feeling his cock stiffen, he quickly tried to divert his thoughts, cursing his decision to wear a tracksuit. He wondered why they were so popular among his peers, given the unsuitability of such leisurewear for disguising their almost permanent erections.

He thought of Griffo's outfits with envy. Chops had told Shane that Griffo drove a BMW 320i, only a year or two old. This didn't spark jealousy – it was well beyond Shane's conception of what was attainable. But he coveted the designer clothes, the easy cash. The coke.

While the teacher continued to chatter ineffectually, he compiled a mental list of the items he'd buy with the anticipated grant money. He'd still have plenty left over for a few nights out. Or he could spend it all on a holiday. Ibiza. Or

Ayia Napa; it was supposed to have nicer birds these days.

The teacher continued talking as the bell rang faintly to signal the end of class.

—Folks, perhaps the most important thing to remember is that as long as you're not in the technology business, business technology is only there *to serve a purpose*. At the risk of making myself redundant, business has not kept pace with technology. It hasn't changed all that much since the advent of the modern era.

As he gathered his papers and switched off the projector, he carried on talking out into the hall and away from the class.

—Ultimately, business is still founded upon the exchange of goods or services for profit. It's the capital and profit you're after. Technology is only the means to an end, only a tool to facilitate the more rapid exchange . . .

They could hear his voice receding down the hallway, still talking. Shane left without having spoken with any of his classmates. Growing up where he did, he'd learned to be wary of talking to new people.

Shane was meant to meet Chalkie the next day, but he ended up not going in at all. The mentality he'd had in school had been directly transposed onto college. He actively worked at avoiding work and avoiding learning. Staying up half the night browsing Bebo and watching Internet porn, he'd sleep for most of the day. He was caught in a cycle of staying awake until all hours and sleeping until near evening.

So it went on for the next couple of months. He made it to less than a quarter of his classes. He'd no chance to bond with his fellow students. Deadlines came and went, and a backlog of essays built up. The only thing he actually handed in was a short assignment for Introduction to Marketing. Shane started to avoid the teachers who pressed him to produce work, abandoning some classes completely.

All Shane learned that term was a trick to get into nightclubs. Usually, all the lads got refused by the bouncers. A load of working-class fellas just turned eighteen weren't considered ideal customers. 'Not tonight lads,' or 'Private party,' were the usual knockbacks they heard. The worst of all was 'Can I help you lads?' As if they were so worthless it was inconceivable they'd have the temerity to even *try* to get in. Shane hated it – it made him feel like a thick, fucked with his head, compounded his constant sense of inferiority.

One of the nights he'd seen his da working on the door though, he'd noticed that he had a list on a clipboard. When people gave a name, his da waved whole groups through. They were mostly pre-booked 'work-nights out', his da told him. So Shane rang up one of the big dance clubs in town. He pretended to be a foreman in the Jacob's factory, and was surprised when it worked. Even if it had to be through fraud, Shane was delighted at the prospect of getting into a proper dance spot, a place with a well-known DJ playing. Six of the lads came: Chops, Mick, Aido, Dotsy, Chalkie, Farreler. Shane made seven altogether.

There was confusion at the door when they arrived though. When Shane gave the name of his 'boss', the doorman told them to wait, scrutinising the list more closely. The lads stood at the side of the door as the other bouncers screened the queue and let people through in dribs and drabs. They were still getting refused after all that, Shane was certain. His face flushed with embarrassment: he'd told the lads he had it sorted and had hyped up the night by telling them all how deadly the club was meant to be, and they had dressed up and trekked into town. But it turned out the doorman just didn't know whether they were marked down to get in for free or just skip the queue, and was trying to radio a manager for clarification. When they said they didn't mind paying, they were briskly waved straight through to the till. They could hear the music inside. They were each only too glad to pay the score in, pushing past one other in their eagerness.

Receipts in hand, away from the doormen, they hustled each other up the hallway, hyper and laughing. The deep throb of the bass mounted as they moved with the crowd toward the heart of the club. The high-hat and snare became audible as they entered the main room, and even though they'd yet to take their Es, they each felt a rush as the melody and vocals floated over their heads.

The place was heaving. The crowd was oriented toward an energetic DJ who stood on stage behind the decks mixing tunes. From time to time he lifted his eyes from the mixer and smiled as he looked out at the crowd, gave someone he recognised on the dance floor a nod. The lads were straight up to the bar, pushing their way to the front. They got served quicker than expected. The night was moving toward its peak. Drink wasn't the focus, it was about music now. And Ecstasy.

—Are ye righ we do these pills? Shane said.

—Wait till we get away from the bar. Don't want to be throwin the eye on ourselves ye know, said Chops.

—Yeah, sound.

After getting drinks they moved through the billowing

crowd as best they could, over toward the far wall. They kept their eyes level as they discretely took out the tablets. Shane placed one in his mouth, gently holding it on his tongue. He took a sip from the pint glass in his hand, then swallowed, feeling the pill as a little bump with the liquid that went down his neck.

Half an hour later, they started coming up. Most of the lads were straight out on the dance floor, but Chops had a few more pills he wanted to sell, so Shane stalled it with him. He watched how Chops worked, keeping one eye out for potential customers, another for doormen. He overheard someone asking if there were any pills around.

—Are yis lookin for little things? Chops asked.

—Yeah, how much?

—How many d'yis want?

—Just two.

—Ah sorry luv, I have them wrapped up. The smallest I can give ye is five for a score.

Chops was a good salesman, and understood consumer psychology instinctively. Limited supply equalled increased demand, and the seller could dictate terms. Offering a discount incentive for bulk purchase was elementary, and customers acquiesced. Gratefully.

—Sound, cheers.

Chops had them pre-wrapped in bundles. He'd place them in cigarette rolling papers in rows of five, wet the lip of paper with his tongue and roll them into neat little packets, tearing off the spare paper at the ends. The bundles looked almost exactly like tiny blank versions of the packets of Lovehearts sweets they'd all enjoyed when they were kids. Instead of trite mottoes like 'Angel Face', 'Be Mine',

'Trust Me', 'All Yours' or 'I Surrender', Ecstasy came pressed with stark symbols: shamrocks, lions, crowns, doves, anchors, stars, roses, hearts, butterflies, Xs, question marks, apples. Or brand logos: Rolex, Mitsubishi, Adidas, MTV, Armani, Playboy, Rolls Royce, McDonald's, Apple.

When the bulk of the pills had been disposed of, Chops and Shane went to meet the lads in the main room where the dance floor was. They found them up front near the DJ box, sweating and pumping their fists in time with the beat triumphantly.

—What's the story boys!

—Fuckin deadly!

—Savage tunes man! Tha DJ's deadly!

Shane and Chops joined them, quickly moving toward the same state of euphoria and inebriation. The DJ rocked back and forth behind the decks in time with the funky-house music. His movements were dramatic, manic even – but precisely to the beat. Twisting the EQ, he took the bass out. He looked at the expectant crowd who put their hands in the air and gazed back at him . . . he waited for exactly eight beats . . . then slammed the bass back in – to cheers.

Well high on the E, Shane danced for a while, then wobbled out through the throng. He climbed up the narrow staircase and got in the line for the jacks. As he reached the door, a big fella skipped in front of him, ignoring the queue. While in the process of taking offence at the big man's boldness, Shane recognised him.

—Griffo!

If he'd been sober, Shane would have been too embarrassed about the missing hours in the Pink Pound to initiate a conversation.

—Ah howye, said Griffo.

He searched Shane's face, eyes flickering then thinning with a glint of recognition.

—Where do I know you from? Sorry kid, I know I know ye, I just can't place ye, he prattled.

—The Pink Pound, d'ye remember? said Shane.

—Ah Jaysis that's righ! Chops's mate isn't it?

—Yeah yeah. Downstairs he is. C'mere I meant to say to ye man, sorry if I was wreckin yer head tha day. Ou of it so I was.

—Ah I wouldn't worry about it kid, I hardly remember the day meself! Everyone in there is in the same boat. Sure it's the only reason we go to tha place are ye wide? The *Pink Pound*? Should be called the *Dog Pound* the behaviour of us all in there!

—Ha ha, yeah.

—Righ man, I'm bustin here, said Griffo.

—No bother.

Shane pissed at the far end of the urinals from Griffo, who seemed edgy. The black fella in the jacks squirted soap onto his hand after he pissed, then passed him a paper towel after he washed his hands. Shane's €2 coin rattled in the dark glass ashtray – it was the only place you'd find an ashtray in a club anymore, since the smoking ban came in a few years previous.

—Thank you Sir.

—No bother.

For that money he was takin a squirt of aftershave too. As he sprayed, he noticed Griffo was standing in the cubicle, door open fiddling with a bag. Poking his head out, he gave Shane a nod. Shane looked at the black fella, who stared back impassively.

—It's alrigh, I know him, said Griffo to Shane.

Shane joined Griffo in the cubicle, pressing against his stiff steroidal bulk as he squeezed the door shut. Griffo used toilet paper to scrub a small area on a ledge above the cistern. He then emptied about a third of the bag onto the area he'd cleaned. He chattered as he mashed the coke with the flat of an Xtra-vision card, before using one of the sharp edges to divide it, chopping at it a few times. The cubicles were illuminated by blue ultra-violet lights. Flecks glowed blue all over their shirts.

—They put these bulbs in to stop people bangin up in the jacks, said Griffo. —Junkies can't find a vein in this light, he continued. —So the idea is, you won't get cunts bangin up and overdosin in yer jacks if ye give it the aul fluorescent treatment.

Shane nodded.

—The thing is though . . . it makes doin coke all the more excitin.

Griffo leaned back and looked at his handiwork. Four lines were laid out, glowing invitingly under the indigo bulbs. Griffo was right, there was no doubt. The lights gave the coke an ultra-pure, ethereal glow – like some futuristic super-drug. The two lads briefly stood motionless, staring at the lines. Too pure to disrupt . . . almost.

—Luminous lines wha? Have ye a note there? Griffo asked Shane.

—Yeah here . . .

Shane pulled a crinkly tenner from his pocket, but Griffo rejected it as too crumpled and, fishing his wallet from his back pocket, chose a crisp fifty. He rolled it into a wide but tightly composed tube, then used it to sniff deeply, moving it slowly along the line. He bent back up, face red, eyes tightly closed.

—Awgh, he snuffled, rubbing his nose before snorting again.

He passed Shane the note without looking. Shane tried to replicate Griffo's technique. The coke hit him straight away, even better than the little sniffs he'd been doing with Griffo in the earlyhouse.

As they left, Shane gave the black fella a fiver at Griffo's behest.

—I always look after him, said Griffo. —Makes a fortune ou of me tha fella does.

—Nice one again man, said Shane. —Are ye buzzin downstairs and I'll get ye a drink? Shane asked.

—No, you go on kid yer grand. Yeh don't need to buy me a drink. I'm up in the VIP anyway.

—Alrigh man cheers.

—Here take me number if ye need anything.

—Yeh gave me a number to ring the other day.

—Ye might as well take me own number now I know ye kid, go on.

Griffo gave Shane his number, then shook his hand and slapped him on the shoulder before bustling off. Shane watched his brawny bulk ascend the staircase to the VIP area, a bouncer pulling back a velvet rope at the top of the stairs.

Shane danced and drank the rest of the night away, ebullient from the mixture of coke, drink, ecstasy and music. Carefree, he kissed three different girls without effort, and lost each one in the crowd without regret. This couldn't be simulated, he thought. This was real, this was the real deal.

He hugged Chops, embracing him with true affection, brimming with love.

—I love ye man.

—I fuckin love you too Shane, and I mean tha, Chops said.

At the end of the night they all waltzed out of the place, tripping merrily through the throng. No aggression, no anxiety. Total confidence, full immersion in the moment. An imposing full moon shone down on them benignly. A selenic spotlight on their performance, they danced arm in arm up the street. In the approving silver light, they frolicked, boisterous.

Chalkie pulled down his trousers and bent over, baring his rear to the sky, two globes of flesh.

—Will ye look at this fuckin lunatic, Chops chuckled.

—Wha? I'm moonin the moon! cried Chalkie.

They wandered off into the night, making their ways home slowly to prolong the moment.

★

Amidst his sporadic attendance at lectures on venture capital and profit margins, Shane continued to daydream about the commodities he coveted. At the end of November, the first instalment of his grant came through. More than €1,100 appeared in his bank account on the Monday. His desires had grown to exceed this amount though.

He pondered what to buy first. Expensive jeans and T-shirts like Griffo wore. Armani, Hugo Boss, Evisu, Von Dutch. The brands had emblazoned their images on his mind, proving their marketing mettle. On the Tuesday, he withdrew €1,000 from his account. He took it cautiously from the teller in the bank, checking it deliberately at the counter before stowing it in his front pocket. He'd never seen – let alone held – so much money before. On the way back out of town, the brightly lit shopfronts seemed to beckon *him*, specifically. They'd never seemed so inviting.

He wandered out of his way, up Grafton Street, past Brown Thomas and toward the Green. He stood between Traitor's Gate and the Stephen's Green Shopping Centre. He imagined slowly choosing garments before trying them on and admiring himself in the plush privacy of the changing room. Christmas advertising was in its full winter bloom, and Shane watched the shoppers hurry to and fro as the sky darkened. Serious, even business-like, they went into shops – then came out with their bags, relaxed. The act of acquisition itself was the main pleasure, not enjoyment of the goods. Shane looked at the logos on their bags, visualising the items inside based upon the type of shop they'd been to. Clothes, runners, CDs, DVDs, Xboxes, iPods, phones, laptops, fragrances, chocolates. He wanted it all. Shivering in the cold under a crescent moon, Shane rejected the lure of the shops and hurried to catch a bus home.

In the house, he checked carefully that he was alone. He picked up his phone, scrolling through the contacts. Ceremoniously he pressed the green button. After a long few seconds he heard a voice.

—Helllllo?

—Griffo? said Shane.

—Yeah who's this? Griffo replied.

—Shane.

—Shaaaaane?

—Chops's mate. I was talkin to ye in the club at the weekend there.

—Ah yeah yeah yeah. What's the craic kid?

—I was wonderin if ye'd still be able to sort me out with an ounce of tha coke? said Shane.

—Eh . . . are ye around? replied Griffo.

—Wha d'ye mean? asked Shane.

—Are ye able to meet up like?

—Now?

—Yeah.

Shane felt awkward, unsure of the protocol.

—Yeah OK. Where?

—I'll see ye outside the Merchant Arms in about twenty minutes.

—Sound.

Aware of the significance of the step and feeling nervous, Shane put on a cap and jacket and then made his way on foot down to the local pub. As he walked into the car park, Griffo pulled out of a space in his navy BMW and pulled up alongside him. Stooping, Shane peered into the passenger window, which Griffo had lowered, the car still running.

—Hop in there, Griffo said.

Shane got into the car and shut the thick door. It clicked plushly, unlike the harsh slam of the cheap hatchbacks his ma and sister drove. Griffo eased out onto the road.

—Sorry kid, I should have told ye. I don't be talkin dirty on the phone any more ye know, too dodgy.

—Righ, said Shane, though he didn't know what Griffo meant.

—If you're ringin me don't ask for coke, just say ye want raffle tickets yeah?

—Sound.

—I'll say 'How many?' and you say 'One' for an ounce.

That's wha ye want isn't it? Forgot to say to ye as well, I have little fellas there too, gettin a good price on these yokes now, so I can give ye a thousand for nine hundred nicker.

—Nice one man. I'm oney after a bit of the charlie for now. C'mere I was oney ringin to ask ye, Shane put in quickly. —Will ye do it for a grand instead of twelve hundreh?

—I can't man, said Griffo firmly. —Not tha stuff, sure it's straight off the rock. I can give ye other stuff for a grand if ye want, it's not as nice now but it'll do the trick.

He knew his consumer psychology too. Instead of an outright refusal, offer a lower quality product at the price requested. The customer was unlikely to accept offer, but it put them in a poor bargaining position.

—Nah man, it's tha stuff ye had ou last time I want.

—Can't go lower than twelve on tha man. Seriously, most fellas wouldn't even give it to ye on tick first time anyway.

This wasn't true. The overwhelming majority of cocaine sold was given on tick. Shane knew this.

—I don't want it on tick. I have cash.

—Ye have the cash there?

Griffo was surprised.

—Yeah.

—Now like?

—Yeah.

He found it hard to believe a youngfella from the area who wasn't already sellin drugs could amass €1,000. Most of them couldn't hold on to fifty quid past the weekend.

—Grand so . . . If ye have a grand. Grand if ye have a grand wha?

Griffo laughed, and Shane did too.

—Sound, said Shane.

The two of them smiled.

Griffo left Shane home, then called back about twenty-five minutes later, ringing him when he was outside. He didn't get out of the car. Shane went out to him and sat in the passenger seat again. Griffo glanced in the rear-view mirror, then pushed his pelvis forward a little. He put one hand down the front of his tracksuit bottoms and pulled out a round white ball. The plastic was thicker and shinier than on the little oner bags Shane had seen before. Completely transparent rather than semi-opaque sweet-bag white.

Griffo tossed it casually to Shane. It was around the same size as a golf ball, a little larger maybe. It was more coke than Shane had ever seen, but it felt light. It didn't feel worth €1,000. *More than gold*, Shane marvelled. In Argos, you could buy an ounce of gold in tacky-bracelet form for €800. And people put this up their noses. People killed over this, people died over this.

Shane tucked it into his sock like Chops had taught him to do with Es, then gave Griffo the cash. It was folded inside one of the small brown envelopes his mother kept in the kitchen drawer.

—Classy, Griffo said. —Like Bertie, wha? I won't ask where the money came from, he smiled.

He eyed Shane, gauging him. Shane smiled back, enjoying the insinuation that he had acquired the funds illegally.

—Have ye got a josey already? Griffo asked.

—A wha?

—A Josey Wales . . . A weighin scales. For measurin it ou like.

—No.

—Righ, well that's the first thing ye'll need kid. Get yerself a little electronic one. Make sure ye stash it well though, cause it's the same as gettin caugh with the stuff itself if the Old Bill nab ye with a scales and there's powder left on it.

—Sound.

—Wha're ye gonna do fer bags?

—Eh, just use bits off plastic bags . . .

—Yeah ye can cut them into squares and tie them up. But they're bulky and it does be hard to open the knots on them. After ye get yer scales ye wanna get yerself down to Tescos. They have freezer bags – not the thick ones in the boxes – they have little rolls of thin ones too, they're better. They're only 65 cent. One roll will do ye until you make yer first million.

They laughed.

—Cut them into squares, and tie them up. Don't forget, after ye have them tied up and ye cut the tops off don't just fuck the leftover plastic in your bin. There'll be coke on it and they can prove your dealin just from the leftovers in the rubbish. Throw tha stuff ou on the road or down a shore or somethin, and stash yer coke somewhere safe and tell no one. Like *no one*.

Shane was serious and attentive, noting everything Griffo said.

—Sound.

—And if yer oulwan catches yeh, ye didn't get it off me!

They laughed.

The next day, Shane went into town to buy the weighing scales. He also bought a cheap ready-to-go mobile phone handset with an unregistered SIM. On the way home, he got the freezer bags Griffo had recommended. He had the coke stashed inside the curtain pole in his bedroom. The tooled ends of the pole came off, and Shane removed one and stuck the ounce inside. The ornamental cap could still fit back on, concealing the coke. The bulky scales was more difficult. He considered just storing it one of the cupboards in the kitchen, but his ma would notice this new addition to her household stuff. She'd ask questions, defo. In the end he settled for the stereotypical under the bed.

After his dinner, he went upstairs and locked his door. There was a simple bolt he'd screwed on for some privacy from his ma and sister when he'd first started wanking. He got out the scales and the coke. After opening the bag carefully, he turned the scales on and scooped some out onto the stainless-steel platform. The display showed '00'.

Shane put a bit more on. Nothing. It looked like nearly a oner bag but the scales wasn't even showing a portion of a gram. He put more on. Still nothing. *There's at least fuckin gram on there now defo*, he thought. *More.*

The display moved, reading '1'. After fiddling with it for a while to no avail, he rang Chops.

—It's only showin me by the gram and even then it's not even accurate. How am I sup posed to be measurin 1.4?

—Are ye usin it righ?

—I dunno! That's why I'm ringin ye! said Shane.

—Lemme see. You're meant to set it to zero before ye put anything on it. Did ye do tha.

—Hold on. How do ye do tha?

—Press 'Set', Chops said.

—There is no 'Set'.

—Wha size is it?

—I dunno.

—Abou?

—Abou the size of a record.

—Wha?

—Abou the size of a record, Shane repeated.

—Is it round?

—Yeah, said Shane, exasperated.

—A single like? Seven-inch?

—No. A twelve-inch.

—Wha colour is it? asked Chops.

—White.

—That's a scales for baking cakes ye dzzzope.

—Oh.

Shane hadn't even started dealing and he was already down €50.

The next day he bought the proper jeweller's scales from a head shop in town, another €50. On Chops's advice, he also bought a box of Teetha, a granular medicine for teething babies. The idea was that it would numb the gums like real coke, so people would be less likely to notice that the coke was adulterated.

He made it into college on the Thursday. He had two classes: Business Law and Maths. Two periods. On the way in, he met Chalkie, who was on his way out.

—What's the story man, did ye get yer grant? Shane asked.

—Nah man.

—What's the story? Are they not payin ye?

—Ah I never filled ou the forms, said Chalkie.

—*Wha?*

—Ah I just never got round to it, ye know yourself. Did you get yours?

—Yeah, I got paid Monday, said Shane, shocked.

—How much was it?

—They pay ye in three instalments, €1,100 first one.

—No way, said Chalkie.

—Yeah but c'mere man, me sister was sayin they can backdate it even if yer late applyin. Ye should send the forms in man, it's well worth it.

—Ah then ye have to wait for it and all. Ah, I can't be arsed.

—Wha?

—Ah the fuckin hassle of it ye know. I want me money now buddy ye know wha I mean?

Shane was incredulous. He couldn't believe Chalkie would let three grand go for the sake of filling out a few forms.

—Jaysis Chalkie, you're a mad cunt.

—Ah fuck it man, I can't be bothered with all this shite, I'm thinkin of fuckin leavin anyway.

—How come?

—C'mere I've been on the radio for years, I know how to do a fuckin radio show. But they want me to learn abou politics and history, all tha shite – would ye fuck off! I mean wha the fuck do I need to know abou Fianna fuckin Fáil for to play dance music? It's a load of me bollix.

—I dunno, ye migh get a job ou of it.

—That's wha I want. A job. On the radio. Playin music. All over Ireland. Not sittin on me hole in the Dáil all bleedin day.

—Mind you tha sounds alrigh.

—Ha ha, yeah I was just thinkin tha after I said it, it does sound alrigh. Vote for Chalkie!

—He'll wipe the slate clean!

—Ha ha, I like it buddy, I like it.

They parted company and Shane headed to his maths class. The teacher set them a few questions and the class got to work. She had suspected Shane of cheating on assignments, and had even imposed a spot quiz to try and catch him out. She'd pointedly told the class, 'Some of the students are at an unexpectedly high standard for this stage of the academic year.' She looked directly at Shane as she said it, hoping he'd betray some sign of discomfort. He was impassive, leaning back on his chair. She was rattled when he passed with flying colours. He was just naturally good with numbers. There was no possibility he'd cheated – she'd watched him throughout.

Shane knew the suspicion was due to his accent, and the tracksuit he'd worn on the first day. *Skanger*, he thought to himself, *that's what she thinks of me. Or what's the other word the culchies use? Scrote. Then the D4 heads: knacker, scobe. The Old Bill: scumbag.*

Branded with an indelible verdict. A tag that stamped itself onto the psyche as deeply and irreversibly as any steaming mark on animal hide. There was nobody like him teaching there, nobody with his accent or clothes, just culchies or poshos. They didn't speak his language. It was the same for all the lads, there was nobody successful who was like them. Anyone from the area who made money or achieved anything moved house and picked up a D4 accent along the way. Sportspeople were the only ones to look up to. Boxers and footballers. Either them or gangsters and drug dealers. Chalkie felt the same. No one talked like he did on licensed radio stations. Except Joe Duffy and Dustin the Turkey.

Shane returned his attention to the problem at hand:

7) Cusack's Camera Shop sells digital cameras for
€120 each. In an attempt to increase profit, they raise
the price by €5.76. Express this increase as a percent
of the original price.'

Cusack's Camera Shop are dzopes, he thought. *If ye wanna
shift volume why up the price from an attractively round
€120 to a difficult €125.76? If that's the buzz ye were on, fuck
it, just go for €130.* But he solved the problem, using the cal-
culator as permitted, dividing the variable by the base
number then multiplying the result. While he waited for the
rest of the class to work it out he imagined a question of his
own:

1) Deco bought an ounce of coke for €1,000, and
added a quarter of an ounce of mix in an attempt to
increase profit. He sold three eighths for €200 each
and a quarter for €300. The rest he divided up into
oner bags and sold for €100 a pop. What was Deco's
net profit?

'A lot,' was the first answer that sprang to Shane's mind.

That weekend, Shane sold three oner bags himself,
giving him a profit of just over €150 for less than an hour's
work. He'd double his money on the ounce if he sold it all
in hundred bags. More than double it, cause he'd mixed it a
bit. The coke Griffo had sold him had come in a solid chunk
– a 'rock' – which was supposed to show that it hadn't
already been cut. In reality, it was 're-rock': the powder had

just been recompressed into a solid again after it had been mixed. But a compressor was an expensive piece of equipment. The solidity proved that the coke hadn't been cut since a higher level of dealer. Probably whoever Griffo bought it off, mused Shane.

It was on the basis of quality that Shane dealt. He was working in a different market than Chops in the nightclubs. The area they lived was saturated with dealers – nearly every youngfella that took coke regularly sold it as well. Absolutely everyone knew someone they could buy it off, even those who never took drugs. Even people's grannies knew someone to ring if they wanted a bag.

To compete, Shane didn't go heavy on the mix. He'd sent out a few texts from his new phone number (which came with €20 free credit), telling people he had stuff there to sell. At first he got no replies. He was worried he'd be left stuck with the whole lot until he got a call from Chalkie on the old phone.

—What's the story man? Chops was sayin ye have nice charlie there?

—Yeah yeah, are ye lookin for a bit?

—No, me mate from up the estate is just lookin a oner bag. I said I'd give ye a ring meself first before I gave him yer number like.

—Don't give him this number, I've another number I'm usin for business. I don't be talkin dirty on this phone anymore ye know. Too dodgy.

After that, more orders came in, and Shane stopped worrying. But he didn't spend his profits. He wanted to make back that €1,000 initial outlay, amass enough to buy the next lot before counting his chickens. He'd seen too many youngfellas get themselves into debt getting drugs on tick. Chasing their tails. The prospect frightened him. Chalkie's ma had had to borrow two grand from the credit union to pay off his drug debts the year before. Fellas had called to the gaff, threatening to shoot Chalkie if they didn't get their money.

Word spread, one customer leading to another. Shane was a decent youngfella in his own way. He was well liked and that helped. People didn't want to buy drugs off psychos unless they had to. In only a couple of weeks, he had less than a quarter of an ounce left. He'd well made his money back. Time to get more in.

Griffo was surprised when Shane rang him to ask for another ounce so soon.

—Fair play to ye kid. Like a duck to water wha!

He was glad Shane looked set to prove a steady customer. Too many dealers were unreliable, out on the batter soon as they got their money. In bits then for the week after. Ringing up at the last minute looking to buy a quarter only, just to tide them over. Shane always rang Griffo a few days before the weekend to organise things.

It wasn't like the newspapers made out, like there was someone at the top controlling the whole thing. It was just an unregulated commercial enterprise. It would have been impossible to control the supply in any area – the thing was to compete. Griffo sold the coke to Shane, Shane sold it to other people, end of story. Griffo couldn't give a fuck what Shane did with it. And if Shane was to take his business to another supplier that was his choice. It was nearly a full-time job for Griffo chasing up the fellas that owed him money, without trying to force people to buy off him as well.

There were costs and benefits in every line of business. Supply was sometimes limited by the efforts of the Garda, but this was what gave cocaine its value as a commodity. And created the high profit margins. Business went well for Shane, and he kept on going back to Griffo, paying cash every time.

—It's gonna be a white Christmas if ye keep goin like this kid! Literally.

Griffo pulled the ounce from his underwear and tossed it to Shane, as had become routine.

Shane bought a packet of five pairs of Y-fronts for himself in the Marks & Spencers in town. Oulfella pants. He felt safer keeping the coke in his jocks if he was going to meet someone. To avoid catching the eyes of gardaí, he stopped wearing tracksuits and caps.

In the run up to Christmas, he made more than a grand a week. He bought loads of clothes – throwing the bags and tags away before he brought them into the house, hoping his purchases wouldn't be noticed. He bought a new phone and an iPod. He got his ma Chanel perfume and a gold necklace at Christmas. She loved jewellery. The girl in the shop had helped him pick it, given him advice on the style – she could see Shane was flustered and embarrassed in the women's section. He got Lydia a pair of Ray-Bans – she was off to Tenerife in January. He told them both he'd gotten the stuff cheap in TK Max. They were too pleased to query. Shane was delighted to see how happy they were fussing over the presents, especially his ma, looking in the mirror with the necklace on her. It didn't take away from it that they didn't know how much he'd spent.

He didn't mind that the presents they got him were

cheap in comparison. He knew they spent what they could afford. The largest whack of his own money went on himself anyway, for clubbing. Neither his ma nor his sister had any way of knowing how much he spent on a night out. Taxis replaced buses, vodka and Red Bull replaced cider – €12.60 for two vodkas and a Red Bull. Shane drank them like water. Faster than he drank water.

He never took drugs when he wasn't drinking, and he only went out once a week, usually on Sunday night. Yokes left him comatose for days afterwards, depressed and lethargic. By the time he'd recovered from the Sunday-through-Monday session it was Thursday, and customers were ringing again. When the weekend ended, so did business, and then time to start the process all over again. The ability to resist lashing into his own coke meant he realised far greater profits than his mates. Although all the lads were now on the sidelines of drug dealing, people like Shane and Chops could make money out of it, while people like Chalkie and Dotsy were likely to end up caught, shot or in debt. Those who would never see a penny of true profit from it were the very ones who'd pay the heaviest price.

After Christmas, Shane lodged two grand in the credit union. His account hadn't been used since he'd withdrawn his confirmation money, so the new deposit lifted the balance to €2,003.12. January was slow in comparison to December, but things picked up again after a month or so. It wasn't anywhere near as busy as Christmas, but Shane was selling just under an ounce a fortnight.

As he sold more and more, Shane had switched from Teetha to Creatine for mixing. It turned out that Teetha was only homeopathic anyway – a load of bollocks despite

Griffo's recommendation. The Creatine, a body-building supplement, was less expensive and less granular, more akin to cocaine.

His customer base kept expanding. A girl from his area who he'd gone out with for a week or two in secondary school, Cynthia, put him on to a friend of a friend, Rory. Some Southside-type fella. He started buying at least an eighth a week off Shane – paying €100 above the odds. In return for the extra cash, Shane would break Rory's portion straight off the rock, leaving it unadulterated. Rory quickly became his best customer, providing a steady income.

Unable to hide his growing expenditure from his ma and sister, he told them he was earning a few quid helping Chops DJ. Both Lydia and his ma liked and respected Chops, so his was a good name to drop. Shane thought about moving out with him, the two of them maybe getting a little apartment or something. Solve their parental problems. His ma went out after work on Fridays, and down the local most Saturdays, so his busiest evenings were safe enough. And Lydia was always in work or over in her fella's gaff now. But Shane was still worried his ma or sister would cop something. Or, worse, his oulfella. It was only a matter of time. Not even that he was selling – they were bound to cop that he was taking drugs, with the state of him after being out. The drug routine was taking over his life, he was missing more and more college days. The accumulating backlog of assignments overwhelmed him.

He used the few skills he had learned in his Communications class to compose a letter informing the college of his decision to quit his course. He hadn't been going to bother saying anything, but his sister pressured him to let them know. She advised him to blame it on 'personal reasons'. If he wanted to go back at some stage, it would look better than just dropping out and saying nothing, she said. Lydia didn't even try to persuade him to stay. She knew that would have been fighting the tide. She didn't have the time to discipline him. His ma didn't have the ability, and his da didn't have the will. Yet.

Shane asked his sister to hold off telling their ma.

—She's gonna cop it eventually Shane, you're better off tellin her. Do ye want me to tell her for ye?

—Ah, I'll tell her meself when the time's righ. I can't be dealin with her moanin at me. It's the summer soon enough anyway.

—It's only the start of March Shane, said Lydia.

—Not tha long, he replied cheerfully . . .

AN ASSIGNMENT

Introduction to Marketing: Shane Laochra Assignment 1

Q7. The Killbargan Arms is a five-star hotel and spa over-looking a lake and mountain range. It features an eighteen-hole golf course and a Michelin-starred restaurant. Write the text of an advertisement for the Killbargan Arms to appear in a national newspaper (100-150 words).

A7. Killbargan Arms Hotel Ad
Why not come and stay in the Killbargan Arms? You're sure to get your hole on our lovely golf course: it has eighteen of them! The chef in our internationally renowned Mitchelin-starred restaurant is so good he could make a Mitchelin tyre taste nice! You'd have to be a spa not to come and enjoy our spa, which is luxurious and relaxing. Soak your cares away in our hot tub, or boogie your socks off in our nightclub. It's all here at the Killbargan Arms Hotel.

Comments: Shane this is a spirited and energetic first attempt. You display a promising command of the English language. I expect that in future you could avoid spelling or grammatical errors by checking your work over before handing it in. Unfortunately, the humorous content, while ingenious, is inappropriate for an advertisement of this nature. I wonder if you took the brief seriously? Five-star hotels generally don't have nightclubs. You also fail to make the word count. Mark: 60 percent (merit). —Gareth Deasy, Course Coordinator

3

A romantic at heart, Shane loved finding significance in coincidence. Out viewing apartments with Chops, he grasped what he took to be a sign, and pressed his friend to take the seventh place they looked at. Purely because of a nautical picture on the bathroom wall.

—Did ye see tha anchor in the jacks? Shane asked.

—Yeah? Chops replied.

—It's a sign, get it? We should put down anchor there! Chops shook his head.

—I'm tellin ye! Shane pleaded.

—A sign? I saw a sign as well. A big one outside. It said 'McCreevy Letting Agency'.

But Chops didn't put up too much resistance. He'd grown weary of searching. Every place had had a slew of people viewing it. On top of that, landlords and agencies were reluctant to let a place to two working-class youngfellas. To get past this they'd courted a girl to come along, hoping it would make them a more attractive prospect. Shane got his cousin Janet to play the part of Chops's girlfriend.

They hadn't been able to agree on any of the places they'd seen, though. Either Shane had a problem with the location, or Chops didn't like it for sound – he wanted somewhere with good insulation so he could play his decks. Or else Janet didn't like the decor.

—Wha the fuck do you give a shite abou the fuckin wallpaper for? asked Shane laughin. —You're not gonna be livin there!

—Oh yeah, she laughed. —I was just gettin into character an I forgot fer a minute!

Shane turned his attention back to Chops.

—Look man, it's nice and new. It's in town. Wha more d'ye want? he asked.

—I dunno, bit of character maybe, Chops replied. —I saw on *Location, Location, Location* tha ye shouldn't take a place if ye don't *adore* it.

—*Adore?* Will you get a grip! We're only rentin, ye mad yoke.

—I suppose.

It was a small but fresh two-bed apartment, in a newly developed block near the back of the Ilac Centre.

—Least it's on the Northside, said Chops.

—Ah c'mon, ring yer man Chops, see if he'll give us it, said Shane.

—Fuck it, I suppose it's as good as anywhere! We prob'ly won't get it anyway. Here Janet, you give him a bell. A fine young lady's voice can work wonders.

—Alrigh . . . I'll just tell him we want it, yeah? asked Janet.

They'd submitted work references and letters of recommendation from other landlords. All fake. Friends and relatives were recruited to supply phone numbers in case someone checked.

When Janet rang the agent, she could hear him shuffling through papers to find the relevant documents. There was silence as he examined the file, but then he made a spot decision.

—OK, have you got the deposit today?

She looked at the lads, who nodded eagerly.

—Yes.

—OK, you've got the place. I can meet you there at half four, he said, not waiting to see if the time suited. —I'll bring over the lease, direct-debit forms, a spare set of keys and we'll be done.

—Great, thanks very much! said Janet, excited.

—See you then.

Rent was €1,500 a month, deposit the same. When the agent turned up with the lease, the landlord's and witness's signatures had been filled out in advance.

In theory, Shane's ma still believed his only income was the €200 or so he got from Social Welfare, plus a few quid from helping Chops with the DJ'ing. In reality, she had noticed he was showing a fair bit of cash. She didn't realise the full extent, though – she turned a blind eye. Deep down, she knew it would have been fruitless to pursue the matter. She sensed in Shane a new . . . will. An energy, a direction that might be diverted temporarily but not stemmed. So she chose to believe the story he invented about getting a place cheap.

Part of her was reluctant to see him go, and she didn't encourage him to leave, but there was relief too. She didn't work at the start of the week, and these were the days Shane would be in the depths of his drug-induced depression. Surly, lethargic, irritable. The low mood seemed to infect the house, draining her too. Then he'd be hyper as the weekend started, making her anxious. The only day he'd get out of bed before three o'clock was his signing-on day.

On Griffo's advice, Shane had started collecting the dole as soon as he'd dropped out of his course.

—Ye need a bank account, said Griffo in his rapid fire manner, —especially if yer movin into yer own place. Unless you're Bertie, wha? Rent, utilities, ye'll need direct debits. But ye can't just be depositing cash, cause if the Old Bill ask any questions, you'll have no explanation and you'll be fucked. So leave the bank account for yer scratcher, and keep the money ye make elsewhere. If ye've any left after them mad ones you do be on!

The Social Welfare office had been deserted, there was close to full employment. But only one counter had been open, so Shane still had to wait ages. Like applying for college, the student grant, his driving licence, the process itself had been bewildering and torturous for him. To top it off, the oulwan behind the desk was an absolute geebag. Shane had read the graffiti while she had gone off and filed forms:

OISIN LOVES TARA '04

PAULY FITCH LOVES COCK

I RODE YOUR MA

SHUT UP DA YOU'RE DRUNK

Eventually, he had managed to get signed on. They weren't asking questions once you had the paperwork.

Although he'd moved in with Chops, Shane hadn't advised them of his change in circumstances. Suspicious of all officialdom, he kept signing on using his ma's address. He'd never have been able to explain how he could afford to live in an apartment in town anyway.

The first night they moved in, Chops and Shane went out to celebrate. It was a Monday, so they just went to a little club off Dame Street, RuailleBuaille. It was always busy with midweek drinkers, mostly restaurant and bar staff on their nights off. A few students as well.

Chops and Shane sat at a little table on their own, the single tea light illuminating their faces as they spoke. They discussed chat-up lines, competing to see who could remember the dirtiest or the cheesiest.

—Is your da a baker? offered Chops. —Cause you've sweet buns.

—Woeful, said Shane. —Ah them chat-up lines, they're gas but they don't work, man. They just look at ye if ye come ou with somethin like tha.

—You have the best lines alrigh, said Chops.

—Wha? said Shane.

—Sure a few lines of charlie'll get half the birds in Dublin to drop their knickers these days! Chop ou a bit of the oul devil's dandruff, next thing ye know you're hockeyin her out of it!

Shane pondered this as he sipped his pint.

—Well c'mere, don't get the wrong idea, but do ye wanna line?

—Sound, Chops smiled.

After snorting two each, they danced to the retro sounds in the club. 'Charly' by The Prodigy felt appropriate. SL2's 'On a Ragga Tip' came on and they gave it loads.

—Fuckin love this tune! Chops shouted.

On the way back from the dance floor, Shane's attention was caught, magpie-like, by a beautiful girl. She had platinum hair, a short, dramatic cut. Without thinking, he stepped in front of her.

—Ah howye! I haven't seen ye in ages! he improvised instinctively.

Her face broke into a smile but her eyes betrayed nervousness instead of recognition.

—Howye! she said, frantically trying to recall his face.

—What's the story. How are ye keepin?

—Grand yeah, you? she asked, still smiling and searching.

—Ah not a bother. Have ye seen Sarah?

—Sarah?

She let her puzzlement show itself.

—Yeah Sarah . . . from the flats, tried Shane.

—My flats?

—Yeah.

—I don't know any Sarahs in my flats, she said frowning.

Chops watched from a discreet distance, supping his pint.

—C'mere missus I don't know ye at all, Shane admitted. —I only said tha so I could talk to ye because you're so goodlookin.

—Aw ye bastard!

She put her hand on her heart.

—You're after givin me a frigh there, she continued, breaking into a smile. —I swear to God I was thinkin to meself, 'Aw shite, who the fuck is this fella? Was I talkin to him some nigh when I was locked out of me head or somethin?'

—C'mere, what's yer name anyway? he asked.

—Elizabeth.

—Shane. Nice to meet ye Elizabeth.

As they shook hands nerves started to creep up on Shane. He'd acted on impulse and didn't know what to do or say next, but she broke the ice.

—Howye Shane. Ye fuckin prick.

They laughed.

—Well listen it was nice meetin ye Shane. Me friends are waitin on me.

—Yis're leavin already?

—Yeah we're goin up to Harcourt Street.

—Well now tha ye know me, are ye gonna give me yer number?

—Mmmm . . . I dunno now. I dunno if I trust ye. You're after lyin to me already, she teased.

—God loves a trier.

—Yeah but he hates a chancer . . . Go on then. 085 . . .

Shane entered her number in his phone, tryin not to let his hand shake. Talking to such a beautiful girl allowed his anxiety to surge past the drink, a process expedited by the hefty lines he'd done.

—Righ, nice talkin to ye Shane.

Elizabeth smiled and gathered herself to leave.

—Goodbye kiss? he ventured.

She looked up at him, thinking. She looked around. She'd only come back to go to the toilet, but her mates weren't looking for her yet.

—Alrigh then go on. Quick one.

—Righ.

His heart beating loud in his chest, he bent in and put his lips to hers. His breath was caught short with nerves before they met, but he composed himself as she pressed her soft mouth against his. Full lips sticky with gloss. She set the pace, gently pinching his lips with hers, rhythmically. Then the deep heat of her tongue, held soft, the way he liked it, flowing back and forth against his. Slippily chafing. The relief in that warmth swept over Shane. Success. All that mattered. Affirmation of the only true kind. Her smell then, a zest of yellow flowers.

As he caught his breath again, he inched forward on his feet, and she copied, pressing herself against him, her form a welcome weight against his body. Their breathing quickened and they pushed together harder, middles meeting. Hearts beating, blood pumping. Pulsing stiffer with each throb, growing eagerly. Eyes closed in a dark world, they tarried. The only intruder was the rhythm of the music heard faintly in the background.

—ELIZABETH!! GO ON YE GOOD THING!

Snapped out of their dream, they pulled their faces apart, still clasping each other, pressed together at the middle. Her mates stood a little away, coats and handbags in their arms.

—Ye said ye were goin to the jacks! one of her mates shouted. —Is tha Jack?

—Fuck off youse!

Elizabeth blushed, looking down and giggling.

—I have to go righ? she said to Shane.

—Yeah no bother. I'll text ye later, said Shane.

—Later? I though ye were gonna bring me out on a date? she said, teasing, but serious too.

—I'll text ye tomorrow and we'll arrange somethin for the weekend then, yeah? said Shane.

—COME ON ELIZABETH WILL YE!

—OK, I have to go. Byeee!

She gave him a quick but firm kiss on the lips, then legged it up to her mates.

—See ye Jack! one waved at Shane.

—See yis!

He waved back, smiling. Chops appeared, slapping him on the shoulder.

—So . . . which line did ye use?

—None man. All natural. Just got talkin to her and lobbed the gob. We just clicked – love at first sight. So much for your cheesy lines. And I don't need to use coke to get me hole either pal.

—Ask me bollix, laughed Chops. —Fair play though man. She was fuckin nice, I'll give ye tha much.

—Yeah she was a little dinger alrigh, wasn't she?

—Where's she from?

—I dunno . . . The flats in town, but I dunno know which ones.

—Oooooh Jaysis, ye have to watch them townies pal! Chops laughed again.

—I'd watch her twenty-four-seven man, said Shane. —No bother.

—Sure, we're townies ourselves now anyway I suppose. Technically. I seen ye gettin her digits there, when are ye gonna text her?

Shane wanted to wait now. Show her he wasn't after his hole. Not *just* his hole. Savour the anticipation. He reckoned she was the best looking bird he'd ever kissed. He was buoyed up by the prospect of kissing her again. More. He was almost glad she was gone so he could relax and chat with Chops, enjoy his achievement. After he texted her there'd be the wait. Would she text back? Plenty of times he'd texted birds and they hadn't texted him back. Some gave bogey numbers in the first place. Usually the ones he actually fancied. Until he texted her, it was stored in the bank, though. Elizabeth. A romantic prospect.

The two lads danced again and got pissed, Shane hyper. He felt like a youngfella after a sporting victory, light and full of energy. Once again, the ever-present feeling of inferiority had been allayed, temporarily replaced by triumph. He went up to the bar to get a round in, slyly pushing his way to the front. The drunkening crowd didn't notice his skipping. At the bar, he found himself pressed next to a pale brunette with no make-up.

—You smell nice, wha're ye wearin? he said, brash and easy after his earlier success.

—It's called 'Sui Dreams', she said in a soft voice, well-spoken.

—Sweeh dreams?

—No, Sui Dreams. 'S-U-I' dreams. It's by Anna Sui. A designer.

Shane found it difficult to decide if she was being very polite or very condescending.

—Oh, he said, feigning disappointment. —Here was me thinking it was your natural aroma.

She laughed despite herself, shaking her head. He chatted to her a bit. She was shy, more sober than Shane, only on the verge of tipsy. They talked about DJs they'd seen play. She knew her house music and that was a green light for drugs as far as Shane was concerned. Everyone who was properly into house did class As.

—D'ye wanna go and do a line? he asked her.

She looked around.

—Where?

—In the jacks. There's only one doorman in this place, he won't catch us.

—I'm not going into the gents.

—The ladies then.

She thought.

—All right.

Close to that stage of drunkenness where there is no thinking, just doing, Shane took her hand and led her quickly down the back of the dark little club to the ladies' toilets. She pushed the door tentatively and looked in, then she nodded to Shane and they entered. Hurriedly, they found a cubicle and bolted themselves in.

She brushed against him while closing the door. Shane felt his desire solidify as he smelt her sweet fragrance again. He looked her up and down while she had her back to him for that second. Glancing away as she turned back, he fumbled in his underwear for the bag. She averted her eyes, giving Shane the opportunity to return his stare lustfully to the full form of her arse. The intensity of his arousal made him catch his breath. Mindful of Chalkie's theorem, he noted that she was wearing flats, a pair of runners just. Her clothes were plain: black trousers and a black top with a little sprig of lace.

—Have ye got a key? Shane whispered.

The landlord's agent had forgotten to bring a spare key, so Chops held the only set.

—My handbag and stuff is in the cloakroom, she whispered back.

—I'll just use a coin.

Scooping a large bundle onto the edge of a fifty-cent piece, Shane chatted in a hushed voice. He snorted first, putting her at ease. She'd heard stories of girls being offered coke that turned out to be ketamine. She sniffed off the coin bashfully, having asked Shane to look away. The coke swept away her reservations though. After they'd each done two coins, Shane kissed her. Maybe Chops was onto something after all, he thought to himself.

Kissing turned the girl's edgy nerves to arousal, and they stumbled as they pushed against each other. They could hear another girl moving about and flushing a toilet in the next stall, but they continued. He noted her svelte waist and pert thighs as he ran his hands over her body, then clutched her arse. He moved his right hand around her waistband to her belly, and there was no resistance as he flattened his palm to push it down the front of her trousers. The feel of hair on her mons stiffened him more, and then he found welcome wetness as he pushed further down. A milestone in a fumbling transaction. That shocking odour, startling and arousing. The sweet smell of success, as Chalkie liked to say. The words resounded in Shane's head as he and the girl did what they could in the cramped cubicle.

—Eh . . . d'ye wanna just leg it back to my gaff? he asked her.

She hesitated.

—I don't know . . . Where d'you live?

—Just at the back of the Ilac. We've an apartment there, he panted proudly.

Back in the body of the club, the music had stopped and the lights were on. Shane found Chops chatting to two girls at an adjoining table. He used this as an opportunity to find out his own girl's name. He'd neglected to remember, when he'd asked her at the bar.

—This is Chops, he introduced.

Chops and the girl shook hands.

—What's yer name luv sorry? Chops said.

—Laura, hi.

—Howye Laura. This is Rachel and eh . . . Fiona? Chops stumbled, gesturing to the two girls at the table.

Everyone shook hands. There was a cute fat girl and a hot blonde who seemed prickly.

—Are yis all gonna come back to the gaff and we'll have a bit of a shindig? said Shane, backing Chops up.

Chops's two girls looked at each other. The fat one was well up for it, but the other one was sceptical. She was a pain in the hole – Chops hoped she would fuck off and leave him with the fat one. They both agreed to come though, after exchanging some unspoken correspondence through telling glances, frowns and eye movements.

Back at the gaff, Shane emptied what remained of the coke onto the table, and then chopped it into lines. Only one each. He wasn't gonna open another bag unless some-one was paying.

Girls rarely paid for it though. Shane had noted long ago that at parties there were always at least as many girls doing coke as fellas, but not a single one of his regular customers was a woman. They'd just take it if it was going. Fellas were as thick for dishing it out though. Birds did well out of coke in other ways too. None of the gangsters' mots risked getting locked up, but they defo shared in the profits, and then some. What was the point of selling it in the first place, the point of buying designer clothes, the point of going out on a mad one – only to get your hole anyway. What was the point of doing anything except for birds?

Chubbygirl abstained from the coke, Chops gladly taking up the extra. Laura drank a bottle of beer with Shane before he took her hand and led her to the bedroom. He'd been less impatient than usual. After their dalliance in the club, it seemed getting his hole was definitely on the cards, so there was no need to pursue it so determinedly. Chops's nattering and Chubbygirl's giggles covered their departure. Even the prickly girl was loosening up and starting to smile, eyes wide, erect in the chair as she flew on the line of strong coke. Shane left his personal supply uncut.

In the bedroom, Laura and Shane kissed eagerly, undressing each other. The place was sparsely furnished, but there were fresh covers on the bed and the room looked clean and new at least. Once naked, she lay back. Shane went down instead of rushing to push inside her – he wanted to relish her body. He prostrated himself before her then lifted her legs. She shut her eyes and relaxed, spreading open.

Pleasing her pleased him. He savoured her taste and smell, immersing himself in the now. He revelled in her, marvelling at the chance to explore a woman's body totally unfettered. He wanted to see, touch, smell, taste every part of her. Every millimetre of her. To worship her carnally. She groaned and moved against him to find her own pleasure. He was glad at how free she was: she'd been a little reserved and awkward when they had talked at the bar. But here there was no pretence, no acting, no attempt to hold anything back. The light was still on as they let themselves go. Giving was receiving in the exchange. They licked and grabbed each other. Squeezed each other forcefully. They fucked roughly and gently. Slowly and fast. The drink abated his spleen – otherwise it would have come quickly to extremes. Even still, he soon had to pull out to rescue the moment.

She lay with legs open, slowly squirming, still enjoying the sense of physicality. Shane drew his hand up her thigh, then gently pressed two fingers into her. She groaned. He worked his hand deep in her vagina, and she put back her head again and closed her eyes. Guttural groans registered her approval when his movements were right. While she validated his actions vocally, he clutched at her faster. Her wetness thinned then spilled. He redoubled his effort at this new sign of approval. She squirted water on his hand, her face contorted, acceding to the event loudly and without shame. Shane moved his hand quicker, the juice splashing now. A sanctifying sprinkle, fragrant rose water. Aspersion confirming his rights in this communion.

Although Shane was unconcerned at the seeping wet patch spreading across his new bed set, he was surprised by the amount that splashed from her. Enthralled at the sight, he wondered what the fluid was. It wasn't piss – it was too clear. He licked her again, tasting it as she pressed herself against his tongue. Feeling even more free after her demonstration, he pushed her thigh up, motioning for her to turn over. She jostled around in the bed, eager to accommodate after Shane's efforts to satisfy her. She lay flat on her stomach.

He admired her lithe, pale form: smooth skin with hardly a blemish – tight on her tall frame, but with a healthy bulk of ripeness. He licked the near invisible gossamer hair at the bottom of her back. She squirmed, shaking in near giggles, mismatched with her serious expression. Shane gauged her reaction as he moved lower, and felt her sudden shifts and moans as assent. He ran his tongue down the centre of her lower back, into that crevasse, shocking himself. Strange sensation on his tongue. Another shocking odour, though faint, followed by more intense arousal. She lifted and pushed back, opening, legs wobbling. A deep moan, affirmation again. He churned his tongue against her, losing himself. It was a sacrament. Deep and sincere pleasure, nothing better. All for this.

Over the night they napped and returned, repeating the same actions again and again, if a little more restively. She stayed until after midday, and then left politely without breakfast. A waitress in town, she explained she had to go home and get changed before work, so she wasn't going to bother taking a shower in Shane's. They exchanged numbers and a dozy languid kiss at his door.

Shane was dazed but happy. One want satisfied completely, he returned to bed, savouring a wank while running the night's experiences through his head. But he found he couldn't drift off afterwards. Lying awake, he wondered if the chubby girl was in bed with Chops. Or the prickly one. Or the two of them even. He'd made too much noise with Laura to glean anything of what went on after they had left the sitting room.

His mind flitted back to Elizabeth, and he considered texting her straight away, but then decided against it. He'd wait until tomorrow. Although his encounter with Laura had been one of the most pleasurable he'd ever experienced, he felt none of the anxiety that signified romance. No trepidation, no connection on that level. He was still delighted with himself though. He had Laura's number, he'd been intimate with her in every way, he'd see her again. But Elizabeth was a different prospect. A prospect of potentially more value.

After a short, intense sleep, Shane pottered into the sitting room. Chops was watching telly. They'd only the three bog stations until the NTL got sorted.

—How's Don Juan? said Chops, not moving his eyes from the screen.

—Look who's talkin. Did ye get yer hole or wha?

—Rode the little fat one, said Chops.

—Grand!

—She went to the jacks, and I nipped in after her on the sly, lobbed the gob and then got her into the room. Got straigh into her, but tha other bitch knocked in, moanin about bein left on her own. Just when I was abou to shoot me load as well.

—So after five seconds then?

—Fuck off you.

—Shite though, tha wagon ruinin it on yis, said Shane.

—Yeah, load of bollix. Cock-blockin tramp.

—Were they Southsiders or wha were they?

—Culchies.

—And wha happened then?

—Yerwan said she'd be out in a minute. I went at her again and was just abou to blow me muck *again*, and yer one starts knockin *again*. Freaked, so I was.

—Ah well. It's still your hole though I suppose.

—Ah yeah. Every hole's a goal, as they say. No need to ask you how ye got on, said Chops. —I'd say half of town could hear yer one screamin. I thought the Garda were gonna come knockin on the door any second, lookin for a fuckin murder victim.

—Was it tha loud?

—We were in stitches in here, so we were. Even tha geebag.

—Jaysis . . . Ah, d'ye know wha, fuck it, I don't give a bollix.

—Yeah, fuck it man, she was nice. Lucky cunt ye. Did ye wear a johnny?

—No man. You?

—Always, said Chops. —Ye'd wanna be careful or ye'll end up riddled.

—Ah, I'll be alrigh. It's not like she was some dirty yoke.

—Dirty or not, wha if ye end up polin her? I don't want any of your little snotty-nosed rag-arsed brats runnin around me new apartment!

—Ah, I didn't cum inside her pal. D'ye think I'm tha thick?

Shane's eyes twinkled. Chops smiled.

—The face? asked Chops.

—You know it.

Chops patted Shane on the back.

—Good man, good man.

That had been the highlight of his encounter with Laura. He'd been pleased when she'd shyly agreed to let him cum on her face. But then, when he pulled out just in time and started to let go onto her, she'd stretched her neck up to make sure it covered her, then opened her mouth and slipped out her tongue to taste it. She'd lapped at it as it spurted onto her, delivering Shane into euphoric ecstasy. Seeing the way she enjoyed it was too much. He almost fainted as his cock spasmed, shooting more and more of his egg-white-thick cum all over her face. It was acceptance: swallowing something that had come from deep inside of him, taking it into herself and liking it. Shane had never felt such a release, such relief.

Chops and Shane chilled out together for the rest of the day, enjoying the freedom of their own space, away from parents and elder siblings.

The next day, their mate Mick gave them a hand moving the rest of their stuff from home. He was the only one of the lads who drove. Or at least the only one who drove legally. There were a few other things to sort out: installing the NTL, setting up the direct debits. Shane had to get a key cut for himself, because he didn't want to contact the letting agent again for the spare. The relationship was tenuous enough, considering the false references. And the fact that Shane and Chops both sold drugs.

Tired that evening, Shane composed a text to Elizabeth. He'd texted the waitress girl, Laura, the day before and had got a reply. Texting Elizabeth summoned nervous tension though. He carefully constructed the message. He read the drafts over and over, changing things around but trying to keep it casual-sounding. Eventually, he settled on a final draft:

Well missus, what's the craic? Sorry about the pretending to know ye thing, but needed an excuse to come over and say hello. How was the head yesterday morning? —Shane(the goodlookin fella)

Cheeky, but nice. Should do the trick, he thought.

He hoped she hadn't met someone else up on Harcourt Street. Some older fella. A culchie. A fuckin Gard in Coppers, even. Sick of deliberating, he firmly pressed 'Send', and then put the phone down on the table. Chops was sitting in the armchair beside him, but Shane didn't mention who he was texting. If she didn't text him back, he knew his head would be wrecked – if Chops knew as well, it would just add to it. He wanted to be able to buzz off Chops, to try and forget about it if Elizabeth didn't get back to him.

For the first few minutes, it was all he could think about. He glanced at the phone every now and then, even though it would have rung if she had texted. He felt antsy, unable to sit still. He even sent himself a text to make sure there was no problem with his phone. After an hour went by, the doubts in his head were confirmed.

Even though he didn't know the girl, he felt foolish and exposed for having thought she'd want to meet up with him, for having texted her at all. It even took some of the fun out of the new apartment. He stayed in on his own that Friday.

Chops had a gig in a little club that night. He'd been practising in the sitting room most of the day.

—Hope ye don't mind the noise pal! he shouted above the music. —Have to practice a bit of Richard Nixon on the Gregory Pecks fer tonigh!

—Ha ha, I like it, said Shane.

Chops was making a mix CD. Shane enjoyed the few tunes, a bit of distraction from his disappointment.

—The best way to get ready for a gig is to record a mix, Chops explained.

—Yeah?

—Yeah, if ye just bang on the decks and mess around, ye just get sloppy, there's no motivation to keep the mixin tigh ye know.

—Ah your mixin is always tigh, said Shane, sincerely.

—So's yer sister's fanny.

—Fuck off you, Shane laughed. —She wouldn't piss on you if ye were on fire.

—I know, I set meself on fire once to see if she would. C'mere did ye text either of them mots from the other nigh? Chops asked.

—Yeah I was textin yer one tha stayed here.

—Laura, is tha her name?

—Yeah, yeah, her. I'll keep her offside as a backup, ye know. Deadly in the sack she was man.

—I know. I might as well have been ridin her meself yis were tha loud, said Chops.

Shane decided to come clean about Elizabeth.

—I text yer one Elizabeth as well, the blondie little mot, but she never text me back.

—Phone probably dead or somethin.

—No man. Delivered and all the message was, said Shane.

—Maybe she'd no credit to text ye back.

—Nah. Blanked I am.

—Well fuck it man! Plenty more fish in the sea. Sure ye got yer hole tha nigh anyway, I wouldn't be worryin bout it pal.

—True, true. Are ye gonna see tha little fat mot again?

—Yeah. Wanna finish wha I started there. Get her ou withou tha other geebag followin us around actin like her fuckin chaperone. I'll probly text her later when I've a few gargles on me. If her mate's not out, I'll meet up with her, try and get her back here. Have to break me seal in the new gaff ye know!

—Fuck it man, go for it. Sexy little yoke.

—Yeah, I like a bird with a bit of meat on her.

—She must like a fella with a bit of meat on him too.

—Fuck off you, ye scrawny AIDS victim.

When Chops left, Shane's mood sank again. He was still disheartened over his rejection. He texted Laura again, and then he was even more downcast when she didn't text back either. Probably working, he told himself. But she'd answered his previous text while she was in work.

He met four customers that night, each getting a oner bag. Two he met on the street, the other two he knew from his area, so he had them call up to the apartment. It was a toss-up: he felt safer in the apartment, doing it behind closed doors where there was no chance of the Old Bill noticing you. But he didn't want to throw the eye on the place either. The neighbours would cop that something was up if there were people calling to the gaff all the time. So he kept it to a minimum.

The best compromise was meeting people in their cars. Most of Shane's new customers were older and driving. He'd hop in, and they'd drive around the block. He'd leave the cocaine down by the gearstick, and they'd have the money out waiting for him so that there was no need to be handing things to each other. That was the best way. He resolved to buy a car himself soon.

He was amassing money more quickly than he could spend it. Even though he was blowing hundreds every time he went out, he'd €1,900 in cash stashed back in the bedroom of his da's gaff, €3,007.12 in his credit union account, a

grand in the apartment to cover the next ounce, and a few
hundred quid from the dole in the bank to cover bills. Now
he also had €400 in his wallet, pure profit. Less than a year
earlier, he'd been unable to imagine what having a grand
would be like. Now it was normal for him to make more
than that in a single week.

But the cash didn't allay the insecurity that gnawed away
at him as he stared at his blank phone. He took it as a judg-
ment of his worth that the girls hadn't replied.

He'd given them his original number, not his new
number, which he kept for customers and Griffo only. He
made no personal calls on the drug phone, because if anything happened, he wanted to be able to deny it was his.

He never sent texts. If the Gards weren't actually tapping
your phone, they couldn't retrieve past conversations, Griffo
had told him. They could only get the times, dates and dura-
tions of calls. But phone companies stored texts indefinitely.

Shane kept telling customers not to text anything illicit,
but they kept on doing it. From the posh fella his ex, Cynthia,
had put onto him:

Hey man. Can you get any e's or do you just sell coke? Rory.

From a number he didn't know:

Hi Shane, Jenny here. I'm a friend of Rory's. He gave me your
number. I was wondering if it might be possible to get a
wonder bag off you tonight? Thanks.

He'd laughed at that one. A 'wonder' bag. She meant a 'oner'
bag. *Sounds good though. Should rebrand them as wonder
bags*, he'd thought.

From Scully, one of Chalkie's mates, at 4 AM:

WATS UP AV U COKE?

Shane hadn't even replied to that one.

He'd tried to get customers to speak in code, even when they were talking on the phone, but drunk people weren't the best at being discreet. One of the gay fellas had rung him only a few days after Shane had told him not to mention coke.

—Hello? Shane said.

—Howye.

—Alrigh . . .

The fella paused as he tried to figure out how to get across to Shane what he wanted, without mentioning the word 'cocaine'.

—Eh . . . Ye know that stuff that you like to *sell* . . . Have ye got any of that?

From then on, Shane gave up on trying to get customers to be circumspect.

Now, one phone was glaringly busy in comparison to the other. Still brooding over the fact that the girls hadn't texted him back, he put both phones on silent and tried to sleep. He fell in and out of consciousness, and couldn't stop himself from checking the personal phone every so often to see if either of the girls had texted. He knew now that he wasn't going to hear back from Elizabeth, and he was unlikely to hear from Laura either.

He was still awake when he heard Chops stumble into the apartment. The chubby girl's voice was loud in the hall before Chops's laughter signalled the close of the other bedroom door. Shane kept his ears peeled, but didn't glean any slagging material, just muffled voices. Eventually, he sank into real sleep, yet the concern over his romantic failures was omnipresent, invading his dreams.

The sun was shining when he woke at ten the next morning, picked up his personal phone and saw that the display read:

1 message received

Satisfaction tempered Shane's anxiety. It was only the night before he'd sent Laura the message, she might have left her phone at home when she went to work. He pressed 'Show', and then felt a flutter as he read the opening lines.

> Hiya Shane, it's Elizabeth (the goodlooking girl). Really sorry 4 the delay! We didn't end up going to Harcourt Street, we met our gay mate (he's a hairdresser too, wouldn't you know) and ended up at a lock-in in some gay bar. Left my phone charging behind the bar and forgot it I was in such a st8! Only got it back now. Sorry! The head wasn't great the next day. How about you? Don't worry about pretending to know me it was funny :-) How did your night go?

At least they had something in common! Shane thought. A lot in common if it was the Pink Pound she lost her phone in. While gleefully composing a reply to Elizabeth, he felt the buzz and ring of another text. It was Laura.

> Hi Shane. Sorry was SO busy last night couldn't text back. Yeah I'd be up for drinks during the week, I'll know my roster Monday so gimme a shout then and we'll arrange. Ciao! L x

All his worries vanished, and an involuntary smile permeated his face. *The two of them!* he thought. *Fuckin deadly!* And a real long message from Elizabeth – she seemed keen.

He felt giddy. In the bed, a wave of elation made him tense his toes with delight. He wanted to see where things went with Elizabeth – she was smart, beautiful. Dogwide as a townie should be, yet without being hard or cynical. Unpretentious. Comfortable in herself. But then she was girly too, she had manners. Class. Elegance even.

He sprang out of the bed and bounced into the sitting room. As he passed through the hall, he could hear Chops and Chubbygirl talking still. *Fair play to Chops*, thought Shane, brimming with goodwill. Not even in the house a week, and they were both banging mots. He switched on the telly, and sat back on the sofa as he thought about what to write back. He texted Laura first, to get it out of the way. Then he replied to Elizabeth:

> No worries Elizabeth. Thought ye fell down a hole or somethin. Yeah we had a good night, we staid on in ruaille buaille then had a bit of a party back in the gaff. Nothin major. We only moved in this week still have to christen the place properly! Do ye fancy meetin up for a drink durin the wk?

Her reply came swiftly and they exchanged texts:

> Ooh u have to invite me to your housewarming so. Who do you live with? I'm off this week, no work. Holliers woohoo! off to playa del ingles 2morro morning with the girlys and gonna try stay off it then for a fortnight. But if u wanna go 4 a meal or something ill be back monday could meet you tuesday night x

> Sounds good missus, I'll book us in somewher for tuesday night so? Just live with one of the lads. Never asked you what you do for a livin? We didn't talk much the other night!

> I know, shocking! Eh do you not read texts? Haha I'm a hairdresser, thought you'd be able to tell by my stylish cut anyway. Only messin luv :-)

I noticed the 'do' actually, very nice. Different than most grls I like it. I thought ye werent gonna reply to me at all when I didn't hear back from ye!

A kisser that good, course I'd text back ;-) Ah I was raging when I left my phone there, all the girls were slagging me. It was shut then when I tried to get it the next day, then with sorting out stuff for the holiday and work I couldn't get it till now. Glad now we got in touch in the end, it will be nice to see u again. Maybe even talk to you a bit this time!

They texted back and forth for a while longer. The speed of her replies and the length of her messages made it clear that she was keen. As keen as he was, maybe. She texted him during her holiday too – every day for the last few days of it. Neither of them held back or played games. They were both too young, too eager. Too alive. He liked the way she wrote. Bright and cheerful. Sweet and feminine.

Life felt good for Shane, with this romantic prospect and the new apartment. Being so close to town meant it was easy to meet customers who rang on the spur of the moment. Plenty of people only got the goo for coke when they had a few jars on them. Shane would run down and meet them in whatever pub they were in – he preferred this to meeting them on the street. He and Chops talked about pooling their resources. Some customers wanted yokes and coke at the same time, so it made sense to just do it all together. They resolved to go in on a joint order of a thousand ecstasy tablets and a couple ounces of cocaine.

Chops put a small bookcase in the sitting room. He read a good bit and had loads of books for college as well.

—What's tha? . . . Brendan . . . Behan. *Borstal Boy* . . . Is tha any good? asked Shane.

—Yeah it's deadly. Take a lend of it there if ye want, said Chops.

—Jaysis Chops, the amount of books ye have. Did ye ever think about writin a book yerself?

—Ah yeah. I'll write an autobiography. I'll call it *Barstool Boy*. Or *Portrait of a Piss Artist as a Young Man*.

Shane didn't get it.

—Are ye dreadin the end of the summer and havin yer head proper stuck in the books again?

—Nah, be deadly when I go back in September man. All them student nights in town, and I'll be the only fella in the college with me own place! All the fanny'll be back here!

—Just as long as you're sharin the wealth pal, said Shane.

Dropping out of college wasn't an option for Chops. He knew what he wanted to do with himself, and that his course would get him there in the end. His ma, a culchie, had gone to university herself. She'd always encouraged him to read, since before he started school even. And she'd read aloud to him since before he could talk. All that had prepared him for his studies.

Chops tried to persuade Shane to go back to college, but it wouldn't wash. It wasn't the same for Shane. He'd never been encouraged academically, beyond being made to be physically present in the school building. His ma and da had never had even that much encouragement, and they had thought that once he turned up at school, he was bound to learn, as if by some sort of osmosis.

Shane did still read the odd time though. He added some books to the shelf. He'd left the kids' ones at home – the Roald Dahls and that – even though he still liked reading them. He lined his books up on top of the bookcase to keep them separate from Chops's. *The Mammy*, Brendan O'Carroll. *The Chisellers*, Brendan O'Carroll. *Martin Cahill, My Father*, Frances Cahill. *The General*, Paul Williams. *Hard Cases: True Stories of Irish Crime*, Gene Kerrigan. *King Scum: the Life and Crimes of Tony Felloni, Dublin's Heroin Boss*, Paul Reynolds. *Terminator 2, Judgement Day: The Book of the Film*, James Cameron and William Wisher. Chops had a glance but didn't borrow any.

As the day of the big date with Elizabeth drew closer, Shane felt like he'd already got to know her, with the number of texts they'd been exchanging. The day before she got home, she admitted that she was nervous about meeting in person, because it had been built up so much. He was relieved when she suggested compromising her 'fortnight off the drink' by having some wine with the dinner. She also suggested going Dutch on the bill:

> Don't think you're going to be paying for me as well by the way, I'm working I have my own money, we go halves OK? I'm not being smart I just hate girls who just expect the fella to pay for everything. I'm not like that myself but I know loads of girls like that, so just thought I'd say it first. Hope you still like me when you see me now, feel like a pig after this holiday! Defo being good for the rest of the summer. Well after our date anyway!

Shane sought some advice from Chops on restaurants.

—Well, it's a fine balance, Chops mused. —Ye don't wanna take her somewhere too fancy on a first date, cause then the two of yis'll just be paro sittin there if it's real quiet an all. But ye don't wanna take her somewhere cheap either, or she'll think yer a waster – *know* you're a waster in this case. Somewhere in between that's a bit lively is your best bet. Would ye not be better just takin her out fer a drink though?

—That's wha *I* said, but *she* said she wanted to go fer a meal cause she was off the gargle after her holiday.

—She's not drinkin? said Chops, incredulously.

—No, she's drinkin now cause she said she'd be too nervous otherwise.

Chops was confused.

—Would yis not just go fer a few pints so?

—Ah, I'm after sayin I'd take her ou fer dinner and all! said Shane, exasperated. —On the bright side, she said she wants to go halves on the bill.

—She's a keeper tha one, said Chops.

In the end, on Chops's recommendation, Shane booked Tante Zoe's, a Cajun restaurant in Temple Bar. It took a little convincing, as Shane didn't really understand what Cajun food was. The only thing Cajun that he'd had before was spicy Cajun wedges from Centra. They were nice but.

Elizabeth asked him to meet her before they went into the restaurant. He'd suggested The Temple Bar itself. Shane knew she'd be late on purpose to make sure he was already there when she arrived. He was early. He just got a longneck bottle of cider while he was waiting. She was only ten minutes late.

—Heye!

She smiled and hunched her shoulders cutely as she walked over to him, high heels clopping on the flagstones.

—Howye! Good to see ye at last.

He kissed her on the cheek, smelling her light fragrance. She fanned her face with her hand. She looked even better than Shane remembered.

—Aw, I was scarleh walkin in, I was like, 'He's not gonna be here.' I got real nervous an all I don't know why!

—Ah, course I was gonna be here! I wouldn't leave ye standin.

—I know, I know, I was just panickin nearly, I swear to God.

—Ah, there's no need to be nervous, I don't bite.

—Ah, I was grand once I seen ye, it was just walkin in ye know.

—Wha're ye drinkin?

—We better head in should we?

—Eh, I booked the restaurant for half.

—Ah grand. Em . . . I'll have a white wine so.

—Sound. Sit down there, he said.

Nerves hit Shane as he stood waiting at the bar with a fifty in his hand. He felt good though. She looked great, her sweetness was charming. She wasn't a complete 'howye', but she was still a real Dub.

—Can I've a bottle of Bulmers and a glass of white wine please? Shane asked the barman.

—Chardonnay or Sauvignon Blanc? the barman asked quickly.

—Eh . . .

The bar was busy. Shane didn't want to go back and ask Elizabeth: he couldn't remember the names the barman had said anyway. He blushed, feeling stupid as the barman hovered and the fella beside him in the queue stared.

—The first one, said Shane.

—Chardonnay?

—Yeah.

The barman twisted the top off the wine bottle before

placing it on the bar. Shane put the little wine bottle in his shirt pocket, then, already holding his cider, he took the wine glass carefully, afraid the stem would snap. He was used to pint glasses, which were more robust.

Because he was going for a meal, Shane had dressed differently than he did when he went out dancing. A button-down collar shirt instead of a clubby T-shirt. Shoes instead of fashionable runners.

—They only had Chardonnay, he said to Elizabeth when he brought back the drinks.

He'd read the name on the label again as he handed it to her, just to make sure.

—Ah that's grand, whatever, I'm not fussy.

—I know. You're out on a date with me sure.

She laughed.

—Ah it's good to finally see ye – it feels like I know ye *ages* now, she said.

—Yeah it's gas isn't it? I was only sayin to Chops there today, it's weird goin to meet ye on a first date. It feels like I know ye so long.

—And wha did your mate say when you said tha?

She sipped from the wine glass.

—He called me a sap.

Elizabeth had copped Shane was up to dodgy dealings of some sorts. The way he spoke and his demeanour kind of gave it away. It added to the attraction. He wasn't too brash with it either though. He'd spun her the same old waffle about making ends meet helping Chops DJ.

They finished their drinks and made their way to the restaurant. Waiting to be seated, Shane had another attack of nerves.

—Hello, said a smiling waitress, a foreign girl.

—Eh, I have a table booked for half eight.

Chops had told him what to say.

—For how many people?

—Just the two.

—What's the name?

Shane didn't know whether to give his second or first name.

—Eh . . . Shane.

The waitress put a line through his name with a yellow fluorescent pen.

—Shaaaaane *Layoh-chah*, she pronounced to herself quizzically. —Follow me.

She looked at them and smiled, taking up some menus. They ordered a bottle of the house white first. The only wine Shane knew he liked was Buckfast, so he was happy to go along with Elizabeth's choice. He'd drink any type of gargle that was put in front of him anyway.

Once he'd figured out that one of the books was a wine list, Shane perused the menu, glad to see that he knew what some of the dishes were. He couldn't choose between Buffalo wings and barbecue spare ribs. Then he thought about the mess. *Fuck that*, he thought, *better have the potato skins.*

It was a toss-up between the steak and the chicken for mains. He picked the steak. The chicken on the menu was 'blackened', and he didn't like the sound of that. Plus, the Cajun wedges came with the steak. She ordered first anyway. Chops had warned him about that.

—I'll have the Buffalo wings and the Tante Zoe Jambalaya please, she said.

It impressed Shane that she was so relaxed. He was nervous

enough at the thought of eating in her company at all. His ma wasn't one for restaurants, and Dubs matches were the only time he spent with his da that wasn't in the pub. His da had never even gone into a cinema, let alone a restaurant, with either of his kids.

The waiter looked at Shane.

—I'll have the potato skins for starters . . . Eh, I'll have the steak for mains . . .

—The fillet or the striploin?

—Eh the sirloin.

—Sorry Sir, it's striploin we have. Is that OK?

Shane had read it as 'sirloin'. He'd never heard of striploin.

—Grand, yeah.

—And how would you liked that cooked, Sir?

—Medium.

—Meeee . . . diiiii . . . um.

The waiter scribbled laboriously. *What the fuck is he writin, his fuckin life story?* thought Shane.

—An I'll have the ice cream for afters, said Shane, snapping the book shut.

—Um, we don't take that now, Sir. We'll come back for your dessert order, is that OK?

Shane flushed as he handed back the menu.

—Grand.

—Can I get you anything else? OK for drinks?

—Yeah, we're grand, thanks very much, said Elizabeth, keen to allay Shane's embarrassment.

The wine soon relaxed Shane, and they both eased up as he felt more comfortable in the restaurant. Elizabeth hadn't started eating out until she'd left school. Her parents weren't ones for restaurants either, but she was naturally confident and self-assured – she had no bother going anywhere. Especially since she'd started hairdressing.

She'd got her start in a local salon: work experience in transition year. They'd kept her on after, but once she was qualified, she'd got a job at a trendy place in town. She loved it – meeting all kinds of different people. Rich oulwans coming in to get styled and coloured, vain young men paying way over the odds for a haircut. The gay fellas she worked with were great craic. She went out to eat with them a good bit, to the poshest restaurants in town sometimes.

As Shane and Elizabeth chatted, it transpired that it *had* been the Pink Pound she'd left her phone in. When Shane told her the same thing had happened to him, she'd been amazed. (He left out the bit about his da pulling him out of the place, and that he'd ended up puking and shiteing all over the kip).

—That's gas but isn't it! she said. —Maybe it's a sign.

She said it in a jokey voice, but a sudden contemplative look revealed that she saw significance in coincidence too.

—D'ye believe in that stuff? Destiny and all tha? she asked.

—Ah yeah, defo.

She was impressed when he told her about the anchor convincing him to take the apartment.

—D'ye believe in star signs and all tha? she asked.

—Ah, I wouldn't really bother with them meself now, he said.

The truth was that with a dull credulity, he always read his horoscope in the *Herald*.

—Oh I believe in tha stuff, she said. —One of the fellas

in work, he does my chart for me and all. Honestly, it'd amaze ye the stuff tha does be true.

—Yeah?

—Yeah. You should get it done. Ye'd be surprised. He told me I was gonna meet you.

—*Me*?

—Yeah!

—*Me* like?

—Well not *you* you – he didn't say I'd be meetin some fella called Shane who was a cheeky little fucker like. No, he said someone new was goin to surprise me soon, and that I shouldn't let the opportunity pass.

—Jaysis.

Shane was superstitious enough to be mildly impressed by the soothsaying. Conversation flowed over dinner, and they enthusiastically agreed to go for a drink after. They went to Gogarty's. Shane brought her upstairs to see the music. His da had taken him there once before.

—D'ye like Irish music? Shane asked Elizabeth.

The band were on their break.

—All that *diddle-e-i* shite? No, I wouldn't be into tha at all now, she said.

—I mean ballads an all? he asked.

—Ah, me oulfella's into all tha. The 'RA music an all. It wouldn't be me now, I have to say. Are you into it yeah? she asked.

—I like a few ballads the odd time like.

Shane loved rebel songs, but he didn't want to strike a note of discord by pressing it. He wasn't into proper trad music. To him, Irish music meant songs that told a story. Traditional tunes sounded all the same to him – musical wallpaper.

The band returned to their positions and lazily took up their instruments before the oulfella on guitar started belting out songs at a furious pace. The crowd was almost exclusively composed of tourists. He sang 'Down at the Red Rose Café', about a little place near the port in Amsterdam. It was one of Shane's favourite ballads, but it wasn't really a rebel song. It conjured up images of red lights and little café bars. White Europeans drinking small glasses of beer. Cocaine and prostitutes. He'd never been to Amsterdam.

—See the ballads don't have to be 'RA songs, he said. —Wha d'ye think tha one?

—Woeful! she said, laughing.

—Jaysis, I took ye to the wrong place. We'll go somewhere else after this so.

—Will anywhere else be busy? she asked.

—Eh, I dunno now, let me think.

Despite the bad call on choosing the pub, Shane could tell she liked him. She'd been impressed that he didn't have any problem telling her that he'd been in the Pink Pound. Her closest friends were gay lads, and it had caused major issues with her last fella.

—D'ye wanna go to the George? she asked, when Shane failed to come up with a suggestion. —Nowhere else will be a bit of craic on a Tuesday night.

—I don't mind, said Shane genuinely.

—C'mon so.

They linked arms and walked over Dame Street. The big purple nightclub had a fluorescent pink palm tree outside. Across the street there was a hair-restoration clinic with a sign that flashed interrogatively: 'Why go Bald?'

It was Shane's first time in the place. He enjoyed looking

around, feeling comfortable with a woman beside him. There were fellas dancing away, big groups mingling and single men at the bar on their own. After a second or two, Shane realised that some of the crowd were actually young women. Boyish-haired and -attired girls in groups together. There were a good few straight girls there with the gay fellas. Some lads were blatantly gay – flamboyant and feminine. Others just looked like normal Joe Soaps. Shane was surprised to see oulfellas there.

Seated on a luxurious purple row, Shane and Elizabeth hadn't got through their first drink before their lips were drawn together. Because it had been built up so much, Shane had been worried about kissing her. In the moment, it came naturally.

Her kiss rekindled the memory of the night they had met – her smell and voice. They were less intense this time around though. They took their time, kissed slowly, and then stopped to sip from their glasses and have a chat. She had vodka and Diet Coke, he had vodka and Red Bull. She'd bought these ones. When it was his round, he bought four vodkas, one Diet Coke and one Red Bull.

She noticed some fellas she knew, and waved them over. They were a little shy around Shane initially, but they made him feel welcome. After just a couple of minutes of banter, they were a confirmed group. Shane was glad of the company – they made the date go easier, reduced the pressure, and he knew Elizabeth was enjoying the craic too. It boded well too, he thought, that she already felt comfortable sitting with him as a couple in the eyes of others.

Just as Elizabeth had copped that Shane was probably selling drugs, Shane guessed that she was probably into doing coke. You could just tell. And going out on the gay scene. Especially the Pink Pound. Defo.

—C'mere, I've a bit of bag there. Just a bit left over from the weekend, he lied. —Do ye wanna do a line? I won't do it if you don't fancy it like.

—Eh . . . yeah I wouldn't mind. Where will we do it though? said Elizabeth neutrally.

—I'll just give ye the bag, you go on up yourself and do one. I'll do one after.

—Are ye sure?

—Yeah! No bother, go on ahead, he said.

When he passed her the best part of a quarter ounce, it was clear that it wasn't just a bit left over from the weekend.

—Jaysis, the size of it! she said.

—That's wha ye'll be sayin later sweetheart.

—Shut up! Fuckin prick! she laughed. —I'll get ye back in drinks for it righ?

—No yer grand luv, it's only a line. Ye don't have to buy me gargle, honest to God. Me and Chops just got it in for the weekend and then ended up not doin it, ye know. Sure yer doin me a favour takin a bit off me!

He had three fresh oner bags on him as well – in case he got a phone call during the night. He worried about losing customers to other dealers if he missed an opportunity to sell. He fiddled around with his phones, which he'd taken out to get at the bag in his pocket. He hadn't kept it in his underwear with the other bags. He'd been planning to give Elizabeth a line, and hadn't wanted to be sticking his hand down his jocks in front of her.

—Oh, two phones. Bogey! she said jokily.

She didn't ask any questions though – she took off to the

ladies. When she came back sniffling, she looked buzzed.

—That's deadly coke! She said.

Shane was glad she was impressed. After she gave him back the bag, he took the gay fellas up to do coins in the jacks. He got them to walk up before him so that they'd be less conspicuous. This place wasn't like the Pink Pound – ye couldn't just run amok and do whatever you wanted. When closing time came, Elizabeth and the gay fellas huddled in conversation.

—Do ye wanna come back to a party? Elizabeth asked Shane.

—Eh, yeah, whatever. I'll go if yis are goin back.

—Righ, we'll go back to Dermo's gaff so.

—Cool.

Shane wondered if a couple and three gay fellas going back to a gaff technically constituted a party, but he was happy enough to go. He didn't expect to get his hole off Elizabeth that night anyway, so he was glad of an excuse to just prolong his time with her. They took the short walk to Christchurch, where Dermo lived. He had a small but fashionably decorated one-bedroom apartment. Shane asked him what he did for a living.

—I work for the Revenue Commissioners.

—Jaysis sketch – I better watch out so, Shane joked, and they all laughed.

Though it wasn't openly acknowledged, it was obvious to everyone what Shane did for a living. They didn't ask him about his work at all, which was enough to communicate they knew he was a drug dealer.

Shane spilt some of the bag out onto the table, and they all did lines with a note Elizabeth rolled up.

—Jaysis that's lovely, Dermo said. —D'ye think you'd be able to get me some of that?

—Yeah no bother man. Here take me number.

Shane got Dermo to buzz his drug phone so he had Dermo's number too. He was starting to get sketchy about taking calls off numbers he didn't recognise – paranoid about the Old Bill.

They all had a great laugh, joking and slagging good-naturedly. The gay fellas accommodated Shane and Elizabeth, making sure the two could sit together.

—Here, d'yis wanna do yokes? suggested Dermo.

—Do ye have some there?

—Yeah I'm just after rememberin.

—Fuck it why not man, yeah.

Some yokes would be nice. A different buzz than coke. Dermo brought them out. He had exactly five.

—Lovehearts.

He put them on the table.

They were very well pressed, neat and clean with a waxy sheen. They didn't have a logo embossed on them – instead, they were actually moulded into little hearts, and coloured pink. Shane had never seen pills that weren't round tablets, he gaped at them through his coke-and-drink haze.

They came up on the pills quickly – definitively – in only about twenty minutes. There was no problem differentiating them from the effects of the coke.

—Jaysis man. They just hit ye like tha don't they? Shane clicked his fingers.

—Fuckin unreal they are, said Dermo.

—Aw I'm fuckin mad out of it! Elizabeth said, her jaw moving and her lip protruding, wobbly.

This made her no less attractive in Shane's eyes, and he leaned in to kiss her. She put her hand behind his head and rubbed his hair gently, opening her mouth and extending her tongue, unselfconscious in front of the lads. Nobody felt awkward, not with the buzz they were on. The gay lads chatted and listened to a funky-house CD – Hed Kandi – while Elizabeth and Shane wore the face off one another.

—D'yis wanna go down the earlyhouse? asked Shane, realising it was already half seven in the morning, opening time.

—Fuck it, I won't be goin into work today anyways. Not in this state, said Dermo. —Let's do it.

Because it was midweek, they were the only crowd of party people in the earlyhouse, though the usual array of grizzly oulfellas were lined up at the bar. There were also two rough-looking townie youngfellas sitting in one corner drinking pint bottles, protuberant jaws showing that they were on E.

Elizabeth's friends got Shane's drinks as thanks for the coke. He'd scooped the remainder of it up and brought it, sticking it in his jocks, where it nestled with the oner bags. Shane and the gay lads did a few more lines together in the jacks. When Shane got back to his seat, one of the townies was sitting there talking to Elizabeth. Shane sat on a stool, since the fella was in his seat on the bench beside her.

—Alrigh, said the fella.

—Alrigh, said Shane.

—Any bag?

—I've a bit there alrigh to sell yeah, said Shane.

He placed the emphasis on 'to sell'. Shane didn't appreciate the fella's brazen attitude, or him pouncing for Elizabeth as soon as he'd got up.

—Wha have ye? Oners? the fella asked.

—Yeah.

—Do us a fifty bag.

He stared at Shane.

—I'll go halves with ye on a bag yeah, Shane said, trying to remain impassive under the fella's stare.

—Go on give us it now, I'll get ye the money off me mate.

—Ah, cash up front, I don't know ye.

—Here you'll be graaaand, the fella scorned, eyes narrowing. —We'll give ye yer money!

—Don't know ye mate, Shane shook his head.

—Give us a tester then.

—I'll do a tester with ye when ye have the cash.

—Tut, hold on.

The fella rolled his eyes before going back over to confer with his mate. Shane reprised his place on the bench beside Elizabeth.

—Scumbags, said Elizabeth.

—Who are they? Shane asked.

—Ah they're just knackers, they're not gonna buy anything off ye Shane.

The fellas came over and asked again about the coke. They also asked Shane if he was with Elizabeth.

—Yeah that's me bird, said Shane, put on the spot.

He wasn't overly intimidated by them. What would they do? He had Griffo to back him up – if they got proper smart, he'd drop his name. The lads took leave of the couple again anyway, disappearing off and allowing the table to relax.

—Fuckin hell those Es are lovely, Shane told Dermo.

—They are aren't they? That coke is very nice as well.

—This cider is lovely too, joked Shane.

—Yeah everything's great today, Dermo said. —The world is just rosey!

—Some first date, one of the gay lads slagged. —The George and the earlyhouse!

—I know how to treat a lady, Shane laughed.

—Sure it was *me* draggin him to the George! said Elizabeth. —C'mere I've to go to the loo, back in a mo.

—Do ye want the bag? Shane asked quietly as she stood up.

—No, I just wanna powder me nose.

The lads erupted into laughter.

—Ah yis know wha I mean, said Elizabeth, laughing as Shane shifted on the seat to allow her pass.

Remembering his hefty pocket of coins after the night's drinking, Shane went up to the jukebox. Since he'd started selling coke, he'd developed the habit of paying for everything with notes, discarding any coins into a jar on his bedside table. The cash he made from dealing was just quick money to be spent.

He loaded the jukebox with money and selected tunes. Chops had been exposing him to lots of new music – different types, not just dance. It was hard to remember what to pick when he was gargled, but he managed to come up with a few: 'Weile Weile Waile', The Dubliners; 'Colony', Damien Dempsey; 'Hold Me', Damien Dempsey; 'Ego War', Audio Bullys; 'I Fought the Law', The Clash; 'Party On', Damien Dempsey; 'Shot You Down', Audio Bullys.

Vocal stuff suited the earlyhouse better than dance. House music wrecked the oulfellas' heads.

Concentrating, Shane tried to recall more songs so he

could get rid of his weighty bundle of change. Snapping him out of this daze, he felt someone push up against him. He turned sharply, frightened. It was only Elizabeth. She took his arm in hers and bent close to him, with a serious expression.

—C'mon we get ou of here, she whispered pointedly in his ear, then looked at him raising her eyebrows.

Still dulled by drink, Shane failed to grasp her earnestness, noticing instead how well-plucked her shapely brows were. Perfect rainbow shapes above her eyes, expressing the neatness and order that typified her appearance. Could eyebrows be a girl's best feature, or was that weird? he wondered for an instant.

—What's up? he said, surprised she wanted to leave already.

He'd been hoping she might end up coming home with him, but suggesting it herself? This was too good to be true.

—Look at me righ? she said quietly, but with significance. —We have to *go* righ?

She spoke slowly and nodded deliberately in an effort to penetrate his inebriated dopiness. Shane knew from her voice that she was demanding that he comply immediately. He could tell there was something the matter, that she wasn't asking him to go back and have sex.

She led him toward the side exit. As he reached to pull the handle, a bulky fella pushed it from the other side, hitting Shane with the door as he burst in.

—Sorry mate, said Shane, looking up at the fella's face.

Shane recognised him. Paddy Lawless. The fella Griffo had warned him about on his first day in the earlyhouse.

He ignored Shane.

—Howye Elizabeth, said Paddy.

Shane thought he could detect a challenge in the tone.

—Heye, she answered.

Lawless eyed the couple, registering them. Shane felt he could almost hear the machinations of his brain. His face betrayed no emotion – apart from the look of calculation he constantly exuded. He brushed past them without further comment, and Elizabeth hurried Shane out the door.

—What's up? asked Shane.

—Wait till we get around the corner, said Elizabeth.

She was rattled.

—Sorry I had to get ye out of there, she said. —I'm after gettin the frigh of me life.

—Wha happened? asked Shane.

He was startin to feel nervous.

—Hold on till I text the lads.

Elizabeth took her phone from her handbag and fired off an explanatory message to the gay lads. She put her hand on her heart and breathed a deep sigh as they walked along the street. Shane directed her unconsciously toward his gaff.

—What's the story? he asked again.

—Aw I was up in the girl's toilets righ? And I could hear someone in the next cubicle, righ?

—Righ, said Shane.

—It was them two youngfellas tha were askin for coke. They were doin a line in the jacks, they had their own the whole time. They were gonna rob ye Shane.

—Wha?

—They were gonna rob ye. I heard them sayin, 'Wait till he's in the jacks, we'll get him in the cubicle. I'd say he's a loada cash on him an all.'

She put on a different voice for the youngfella's bit.

—Wha else were they sayin?

—I dunno, I snuck ou then. I wanted to get ye out of there before anything happened.

—Jaysis.

Shane pondered the situation. His illusions were under threat of collapse. He was surprised that the two youngfellas would consider such a move – he'd thought they would have assumed he was connected, selling bag. The state of the youngfellas, they looked like they didn't have a washer. Where would they get the neck to try something like that?

It frightened him, but he didn't want to let Elizabeth see he was rattled.

—Well fair play to ye for givin me the heads up. I'll see them again with the lads sometime and see what they have to say for themselves.

—Ah you're better off leavin it Shane. The likes of them'd stab ye soon as look at ye.

—They'd want to have serious backup, Shane said.

—They're just knackers, Shane, seriously, there's no point. Just stay away from them, please. Jaysis I'd feel terrible if anything happened after me tellin ye that.

The bravado hadn't had its desired effect, and he didn't know what else to say about the youngfellas.

—Do ye know tha Paddy Lawless fella? he asked.

Elizabeth looked straight forward.

—I know him to see, from around town, she said, frowning.

—I heard he's a major bogey.

—I dunno, said Elizabeth, scrunching her face, still looking ahead. —He was in the papers a few times and tha.

Shane changed the subject to try and spark her interest.

—What abou the lads?

—Ah I just text Dermo and told them we had to leg it. Told him to say nothin and watch ou for them two youngfellas. They're leggin it back up to the gaff. He's dog-wide. Tha other gay fella they met at the bar is comin up with them an' all! she laughed.

—No way, Shane smiled.

—Aw, I'm tellin ye, the things tha they do be doin. They do be tellin me in work, ye wouldn't believe it.

—Do I wanna know? Shane laughed.

—I wouldn't tell ye. I couldn't bring meself to say!

Elizabeth laughed too.

—Are ye gonna buzz up to the apartment with me? Shane asked.

Elizabeth looked thoughtful.

—I dunno . . .

She squinted, looking up at Shane, fixing her fringe.

—Is there anyone else there?

He looked at his old plastic-strapped sports watch, self-conscious in front of her. It clashed with his neat shirt. It said, '9:08'.

—Chops is probly there, but there's no way in a million years he'll be up at this hour. He hasn't seen 9 AM in years. Except when he's still up from the nigh before.

She thought about it.

— Alrigh so, she said eventually.

It was only around the corner.

—I'm not havin sex with ye now, she said when they got to the outside door of the apartment block. —Just so ye know.

—Ah no bother, we'll just go up and chill ou, Shane said unconvincingly.

The apartment was quiet when Shane entered. They could hear Chops snoring as they passed his room, and Elizabeth giggled, holding her hand over her mouth and tiptoeing up the hall.

—C'mon in here, Shane whispered.

—Is this your room?

—Yeah.

She walked through the door he held open for her, then sat down on the bed. She was relieved to kick off her heels. Her short platinum hair stood out boldly and brightly against her tan, and her colourful clothes were untarnished from the night of partying. She looked beautiful.

Shane joined her on the bed and they kissed. She gently opened her mouth wide and he felt her relax as they held each other. He got her to lie down with him. They lay across the bed, parallel with the headboard, their legs sticking out over the edge. He felt her thigh, then hugged her to him and drew his hand down over her bum. Lovely, he thought, her body seemed perfect to him. Small tits, but daintily shaped – pert and blooming. Breast size wasn't a deal-breaker anyway, big tits were just a bonus. A nice face was the must-have. And a nice arse. Personality was a slippier one to quantify.

Elizabeth wore a thin, low-cut top with flowers and lace around the bust. Underneath, she had on tight black jeans. Finished off with a black handbag and stilettos. Shane put his hand up her top, but didn't go round the front for her tits. Instead, he felt her back, brushing over her bra straps. She kissed him eagerly, moaning. She held her breath for a moment, and they felt a sudden mount in arousal and kissed more quickly. The tipping point had been reached. Elizabeth grabbed him, making it obvious.

He kneeled on the bed and pulled at the front of her jeans. The button sprang open, and she hurriedly undid the zip herself, pushing up her pelvis so he could get them down. He pulled them off her fervently. He noted bright yellow knickers that matched her hair. Her plush figure supplied a healthy bulge around the elastic edges of her underwear. Shane unbuttoned his own shirt, breathing heavily as she took her top off. Her panties were see-through, and he could see only a thin strip of light hair – the rest had been waxed. A little damp patch on her crotch caused a further surge in his desire, and he ripped her underwear down as she moaned, leaning her head back.

Shane licked her out for only for a few moments before she pulled him back up to kiss him on the lips. He could still smell her on his face as they kissed. He used his hand to push himself into her. Tight resistance was followed by a sudden spring which yielded into a hot, wet sanctum of . . . bliss.

They suited each other in bed, pleasing themselves as they made love. As she made herself cum underneath him, Shane could barely hold himself back, the intensity almost frightening him. She relaxed then, still enjoying the sensations, holding Shane with her arms and wrapping her legs lightly around him.

—Are you on the pill? asked Shane softly, looking into her eyes.

—Yeah, she nodded quickly, looking back at him.

—Can I cum inside ye?

—Yeah, she said closing her eyes and holding him tighter, pressing her face against his.

Shutting his eyes and moaning with anticipation, he settled

into a rhythm to make himself cum. It felt appropriate to let go inside of her. Not on her face like with Laura.

He was pushing it into her, working to get over the edge, feeling it all well up inside, ready to be released. The thought of his seed spilling into her encouraged him. A beautiful thing. Love.

Then he felt a hot gush of wetness from *her*. He moaned again at the sensation, familiar from his experience with Laura.

—Oh wait! she said, abruptly pushing him off .

She stared down between her legs, and Shane looked at his own crotch. There was wet blood on his cock, a patch of on the sheets too. For a millisecond, he wondered if she was a virgin.

—Aw, I think I'm after startin something, she said, biting her bottom lip, concerned.

—Are ye alrigh? asked Shane.

He was worried that he had hurt her – or himself, he'd heard stories.

—Yeah, it's just embarrassin, she said.

Shane realised now that it was her period. She looked away, downcast.

—Ah don't worry luv, he said and went to kiss her.

She brushed him off again, firmly, pulling away from him and putting her hand like a visor over her eyes. He thought she was angry and leaned back, shocked. Then he saw her lip tremble, heard a sniffle and saw a tear track down her face.

—Aw sorry, she managed, —you're gonna think I'm such a spa now, I'm after ruinin everything.

Her face was burning red.

—Don't be silly, you're graaaand! he said, putting his arm back around her.

She closed her legs and picked up her top, still crying a little, unable to stop.

—Aw sorry, I'm not usually like this. It's just I had such a good nigh last nigh, and now I'm after ruinin it. I can't believe this is after happenin. And now I'm cryin an all like a thick. You must think I'm a weirdo or somethin. I'll get meself together and go before I start wreckin your head completely.

—Don't be silly, c'mere luv, Shane put his arms around her.

She allowed him to comfort her.

—Seriously don't worry about it missus. They're only oul sheets, he lied. —It's nothin, it doesn't matter. These things happen, it's grand. I had a deadly nigh too, I'm not gonna change me mind over somethin like tha!

—Aw I'm just bein stupid, I'm sorry.

She was still crying.

—It's cool, you're just upset. It's probly the yokes and all makin ye emotional too.

Shane almost had tears in his eyes himself now.

—Yeah, sometimes ye get a bit weepy the next day alrigh, she sniffled.

—Seriously missus, don't be worryin, it's grand.

—Are ye sure?

—Hundred percent. I can't wait to meet up with ye again sure.

—Seriously?

—Yeah.

—I better go now though. —Sorry for gettin ye all worked up for nothin, she said.

—Don't be stupid, we can just chill out.

—No . . .

—C'mon it's cool, I'll get ye a pair of tracksuit bottoms – dark ones.

She laughed and sniffled.

—Are ye sure it's alrigh like? I mean, I'm embarrassed.

—There's no need missus, honest to Jaysis. Sure wha the fuck! It's nothin, said Shane.

—Alrigh. Only if you're sure.

—You're grand!

He got her a pair of boxers and tracksuit bottoms and she disappeared off into the bathroom. He got the spare set of sheets and covers, and he changed the bedclothes while he waited for her. She got into bed, and he had a shower before joining her. They cuddled and chatted for the rest of the day – after she'd given him a wank. Just to get rid of his horn.

Around five in the evening, she got him to call a taxi for her. She didn't want to be seen walking home in his tracksuit. The walk of shame. They set another date for that Saturday – some food again, and the pictures instead of a night out. Shane was glad to keep his Sunday free for going out with the lads.

From that first date, they became boyfriend and girlfriend straight away. They'd ring each other every day, and she'd stay over two or three times a week. Elizabeth was great with people. She never made Chops feel awkward at all. He had no bother that she was spending so much time in the house. He was still riding Chubbygirl, but it was only casual. He'd only text her after being out drinking. If he hadn't got his hole elsewhere.

Shane was open about his drug dealing – there was no

concealing it anyway. He'd pop down to meet customers while Elizabeth waited in the apartment. But they didn't discuss it much. Shane idealised Elizabeth. Idolised her. He took delight in her attentions, elated that she'd chosen him. Of all the people she could have been with, she'd picked him. It seemed so unlikely, nearly impossible.

Yet, while he didn't meet Laura as agreed, he did leave it open by texting her to ask for a rain check. He saw no contradiction between this and the purity of his affection for Elizabeth. The relationship had split his psyche in two. On one side, there was the hard, cold world of slagging and banter with the lads. Taking drugs, dealing coke, and trying to fuck women he met in pubs and nightclubs (a habit he pursued with increased success – his strike rate increasing with his lack of need). On the other side, there was the warm cosy world of food, bed, hugs, companionship, affection and making love that Elizabeth supplied.

Contentment begat complacency. He became reliable only for his more regular, wealthier customers – neglecting the youngfellas from his own area. They only ever wanted oner bags, anyway, and even then on tick. Shane couldn't even be bothered leaving the sanctuary of Elizabeth's arms to deal with the hassle of *collecting* these debts, let alone issuing more.

Luckily, the good customers he did have began to increase the amounts they were ordering. They were from backgrounds that didn't afford easy access to drugs, so they started to pick up coke or pills for their mates at the same time that they were getting their own stuff, taking advantage of bulk-purchase discounts. The arrangement between him and Chops worked well, neither trying to glean a few extra quid for himself from the combined profit. Chops got his pills from Griffo now too, so there was only one re-up between the two of them, every few weeks or so. They took turns collecting it. That was the most nerve-wracking part of the job. Getting caught with a oner bag or a few yokes was one thing. Getting caught with an ounce of coke, or even worse, a thousand yokes, was another. That was likely to bring a custodial sentence.

One day, Shane arrived back at the apartment and found Chops sorting out the latest order on the coffee table. The routine was that Shane mixed and measured the coke, and Chops wrapped the Es into bundles of five in Rizla cigarette papers and then put the bundles into plastic bags, twenty bundles to a bag. Sometimes they sold these bags whole to youngfellas from their area who sold E themselves. They'd give them the hundred for two hundred and fifty quid, leaving around the same profit margin on coke. The rule of thumb was always to *just over* double their money. This allowed for unpaid debts, petrol costs and any other expenses. And for any stuff they ended up doing themselves. They had ideas of eventually moving up, only dealing to other dealers the way Griffo did. But they were making so much money as it was that they felt no rush.

This day, Chops was having trouble of some sort, fumbling with a cigarette paper as he tried to create a cylinder of five Es. He slipped and dropped them.

—FUCK!

The Es rattled like skittles across the hardwood floor of the sitting room.

—Bollix it anyway! said Chops.

—What's the story? asked Shane as he put his food away in the fridge.

—It's these new yokes man, I can't get them into the papers. It's fuckin wreckin me head.

—What's wrong? Have ye the shakes or something? The aul DTs?

Chops was too stressed to have the craic.

—No man, it's the fuckin shape of them, they won't stack.

—Give us a look.

Bending over, Shane picked up one of the tablets that had rolled across the floor close to where he stood in the kitchen part of their main room. He smiled as he felt its familiar shape in his hand: a little pink loveheart.

A Card

To Elizabeth (the goodlooking girl)
From Shane (the goodlooking fella)
Happy Birthday babe, hope you have a deadly one
In another year it will be me giving you 21 kisses!

A Letter

Dear Shane,

    I wanted to tell you how I feel about you, but I'm not good at things like this, so I thought I'd write you a letter instead. I know we've only been with each other a while, but since I've been with you I'm so much happier in myself. From that first date when you were so good about what happened, you've really treated me so well, better than any other fella has ever treated me by far. I know I said it a million times, but thank you so much for the watch, it was the best birthday present I've ever had. I can use it to mark the time I spend with you, and I hope there will be lots and lots of it – at least until the battery runs out. Ha! Seriously though, I'm so lucky to have a boyfriend like you, and I want you to know that I appreciate it so much. You're so important to me, Shane and I'm really really glad that I have you in my life now.

Your girlfriend,
(the goodlooking girl!)
    Elizabeth x x x

4

—Shoot! Chalkie shouted to Shane. —GO ON! . . . SHOOT!

Shane shot and missed.

—AH! . . . Fuck it anyway, he said.

—Bollix, said Chalkie, disappointed.

The lads were all playing football in the shadow of the Wellington Monument in the Phoenix Park. The unexpected September sun scorched them as they swore and blasphemed, chasing the ball in herds. Through the trees in the distance, an army in white played cricket, and they could hear the occasional pock of the ball followed by the echo of claps. Deeper in the park, just out of their sight, a cavalry of horsemen lined up for polo.

Chops's shaved head was very obviously sunburnt. Rubbing the ankle he'd mildly twisted in his attack on the goal, Shane watched an energetic Chalkie run after a long ball. It went far wide of the two jumpers signifying goal posts.

—Are ye alrigh? Chops asked Shane.

—I'll soldier on, said Shane smiling.

They were only playing five-a-side. The pitch they'd marked out was small, and tourists wandered across it now and then. Chops and Shane had persuaded the lads to come into town for the informal game. Shane had given them a lift in the car he had bought a fortnight earlier: a Mitsubishi Colt hatchback, dark green. He'd only suggested playing ball in town as an excuse to drive the lads around.

—ATTACK! ATTACK! shouted their mate Mick.

While Mick always kept fit and healthy, Shane had no idea where the dissolute Chalkie's endless vitality came from. Chops, on the other hand, traipsed around slowly in the track of the ball, his bulkier frame a burden. He was the only one who *liked* being in goal.

—He's a bleedin donkey, tha Chops fella isn't he? said Chalkie to Mick.

—Ye shouldn't be talkin abou yer own teammate like tha, said Mick, laughing.

—It's true though, said Chalkie. —Look at him sure.

They watched Chops rest his hands on his knees, trying to catch his breath, while Shane ran after the ball. Both Chalkie and Mick could have passed for footballers – they were fast, lean and sinewy. Chops, on the other hand, could have passed for thirty.

One by one, their energy dwindled, and eventually they all marched off the field, weary of the contest. No one had bothered to keep score, but the fact that it was a futile exercise hadn't dampened anyone's ardour.

—VICTORY! cried Chops, jokingly, arms in the air as he strolled off the pitch under the shadow of the monumental folly.

Spying Griffo's navy BMW, Shane broke from the ranks. There was a youngfella he didn't know in the front with Griffo, so Shane got in the back. Once inside, he coolly passed his customary brown envelope to Griffo.

—Nice one kid, said Griffo. —Give him tha there, he said to the youngfella.

The youngfella passed Shane a paper bag from Boots. Shane assumed it contained a thousand pills and two ounces of cocaine.

—Very appropriate wha? said Shane.

—What's tha? said Griffo.

—The chemist's bag. If the Garda stop me, I'll just say they're a load of paracetamol.

—Ha ha, that's righ kid. I don't think you'd get away with it though. I never seen green aspirin with shamrocks stamped on them before.

Meeting at the park was a change in routine. It had been Shane's idea. He'd thought it would be inconspicuous, but now Griffo pointed out that Garda headquarters was also in the park. The dangerous part about collecting so many pills was that they wouldn't fit down your underpants the way the coke would. Still, Shane supposed, now that he and Chops were taking turns, the chances of getting caught were halved.

The rest of the lads were going to The Hole in the Wall for a pint, but Shane wanted to get the stuff stashed. He drove back to the apartment carefully, obeying all the rules of the road. When he didn't have drugs on him he was a reckless driver – youthfully oblivious to his own mortality, he'd speed aggressively. He had thought about getting a more conservative-looking car. A family car. Less likely to draw the eye from the Gards. Even with his burgeoning income though, he couldn't afford the premium on anything larger.

The car he got was only a 1.3-litre, and insurance had cost him four and a half grand. For one year. The car itself had only cost four grand. The salesman didn't bat an eyelid when Shane paid cash. Everyone was throwing money around at the time. A less-boyish hatchback – a little Volkswagen Polo or something – might have been better. But Shane didn't want to drive a girl's car.

After he cut the coke and wrapped and stashed the pills, Elizabeth called over with Marks & Spencers food. She came straight from work.

—Heye, what's the story? she greeted Shane.

—Wrecked after playin ball, said Shane.

They cuddled on the couch, watching *The Departed*. It was only just out in the cinemas, but Shane had bought a snide copy on DVD off the Travellers. Even though they were tired, they had to contain themselves from having sex. After the film was over they went straight into the bedroom. In the midst of it, they heard Chops come home from the pub. They paused as he moved about in the hall.

When they heard Chops go into his room, and then the shower starting up, they went back at it. With other girls, Shane'd make loads of noise – subconsciously, it was to impress the lads – but he was protective of Elizabeth and didn't want anyone hearing them. Afterwards, they cuddled, and Elizabeth smiled up at him.

—D'ye wanna do something tomorrow nigh?

She had Mondays off, so she was free to go out Sundays. She usually stayed in on Fridays because she worked Saturdays, but she'd often spend her Saturday night with Shane, instead of going out with the girls. In Shane's mind though, Sundays were for going out with the lads. Reaping his rewards, the fruits of his labours. Sunday nights clubbing, hairdressers and drug dealers. Hairdressers didn't work Mondays, and coke dealers would wait to Sunday to go out because Friday and Saturday they were too busy. Like gardaí and nurses, they were a match.

—Ah I'm already after sayin I'd go ou with the lads, he lied.

There was nothing organised, but his expanding client base and list of friends meant there was no shortage of people to go drinking with. Especially when he was doling out coke.

—Alrigh, she said.

She continued to cuddle him but looked down.

—We'll go for a meal or somethin durin the week yeah?

—Yeah. Alrigh, said Elizabeth.

—What's wrong? asked Shane.

Her manner had changed abruptly. It happened a lot lately. She'd go quiet and stay like that for hours while Shane tried to manoeuvre her into her normal chirpy mood.

—Nothin, she said.

—Go on, wha is it? Shane asked.

—Nothin.

She buried her head deeper into his chest, avoiding his gaze.

—C'mon, tell me. Somethin's the matter.

—It's not, it's nothing, she said petitely.

Although it seemed like she was striving to avoid reveal-ing what had upset her, she knew just what tone to strike to inform him of her displeasure without being accused of get-ting snotty. She was toying with him like a cat with a mouse.

—C'mon, ye might as well tell me.

—No, there's nothin wrong Shane, just leave it.

The change in mood sucked all the contentment out of him. He couldn't relax at all when she got like this. He'd jump through hoops to try and get her back to normal. A few silent moments later, he asked her again. Then again. Then again.

—C'mon just tell us. What's the matter?

—Aw nothin, she began. —It's just tha I wanted to go fer a few drinks with ye or somethin. We *never* do anymore.

—We go ou all the time!

—Yeah but only durin the week. And ye never want to stay ou then, you're always wrecked from the weekend. And I do be workin in the mornin anyway. And town does be shite.

Shane was caught. He knew it was true, but his Sunday nights – leading to earlyhouse Monday mornings – had become a routine that excited him so much he found it hard to even sleep the night before.

He did his best to placate her by promising that they'd go out together some Saturday soon. Telling her he'd get Chops to look after his customers for a night, he promised to go dancing with her. But he put no firm date on it. She snapped back into her usual talkative self though, as if nothing had happened.

It was the drug phone that ended up interrupting the

evening. Shane had to run off to meet customers every hour or so. By bedtime, €600 bulged in his wallet. He stashed €350, and left €250 for his night out, increasing his anticipation. He'd bring a few oner bags to sell too, tucked into his underpants alongside his personal bag. Before the session was over, all of it would be spent, sold, snorted.

When the night arrived, it flew over as usual, ecstasy speeding the passage of time incomprehensibly. Somehow finding himself back at a session with a mixture of gays and party people, he shared out coke and talked the ears off randomers. The E helped, breaking down barriers, encouraging strangers to bond. Temporarily. Shane marshalled them all off to the earlyhouse, managing to persuade everyone in the end, despite the characteristic drunken reluctance to move on.

In the earlyhouse, Shane befriended a giantish Dublin man of about forty. Deep-voiced, with jet-black hair and blue Connemara eyes. The fella chatted freely to Shane, who shared coke with him. They snorted from the tip of a key in the jacks – just like Shane and Griffo had on Shane's first morning in that very same pub.

—What's yer name man? Shane asked.

—Robert. Bob. Bobby, Robbie, wharever ye prefer yerself, said the big man jovially.

When Shane returned to his seat, one of the gay townie youngellas he'd gotten to know from the Pink Pound tapped him on the shoulder.

—D'ye know yer man you're talking to there? he asked Shane.

—Just to buzz off. Why? said Shane guardedly.

—That's *Robbie Boyle*, said the youngfella, with significance.

Unimpressed, Shane looked over at the man, who was standing at the bar with one hand on his pint glass, holding court with a group of oulfellas. With bulky muscles, his large frame dominated the bar, his broad belly sticking out, providing an axis around which the other drinkers circled.

—Who is he? asked Shane.

—Ah did ye never hear of him? He's from my flats.

—Is he a bogey?

—Ah yeah. Everyone used to be afeart of him around the area. He used to be into armed robberies an all. But he's sound. Me da does be drinkin with him down the local an all, the youngfella said knowingly.

Drunk, the youngfella sidled up close to Shane, who sensed that a pass was about to be made. With the joint aim of deflecting the expected come-on, and sobering the youngfella up so he wouldn't get sleazy, Shane gave him a pill for free.

Sliding over to the bar, Shane puffed himself out next to Robbie Boyle. His wiry frame didn't cast a shadow on Boyle's brawn. Shane had to catch his attention by offering to buy him a pint.

—Eh yeah, go ahead there, nice one Shane.

Glad that Boyle had remembered his name, Shane invited him into the jacks for another line.

—Jaysis, fair play to ye youngfella, said Robbie between snorts. —Just wha I needed. You're after sorting me out. On the batter all nigh, ended up gettin a lock-in in me mate's boozer. Ridin some yoke in the jacks, so I was. Had to do a legger on her so just came down here. Dyin! But tha stuff's after sortin me ou. Fair play to ye.

—No bother man, no bother, I've loads there sure, said Shane.

—Put it there youngfella, said Robbie. —There's me hand and there's me heart. I appreciate tha brother.

He was high now, speaking earnestly and staring into Shane's eyes. The personal phone beeped, and Shane took it out of his pocket to find a text from Elizabeth: 'Hiya hun, just awake here thinking about you. Text me when you wake up/get home, and we do something later x.'

His new friend interrupted him in the middle of firing off an appeasing text.

—D'ye wanna go round to me mate's boozer pal? It's just around the corner in the Markets, said Robbie Boyle.

—Yeah, no bother, said Shane, glad to figure in his plans.

—I know the fella tha owns the place – well it's just the lease he has on it. He throws me a few gargles and I keep an eye on things. Make sure there's no hassle ye know, said Robbie. —Don't tell any of these cunts though, he continued.

He was referring to the gays, gangsters, transvestites, party people and alcoholics in the earlyhouse.

—It's like bleedin Fraggle Rock in here. We just leg it ourselves, yeah?

—Sound, no bother, laughed Shane.

They left their drinks and ambled round past the wholesalers unpacking their wares. Forklifts zoomed by dizzily. In the gutter lay nets and empty boxes. Onion skins and dirty lettuce leaves. The zing of veg filled the air.

There was a loud crackle followed by an electronic squawk, startling Shane. The shock deepened as an unmarked squad car pulled up alongside the pair.

—Well Robert . . . How are *you* doing today? drawled a young plainclothes Gard from the car.

—Mind yer own business, said Robbie.

He winked at Shane but otherwise kept a straight face.

—Your usual charming self. And who's your new boyfriend here? said the Gard.

He was young and fairheaded. Stout. Fashionably dressed. The accent and the demeanour would have given him away as a Gard anywhere though. Something about the clothes too.

Robbie shrugged his shoulders. The Gard stared at Shane open-mouthed, with a typically bovine demeanour. The other one, in the driver's seat, leaned over to look too. They both fixed their eyes on him unabashedly while he stood there with his hands in pockets. Shane knew what they were up to. Memorising his face. He squirmed a little under their gaze.

—Have ya anythin ya shouldn't have on ya there? the blonde Gard in the passenger seat asked, noticing Shane's discomfort.

—No, said Shane, taking his hands out of his pockets.

He tried his best to disguise the rush of panic.

—What's your name?

—Shane.

—Shane what? said the Gard with disdain.

—Laochra.

—What kind of a name is that? the driver smirked.

—What's your date of birth? continued the blonde Gard functionally, ignoring his sidekick's comment.

Anytime the Gards stopped Shane or his mates, which had happened a lot when they were younger, they had always demanded their dates of birth. Once Chalkie had given his as '22/25/1987'. The Gard had taken it down, slowly mouthing the nonsense numbers as he noted them in his leather pad.

Since then, Shane had learned from his Business Law teacher during a digression in class that you didn't have to give your date of birth under most Acts. It was probably the only piece of information he'd retained from college.

—Which Act are you stopping me under? Shane asked.

The blonde Gard stopped and glared at Shane even more intently. The only other time anyone had ever looked at Shane that way, it had been just before he punched him.

—The . . . Mis . . . use . . . of . . . Drugs . . . Act, the blonde Gard said slowly.

The way he deliberately pronounced each syllable separately was sinister. Menacing. The other Gard smiled.

—Right, said the blonde one, opening the car door and stepping out.

The other Gard took this as a cue, stepping out toward Robbie Boyle.

—Lift up your arms, said Blondie.

—Woah, said Shane stepping backwards. —Show me your ID first.

Shane also knew that if you were stopped by a Gard in plainclothes, they had to present their ID to you when asked.

—MY ID IS IT? Blondie shouted in a Munster lilt. —Here's my ID. Look!

He pushed the little navy leather wallet that contained his badge and photograph hard against Shane's face.

—Go on look at it! LOOK AT IT!

The situation was developing more quickly than Shane had anticipated. Blondie pressed the ID into his face so hard that he felt the cold metal of the shield dig into his cheek before he began to fall backwards. Blondie grabbed him roughly by the shirt and pulled him back upright, before slamming him against the wall. The other Gard stepped in front of Robbie Boyle, holding out his arms to stop him from intervening on Shane's behalf.

Boyle was in stitches laughing though, his eyes scrunched and watering, holding his hands up. Shane was confused and nervous. Blondie was still furious.

—Get a good look at it did you? DID YOU? he shouted in Shane's face.

Repelled, Shane leaned back again, but pressed against the wall he couldn't get away. Flecks of spit were landing on him as the Gard shouted. He searched Shane with vicious roughness, while Robbie Boyle and the other Gard looked on. Luckily the coke was in Shane's underpants. He only had €150 in cash left on him, which didn't arouse too much suspicion. The Gard jumped on one detail though.

—Two phones eh? Now why would you have two phones? he asked triumphantly, staring into Shane's eyes again.

—One of them is me sister's phone, said Shane, surprising himself with his quick thinking. —She left it at home an I'm just droppin it up to her.

—Which one is your sister's? asked Blondie tersely.

—Tha one, said Shane nodding at the drug phone.

The Gard accessed the messages. Thankfully, Shane had erased all the texts. It would have been full of messages from drunkards asking for coke otherwise. He felt blessed he'd thought ahead for this eventuality. But the Gard still viewed him with suspicion for having two handsets, especially in the company of Robbie Boyle. He spent a while scrolling through the phone before handing it back to Shane. He then took Shane's name and address briskly. Shane gave them his old home address, not the address of the apartment. They didn't even bother searching Robbie, just retreated grumpily back to their car.

—Look after yourself now, the Gard said sarcastically as he slammed the car door shut.

Robbie Boyle waved at them before they sped off.

—See yis now, he taunted.

—Fuckin pricks, said Shane under his breath.

—Ah don't let them get to ye brother, said Robbie. —They're only geebags. Fair play to ye stickin up for yerself. I had to laugh though when he got ye in the face with the ID. Gas.

The pair talked about the incident as they walked to the pub. The Mercury Lounge. A scaldy little old kip with a tiled front. The shabbiness of the building made it look as if the pub had itself taken to drinking, and gone the same way as its clientele. It was busy enough inside: a few middle-aged hardcore drinkers reading the racing pages, and older ones wobbling about the bar. They weren't quite as far gone as the wizened oulfellas who populated the earlyhouse. These men looked like they still had homes, maybe even jobs. But they were on the same path.

—Howye John, said Robbie to the barman. —Give us a pint of Smithwicks and . . .

He turned to Shane.

—Wha're ye havin?

—Bulmers, said Shane.

—And a Bulmers when yer ready, said Robbie.

—No bother, said the small, busy man.

He passed them the pints without asking for payment.

It looked like he'd have trouble maintaining order in the place on his own. The customers looked rough and drunk. Not a great combination.

Eager to capitalise on his contact with a fella who had a reputation, after a while Shane allowed his drunkenness free reign and put a question to Robbie.

—D'ye mind if I ask ye something? said Shane.

They were alone in the men's toilets.

—Go ahead brother.

—Eh . . . would you know where I'd get me hands on a shooter?

Robbie Boyle's mean eyes flickered, interrogating Shane.

—Wha d'ye want it for?

—Ah, just in case ye know.

—Who's botherin ye?

Lately Shane had grown more and more nervous. He felt like something terrible was going to happen at any moment. He coveted a gun for the feeling of protection he thought it would lend.

—Ah no one. Just a bit of . . . insurance ye know.

—I migh be able to put ye in touch with a fella who has steel, alrigh . . . but ye better not be settin me up, said Robbie, staring aggressively at Shane. —It wouldn't have anythin to do with me righ?

—Sound yeah.

—Alrigh brother, take me number. But don't mention anything over the phone. An ring me from a payphone if yer ringin me righ? This phone is blemmin.

—Sound.

—No bother brother, said Robbie.

The free drink poured as the pub grew busier. A group of women from the flats came in to drink the day away, some in their pyjamas. Robbie chatted with them when they came up to the bar, but he didn't try it on with any of them.

—Tha crowd? More trouble than they're worth, Robbie explained. —They all have husbands or boyfriends. Most of their fellas are locked up. Get ye killed so they would, the women.

Matching Robbie pint for pint left Shane full and tired. He wobbled down to the jacks to ease the pressure on his bladder. He glanced in a toilet mirror and found that a drunk Robbie had followed him.

—Have ye anthin for the head there brother? Robbie slurred.

—Yeah no bother, managed Shane.

There was only a few lines left in the bag, and Shane pressed it into Robbie's hand.

—No man, it's your coke, you dish it ou. I'll get greedy if ye leave it to me, Robbie said.

A young man came in and nodded at Robbie, who stared him down as he entered one of the cubicles. The fella didn't notice Shane, but Shane recognised him straight away. It was the youngfella who had approached him in the early-house asking to buy coke. The youngfella who Elizabeth had overheard plotting to rob him.

Shane grabbed Robbie's shoulder and pulled his head down to whisper in his hear.

—Tha youngfella was gonna rob me in the earlyhouse one of the mornings, he hissed urgently.

151

—Tha fella there after goin into the jacks? asked Robbie, quiet and businesslike.

The noise of the extractor fan covered their conversation. But they were so close they could hear the youngfella's piss splatter.

—Yeah.

—Are ye sure it's him now? Robbie asked.

—Hundreh percent man.

The youngfella had a pudgy frame with skinny arms. A distinctive ratty face. He was even wearing the same clothes he had been the day in the earlyhouse when Elizabeth had warned Shane about him. Blue jeans with worn loafers. And a snide-looking Lacoste polo shirt with multicoloured stripes.

—Righ, said Robbie, as Shane heard the youngfella unbolting the lock.

Brawny-handed, Robbie used the side of his large fist to slam in the cubicle door just as it opened. The youngfella stumbled back against the jacks, eyes wide in fright as Robbie filled the doorframe, broad-shouldered.

—Alrigh? said Robbie.

—Wha? What's up? said the youngfella.

He was frowning, trying to hide his panic.

—D'ye know me mate here? said Robbie, gesturing to Shane.

The youngfella looked at Shane but didn't recognise him.

—No, said the youngfella, scowling. —What're ye after pushin in the door for?

His breathing was fast and heavy, he knew what was coming.

—Cause I want to talk to ye, said Robbie. —Did you try and rob this youngfella?

—No I fuckin didn't!

—Ye were fuckin goin to though, said Shane, savouring the moment.

—Wha're ye talkin abou?

—Yeh fuckin were! Me bird heard ye talkin abou it with yer mate in the jacks in the earlyhouse.

—Shut yer mouth you, ye spoofer, said the youngfella, opting for a more robust defense.

—Don't get cheeky now, Robbie warned.

—I'm not gettin smart with *you*, said the fella. —This youngfella's wafflin ou of him. I never even seen him before in me life!

—Are ye sure that's him Shane? Robbie asked again.

—Defo, said Shane.

BOOM! Robbie punched through the youngfella's face. The fella's legs went from under him, his hands slipping over the flat partition of the cubicle as he grasped fruitlessly to steady himself. Adrenalin soared through Shane, but he felt a lump in his throat.

BOOM! BOOM! BOOM! Three more punches, full force. The youngfella slipped in the piss on the floor, groaning sickly.

—Go on. Get him, said Robbie, stepping calmly out of the doorway.

The bloody and broken youngfella slid further down, crumpling onto the cubicle floor. Shane felt more anxious than angry. The blood pulsed in his ears though, and after a moment's hesitation he began kicking the fella, swinging back to boot him ineffectually in the sides and the legs. He could hear Robbie breathing intensely beside him. After a couple of seconds, Robbie grew frustrated and pulled Shane away roughly.

—Here, move over, he said.

Robbie took his turn at kicking, stamping on the youngfella's body with his tree-trunk legs. A dull thud signalled the sickening force of each blow. Shane's football-style kicks were weak in comparison to the barrage of stamps Robbie meted out. Without speaking, Robbie continued. The youngfella was now emitting a strange guttural groan. It seemed involuntary, alien almost.

Shocked at the violence of the attack, Shane felt sick. Nothing like the films. He pulled at Robbie's shoulder to catch his attention.

—C'mon, we better leg it.

Saying 'He's had enough' would have seemed weak. Robbie dished out a final stamp, then spat on the prostrate form. He looked at his handiwork for a moment, breathing heavily now from the exertion of issuing the savage beating.

—Cunt.

As the pair turned to leave, the barman walked in, quickly gauging the scene.

—Ah Jaysis Robbie, said the barman.

—Sorry John but it had to be done. Ye'd wanna watch who ye do be servin.

—Ah Jaysis.

The youngfella slipped around on the wet floor, barely conscious, piss from the tiles soaking into his clothes. Along with his blood. He made no attempt to get up. He just lay there twisting and bleeding.

—Ah Jaysis.

—In fairness John, it had to happen eventually with the crowd tha does be in here. Don't worry. It'll send a message.

—Ah Jaysis though, said John shaking his head and staring down at the bloody mess on the floor. —Wha am I going to do with him? he asked, trembling.

—D'ye want me to throw him ou for ye? asked Robbie earnestly as he wobbled, locked.

—No, no. Ah Jaysis, said John.

—Righ. We better get ou of here. Sorry abou tha John but it had to be done, Boyle said cheerfully.

He tapped Shane on the shoulder, snapping him out of a daze. Shane had been staring transfixed at the youngfella, worried he was going to die. He'd never seen anybody battered so badly. But he legged it with Robbie – they walked down Capel Street quickly, then into another pub. The barman eyed the pair unwelcomingly. But under Robbie's penetrating stare, he served them pints without question. An oulfella tha knew Robbie joined them at the bar.

—Have ye another bit for the head there? Robbie slyly asked Shane.

Aware that Robbie had new company, Shane grasped his opportunity to leave. He fumbled for the bag, and then pressed it into Robbie Boyle's hand.

—Go on you take tha. I'm gonna leg it man.

—Ah here, stay brother! Come on, I'll get ye a pint.

—No yer grand, said Shane. —I'm fuckin bollixed. I've to meet the missus too, or she'll be in the horrors. Go on, there's only a little bit left annyway, take it honest to God.

—Are ye sure brother?

—Yeah, serious man. Sure Jaysis, thanks for helpin me ou with tha other thing earlier on, said Shane grasping Robbie's hand.

The grip was returned and they shook hands earnestly.

—No bother Shane. Look after yerself, I'll see ye down there one of the days anyway, Robbie slurred.

—Ah yeah. I have yer number sure, said Shane.

—Ah . . . tha other thing ye were askin me abou yeah . . . Robbie winked.

—Yeah.

—Righ, go on, I'll talk to ye soon brother. Thanks fer tha, righ.

Taking his leave, Shane stepped out of the bar. A scorching sun blazed on his face. Disturbed and disoriented, he rang Elizabeth. Eager to bypass the frustration in her voice, he tried to grab her attention straight away.

—There's after been murder in the pub.

—Why? Wha happened? she said, alert.

—I was drinkin there with Robbie Boyle—

—Robbie Boyle? From up my way? said Elizabeth. — D'you know him?

—Ah yeah I just know him from around, said Shane concocting an air of mystique. — Then who walks into the jacks, only one of them youngfellas tha was in the earlyhouse.

—Wha youngfellas tha were in the earlyhouse? she asked.

—The ones tha were gonna rob me. The day me and you were there. After our first date.

—One of *them* youngfellas?

—Yeah.

—An wha happened?

—Me and Robbie got in a row with him down the jacks.

—Ah, how? said Elizabeth.

—I put it up to him over wantin to rob me an all—

—Ah Shane, ye should have just left it!

She sounded dismayed.

—No fuck it. Little cunt. He started gettin smart so we gave him a hidin. We had to leg it an all there.

—Ah Jaysis Shane. Ye don't know who them fellas are—

—Fuck them, he said.

—It could come back on ye!

—Yer man won't mess with me again, the state me and Robbie left him in.

—How d'*you* know Robbie Boyle anyway?

Her tone was urgent.

—I don't wanna be talkin dirty on the phone. I'm goin back up to the apartment now. Are ye comin up to me?

She hesitated.

—Alrigh . . . I've to have a shower an all first, she said quietly.

There was no sign of Chops when he arrived back at the apartment. Shane's face was green when he looked in the mirror. There was a strange disconnect between himself and the image gazing back at him. The discordance amused and troubled him. He stared at the reflection, transfixed. Happily he noted a beard of light stubble. Until then his facial hair had been fluffy, he'd had to shave it to avoid being slagged.

His personal phone rang, awakening him from this meditation. Its screen flashed 'DA'.

—Alrigh, Shane answered.

—I'm alrigh, are you? his da asked.

He had a nasty, sarcastic tone.

—Grand yeah, said Shane.

—Where are ye?

—I'm up in Chops's.

This was how Shane referred to the apartment to his ma and da. Neither of them had been up there yet, and Shane wanted to keep it that way.

—Not in the pub no?

—No I'm at home. I was ou for a few last nigh that's all.

He felt unsure why he was lying. Maybe because nobody went out drinking on a Monday morning unless they were out from the night before. It wouldn't be too much of a leap from there for his da to guess that he'd been doing E or coke.

—That's funny, his da said slowly. —I drove past ye half an hour ago and ye were comin ou of the Mercury Lounge.

Fuck, Shane thought.

—D'ye wanna explain tha to me?

—Ah I was just ou fer a few pints . . .

Shane had used up all his quick thinking on the Gards.

—Fair enough, said his da. —Wha the fuck were ye doin with tha degenerate fuckin cokehead Robbie Boyle though? Tell me tha.

His da was toying with him, Shane knew it.

—I do drink down there sometimes, he does be in there that's all.

—Yis looked like yis were in a hurry. Where were yis goin?

There was a strong sense that his da could go ballistic at any second. The adrenalin made Shane get his shit together.

—Ah we just went round to another boozer on Capel Street for a pint. Yer man Robbie had a bet on, and he wanted to watch the race.

—An wha? He needed you to hold his hand?

—Ah no, I just went round with him. It was shite in the Mercury Lounge.

More than anything else Shane's uncharacteristic compliance told his da he was still hiding something.

—Tell me the fuckin TRUTH! I'm deadly serious.

—Tha is the truth Da! Shane pleaded, childlike.

—Are you sellin coke for tha fuckin waster?

—No Da!

Shane was shocked at the sudden jump in his da's chain of reasoning.

—I'm fuckin tellin ye, I'll bate the bollix ou a tha cunt if he has you sellin drugs. I don't give a shite how hard he thinks he fuckin is.

—Ah Jaysis Da, I only met him today, he was just drinkin down there.

—A minute ago ye said ye knew him, tha ye do be drinkin down there all the time?

—Ah ye know wha I mean. I know him to see, I was only drinkin with him today but.

—Fuckin scumbags like tha you're hangin around with now! Sellin drugs *as well* as takin them. An wha d'ye think me mates are gonna say when they find ou me own fuckin youngfella is sellin coke for Robbie Boyle?

—I'm not sellin coke for him, Da! I swear on Ma's life!

This strange oath was the only one Shane knew his da would take seriously. It gave him pause.

—Hmmmm . . . Well if yer not sellin it, you sure as fuckin hell are on fuckin somethin – an you're up to no good hangin around with the likes of tha cunt.

—Ah Da, leave us alone will ye!

—I'm tellin ye, when I see him, I'm gonna have words with him an get to the bottom of this. Ye better hope you're tellin the truth.

—Ah Da leave it will ye? I was oney talkin to him!

—An when I see you, ye better watch ou an all. Fuckin wastin yer life son, it's not on. I'm gonna ask around – if I find ou y'are dealin, there's gonna be big trouble Sonny Jim. You mark my words.

—Da, you're just gonna cause me trouble if ye start goin around like tha.

—I'm not afraid of the likes of tha Boyle cunt. Sure he's only a dirtbird.

—Ah Da!

—An I want to come up to tha apartment yer stayin in an have a look around for meself. See what's really goin on with you an tha Chops fella.

—Wha d'ye mean?

—You *know* wha I mean!

—I'M NOT FUCKIN GAY DA! Will ye get over it? For Jaysis' sake, how many times do I have to say it . . . Sure I have a bird for fuck sake!

—Tha could be a smokescreen.

—Ah you're paranoid to bits.

—I fuckin have to be with a son like you!

—Ah . . .

—I'll be on to ye durin the week an I wanna come up there. Good luck.

His da hung up, leaving Shane left drained and panicky. Out of habit, he checked the drug phone for missed calls. He noticed something strange. There were no messages or calls, but there was a strange number in the *dialled* list. All the numbers Shane would ring from the phone were saved in the memory under a name, but now there were unfamiliar digits.

Shane tried to figure out whose number it was – then

cursed himself as he looked at the time of the call. An hour and a half earlier. It was the Gard. He'd buzzed his own phone so that he'd have Shane's number. Shane winced, berating himself for being cheeky with him. Thinking of the possible consequences of this, of what this meant, ratcheted his nerves up another notch. They had his number now. He was known to them.

When Elizabeth came up to the apartment, they didn't do much talking. Hangover setting in, Shane's nerves turned to frantic sexual energy. They had rough, almost violent, primal sex before falling asleep.

Totally spent, Shane descended into a near-comatose slumber. Elizabeth's sleep was disturbed by his snoring, and her concern over the incident he'd been in. She didn't want to see him getting into trouble like that. She didn't want to see him getting hurt. She wanted to talk to him about it then and there, but she could tell there was no way she'd be able to get him properly awake.

Early in the morning, she roused herself reluctantly, then showered and went to work. In comedown mode, Shane only woke up enough to limply return a kiss from the bed and say goodbye. The sleep he returned to was fraught with horror and half-memories from the two-day session. Images of Robbie laying into the youngfella. The Gards making further investigations about him after the stop.

When he awoke an hour or so later, he saw that his drug phone had 18 missed calls. This wasn't unusual. If someone was pissed and looking for coke they'd ring and ring and ring and ring and ring. But it didn't usually happen on a Tuesday. When he saw that his personal phone had 29 missed calls, he got a real fright. He grabbed it and rushed to check who the calls were from. His hands shook as he pressed buttons. The Gards must have raided his ma's gaff.

The missed calls were from Chops, Dotsy, Mick, Aido, a few landlines – then a final one from Elizabeth. The drug phone too had Chops, Dotsy, Aido, Mick and then Elizabeth again. And loads of calls from each of them. There were texts too.

Elizabeth:

Ring me.

Chops:

Ring me soon as you get this pal it's important.

Mick:

Wats up man ring me back asap.

Aido:

Call me.

Dotsy:

Ring me wn u get dis.

Panic swept over Shane, exacerbated by the drug comedown and the events of the previous day. Choosing Chops without thinking, he pushed the green button and pressed the phone anxiously against his ear. It rang for a while. Then Chops answered, with a flat voice.

—Howye.
—Chops? What's goin on? What's up?
Chops sighed.

—Look man, there's no easy way to say this . . . Chalkie's after dyin.

—Wha?

Shot, thought Shane, and felt his heart falling. Owed someone money or got in a row. Lost drugs on someone and couldn't pay them back. Suspected of ratting on someone. Something. He's been shot.

—They oney found him this mornin, said Chops.

Shane looked at his watch. Quarter past eleven.

—Wha happened? said Shane, confused.

—His ma found him in his room. Dead in the bed. He could have been like tha since Sunday nigh.

Overdose thought Shane.

—Was it coke?

—Yeah. They can't say yet for defo, but they're sayin drugs anyway.

—Who told you?

—Dotsy rang me first thing this mornin.

—Do all the lads know?

—Yeah everyone knows. You're the only one we couldn't get through to.

Shane felt guilty.

—Where are ye? he asked.

—I'm up in me ma and da's, said Chops. —I'm here since Sunday. We were all down the local Sunday, Chalkie as well. We were doin a bit of bag, but most of us were bollixed after the weekend. We didn't stay ou late. Him and Farreler went on to a session and got more bag. Farreler is in bits over it.

—I'd say so, said Shane.

—Apparently they were doin it off the table and Farreller

spilled a drink. The coke got all wet, but Chalkie done it anyway. Dotsy was talkin to him, said he was bawlin, cryin down the phone, blamin himself an all. He thinks that's wha done it.

—I didn't know tha was dangerous.

—Wet coke? So they say.

—I can't believe it man, said Shane.

—Yeah I know. One minute you're here, the next you're gone. That's it, Chops said.

—So what're we doin? Shane asked.

—Nothin we can do. That's it. There's nothin ye can do. Just fuckin gone man. It's mad isn't it? Aw the thought of him fuckin lyin there all day Monday, I can't fuckin believe it.

—Did his ma not check on him? Shane asked.

—Sure she thought he was still ou! Didn't hear him comin in. Ah ye know him anyway, ou for days – then in bits comin down. He'd go mental at his ma if she did bleedin knock in for him. She only went in to get laundry ou of the room.

—Aw man, I'd say she's in a heap!

—Stop. Fuckin devastated she is. Listen we're all goin up to Dotsy's gaff now.

—When's the funeral gonna be?

—Ah they haven't anythin like that sorted yet, oney really a few hours since they found him like. It'll probly be before the weekend though. Get a few bottles or whatever and follow us up to Dotsy's right? I'll see ye up there. Ye better text the lads to say ye know too – oh and when I couldn't get ye, I rang Elizabeth, so she was probly ringin ye as well.

—She was, yeah.

—Well give her a ring an follow us on up righ? See ye man, said Chops.

—Alrigh see ye soon.

Shane stayed there frozen, sitting up in the bed. Not even thinking, just numb.

Although he was panicky and didn't feel like drinking, Shane bought a crate of cans in the Spar outside the apartment before driving out of town to his old area. He had to pass Chalkie's house to get to Dotsy's. Although the door was closed and there was no activity around it, there were little groups of neighbours gathered at intervals on the road. Women, huddled in sombre conversation.

In Dotsy's gaff, the lads drank, listening to rebel songs with Dotsy's da. 'Sean South' and 'Follow Me up to Carlow'. Songs about fallen comrades felt appropriate. They stumbled into their beds that night, Shane back in his childhood bedroom in his ma's. They all woke up rough the next morning, a startled anxiety penetrating their hangovers.

Still Shane didn't feel grief so much as a vague awkwardness. They were all unsure how they should behave, how they should feel. Their own mortality was still unreal to them. There was even an element of interest in the fact of someone they knew dying. They imagined their own funerals – the songs they would want played at the Mass, the faces of the mourners. But they had no feeling that death would be accompanied by a permanent cessation of consciousness. The scenes they imagined after their deaths were more vivid than their memories of life. The pain associated with the act of dying held fear, but the state of death was seductive. The elevation of the departed in the eyes of the living. They craved it.

Elizabeth rang Shane that evening.

—Are ye alrigh? she asked him.

—Yeah. Ah me head's just a bit wrecked ye know.

He didn't really know how he felt, but he appreciated the attention and consideration Elizabeth was showing. Enjoyed it almost.

—C'mere Shane I'm a bit worried about you as well.

—Why?

—Aw, just you've been goin on more and more mad ones lately . . . And the mad ones are getting madder . . . and . . . and tha thing tha happened the other day with Robbie Boyle an all.

—Don't be worryin abou tha.

—No seriously Shane, tha youngfella is a dirty knacker, yeh don't know wha they migh do.

—Yer man's not gonna do anythin.

—Ye don't know tha Shane, I told ye ye were better of leavin it with the likes of them.

—You're goin on as if they're big fuckin gangsters or somethin.

—They are gangsters Shane! They're bogey cunts! They're meant to be into armed robberies an all, said Elizabeth.

He was unsettled. Armed robbers were a few leagues up in Shane's mind.

—Wha d'ye mean?

—How do you know?

—I just know the likes of them, she said more quietly.

—Do ye know them?

—Aw look I don't *know them* know them. Well I kinda know yer man tha came up to the table. The fella tha was askin you for the coke.

—That's the one we battered . . . How d'ye know him?

Shane was worried now, and puzzled. He knew she was holding something back. Elizabeth paused, then sighed.

—Aw look Shane I didn't want to talk abou this . . .

Her voice fluttered with nerves.

—I just wanted to forget about it all. But I don't want to be lyin to ye either. D'ye remember ye asked me how I knew Paddy Lawless?

—Yeah, said Shane confused.

—Ah well look, I migh as well tell ye. I used to be with him.

—Wha d'ye mean?

He felt nauseous.

—I used to go ou with him like.

Sick dizziness cascaded over him.

—When?

—Until last year.

Elizabeth could tell from Shane's voice that he was upset, and she went quiet.

—How long were ye with him for?

—Aw for a couple of years on and off. Since I was in school like. I was only a kid Shane, I was fuckin stupeh.

—Why did yis split up?

He wanted to hear that she'd left him.

—Aw he was off ridin other birds an all. Look Shane he's just a fuckin scumbag, I don't really wanna talk abou it.

—Were ye ridin him?

Silence. Shane knew the answer. It hurt him and he didn't know why.

—Well? he pressed, to hurt her back.

—Well I was goin ou with him for two years, wha d'ye fuckin think Shane? asked Elizabeth.

She was angry herself now.

—What's all this got to do with tha youngfella? Shane asked.

—Paddy had a load of youngfellas hangin around with him. Dogsbodies. And yer man was one of them.

—What's his name?

His mind was flashing forward, thinking he'd ask for Griffo's advice. And help.

—Andy somethin I think. I don't know.

Shane processed all the information, adding it to his list of woes. It felt like bearing yet another ton weight.

—Ah bollix . . . Why did ye not fuckin tell me this before?

—*I* didn't know ye were gonna do anything Shane! I just wanted to forget abou Paddy an all them scumbags.

—For fuck sake Elizabeth, this could get me bleedin *killed*! An on top of it I find ou ye were ridin tha scumbag!

Silence. Then Shane heard Elizabeth sob. This roused a surge of anger rather than pity. Lately, Shane had grown quick in quarrel. She was worrying about herself, expecting him to comfort her. Him to tell *her* not to worry, everything was going to be all right. When he had just found out that she'd been hiding the fact she had been with that scumbag. And hadn't even told him that she knew those fellas. Knew what they were capable of. It was his neck on the line, he who had unwittingly stirred up a hornet's nest. It was her that hid the truth from him, who didn't warn him about what he was getting himself into. The thought of her with Lawless riled him and intense blood pumped through his veins.

—Wha're *you* fuckin cryin abou? . . . Selfish bitch!

Shane heard a prolonged bawl before he hung up the phone.

Chalkie's removal was on the Thursday, the funeral Mass on the Friday morning. Fewer people turned up for the Mass, even though the removal was just a perfunctory ceremony. Too early in the morning. Griffo didn't make an appearance either.

On the day of the funeral, the lads donned uniform black trousers, white shirts and black ties. An informal guard of honour. Poor Fareller had difficulty maintaining his position in the file as he trembled and cried.

The Mass itself moved Shane, although he only vaguely heard the recited prayers: 'Deliver me, O Lord, from death eternal on that fearful day . . . '

Inside the church was winter-morning gloomy, but the blush from the electric fires on the wall felt like sun on their skin. The smell of fresh incense and lingering furniture polish sparked memories. The soporific routine made Shane drowsy. The song Chalkie's sister chose roused him though, made the hairs stand up on the back of his neck. It was the 'Green Fields of France'. The Fureys, Davey Arthur singing. The balladeer crooned slowly of funereal pipes and beating drums, his voice echoing in the cavernous church.

Music seemed more resonant, more profound at that moment than it had at any other time in his life. Other than on E. The harmony between music and emotion, a touch of the divine. The words didn't all suit the circumstances, but the tone of futility was right. It touched everyone in the church.

Shane's ma had come along. She knew Chalkie's ma from around the area – they used to go to the bingo together.

Lydia was there as well. She'd been in Chalkie's class in primary school. Until he'd been held back. Their da wasn't there, but he'd rung Shane. Berating him, citing Chalkie's death as further proof of his involvement with drugs. There was a note of concern in his voice that was usually hidden though, and Shane didn't whip against the sermon as he usually did. He tried to appease his oulfella instead of just patronising him. They agreed to go for a few pints together soon. Shane ruminated on the prospect of a night's drinking without coke or E.

After the funeral, everyone went to the local. Soup and sandwiches were laid on. Chalkie's ma took a turn as soon as she walked in, standing up and running toward the door before getting sick on the pub carpet. Her sisters and daughter led her outside to get some air. The food was largely ignored – most people were quick to get stuck in to a few pints. Shane had a bag of coke in his underwear. He could feel its weight next to his balls, conscious of the burden the second he sipped his first pint.

He'd asked Elizabeth not to come, brooding over the revelation that she'd been with Lawless. He disguised this as anger that she hadn't been honest from the start. These things lay heavy on his mind, precipitating a sense of foreboding. Elizabeth gave him 'space'. She didn't draw attention to the issue openly, but when they did speak, she was noticeably off with him. She punished Shane with emotional absence. Simple but effective. His comedown anxiety had become constant. He felt an ever-present aura of impending doom.

Despite the solemnity of the occasion, once the drink kicked in the lads were soon making trips to the toilets, two by two. In fairness, Chalkie wouldn't have disapproved. Eventually they trooped out of the local before bundling into taxis. They went on to a spot called Legion, a new little dance club in town.

Coming out of the jacks in the club after doing a line, Shane saw Robbie Boyle walk in with another big fella. Shane nodded and caught his eye. A comparatively sober Boyle bounded over to him, smiling.

—Alrigh brother, what's the craic with ye? he said extending his hand.

Shane was glad of the warm welcome. Boyle introduced him to his mate, and they shook hands.

—Me and this youngfella got in a bit of a scrape last week didn't we? said Robbie, laughing.

—Jaysis stop. It was a bit mad alrigh, said Shane.

—Ah fuck it he deserved it, Robbie said, a twinkle in his eye.

Robbie was in great form, cracking jokes and slapping Shane on the back heartily. He offered to buy drinks, but it was his mate who ended up paying for them. Shane was glad of the company as the night wore on and his own mates got messier and messier. Aido and Dotsy were turfed out for starting a pointless fight with some culchies. Chops legged it off to meet Chubbygirl. The remaining lads could hardly talk they were so locked.

Shane offered Robbie and his mate a line, and they went toward the jacks, crossing the dance floor on the way. As they walked through the circle Shane spotted a pair of eyes tracking them in the gloom. Instantly he knew the silhouette. Paddy Lawless. Flanked by a gang of youngfellas as usual. As the disco lights traced the little club, Shane clocked that one of the company was the other youngfella from the earlyhouse – not the one Robbie had battered. He thought of Elizabeth and Lawless having sex, and his stomach tensed, a swirl of unwanted images reverberating through his head.

Shane knew it had been bound to happen. Dublin was a small city. He was relieved to be in Boyle's company. But lurking ominously beneath this was the old fear. That ancient, dark emotion that Lawless had inspired in him since that first morning in the earlyhouse. Terror. Impotence. Shane felt like prey. He couldn't shake it. He knew he'd never feel safe with those glaring, hungry eyes in the same *country*, let alone the same room.

They did coke in the jacks, and then Shane swaggered out ahead of Boyle and his mate. His unconquerable fear paradoxically compelled him to challenge Lawless in some way – not to do so would have been to admit his worthlessness. The effects of the drug amplified the fancy of confidence that Boyle's presence lent. This was further augmented by the copious amount of drink he'd poured down his neck since the funeral that morning.

But, as it happened, Shane didn't need to make the first move. As he walked back to the bar, Lawless came over from the side of the dance floor, accompanied by the other fella from the earlyhouse and two more wily youngfellas. He didn't stand in Shane's way, but made a show of nodding toward him. From anyone else it might have been taken as a greeting, but to Shane it was clear that Paddy was pointing him out to his lieutenants. And that he wanted Shane to know this.

One of the lads caught Shane's eye. Rough-looking and freckled, his red hair stood out in the dark club, his penetrating stare a duplicate of Lawless's. Shane could feel his image being stamped in the fella's mind. He knew this fella would recognise him if he ever saw him again. Likewise, the shock of the scarlet tousle etched itself into Shane's memory.

He guessed that Lawless must have felt threatened by his appearance with Robbie Boyle in order for him to make this chess move.

—Alrigh, he said to Lawless, in a challenging tone.

He could have walked straight past him. Lawless wasn't blocking the way. But the more fear Shane felt, the more eager he was to impress upon Lawless the message that he wouldn't be intimidated.

—Alrigh, said Lawless, head back, relaxed.

The image of Lawless fucking Elizabeth fuelled Shane's temper.

—Is your buddy there alrigh is he?

—Who's tha? asked Lawless.

—Tha youngfella there.

Shane nodded at the youngfella from the earlyhouse.

—Ask him yourself, said Lawless.

—I though they worked for you? said Shane boldly.

—No, said Paddy, shaking his head, scowling for the first time. —Sure I'm unemployed.

—Is tha righ yeah? How's yer other mate?

—Who's tha now? said Paddy.

He didn't break eye contact with Shane. The redhead was staring hungrily at the verbal sparring, willing it to turn physical.

—Andy. Is tha his name? Heard he had an accident, done himself a bit of a mischief. Ye know who I'm takin abou anyway, said Shane.

—Ah we know a few of the same people, said Lawless. —How's Griffo?

There was something triumphal about his tone.

—Not a bother, Shane said defiantly.

He got a vague sense that something had happened between Lawless and Griffo, something that Griffo wanted to avoid. He wondered if Lawless was after Griffo, if Griffo owed him money. Maybe Griffo hadn't bothered paying for something when Lawless got locked up. The thought rattled him.

—How's Elizabeth? asked Lawless.

Shane had no retort.

—Tell yer mate I was askin for him, he said coolly, before walking away.

Redtop was still staring pointedly. Lawless made a remark and the lads around him giggled. Shane had lost face and he knew it. Back at the bar, Shane complained to Robbie Boyle about Lawless. Boyle listened not unsympathetically, one eye on the waitress. There was to be no immediate violence this time though, not against this more powerful enemy.

—Don't let him bother ye . . . these youngfellas, they're just cardboard gangsters. Water off a duck's back take it brother. You're better off.

The inner city was incestuous. Everyone knew or 'knew of' everyone else. Boyle was huge, he'd batter Lawless in a straightener, no bother – but Lawless wasn't the type to accept defeat. Boyle had no desire to get involved in a row with him.

Paddy Lawless's renowned ruthlessness was selfish in origin though. There was scant motivation for him to bother seeking revenge on a behalf of a 'friend'. Yet. But Shane knew they weren't 'cardboard gangsters'. They were the real deal. Youngfellas of the type Lawless surrounded himself with had no fear. They'd committed suicide long ago, just deferring the result. Every drink, every sniff, every pill, every ride, every minute not locked up – every minute still alive – they were all just bonuses. Until the day of reckoning would finally arrive.

While a defeated Shane drank at the bar with Boyle, Lawless swanned around the club with his troops. The alcohol-and-drug mix mingled with the anxiety induced by his nemesis. Chalkie's death was playing on Shane's mind now too, fucking with his head. After a while he left, but not before pressing once more the remnants of a bag into Robbie Boyle's hand. He *needed* the friendship. He'd now challenged Lawless publicly, in disregard of his primal fear. It had been a hot-headed act, and Shane rued it, even before he sobered up.

He walked drunkenly home to the apartment by a circuitous route, checking now and again that he wasn't being followed. Once home, he rang Griffo from the drug mobile.

—Griffo?

—What's up?

It was unusual for Shane to call at this hour. Although they were friends of sorts, Shane only really ever rang him for drugs. There was tinny music in the background, just a stereo in a gaff. Shane was glad to hear it – it indicated that Griffo hadn't been asleep anyway.

—C'mere man, I have to talk to ye bou somethin.

—What's up kid? said Griffo, with concern.

He sounded coked up.

—We're after been at me mate's funeral—

—Ah yeah that's righ! I heard abou tha. Chalkie from around the Close there. Didn't know the youngfella well like . . . sorry to hear abou tha.

—Yeah . . . We all went into town after . . . and I bumped into tha Paddy Lawless fella.

Silence.

—Yeah? said Griffo eventually.

—Nothin happened. He was just shapin, givin it loads ye know.

—Yeah, said Griffo. —He's always like tha. So wha?

—No but somethin happened the other week. D'ye remember them two youngfellas I told ye abou ages ago, the ones tha were in the earlyhouse?

—Tha were gonna rob ye?

—Yeah, said Shane.

—Yeah. Go on.

—Me and Robbie Boyle battered one of them in the Mercury. Gave him a good hidin now. Hospital job.

—You an *Robbie Boyle*? Wha?

There was no talk of avoiding discussing such matters over the phone. Maybe Griffo felt safe because he changed his number so often now. Maybe he was just too keen to get the info.

—Yeah, I don't even know him, I was oney buzzin off him in there.

—Righ . . . said Griffo.

—Turns ou the fella we battered is workin for Paddy Lawless or somethin.

—Ah for fuck sake! Griffo hissed. —Does Lawless know it was you?

—Yeah, the other fella was there with him tonigh. I think he pointed me out to Lawless. Lawless came into the early-house tha morning they were gonna rob me annyway – just as I was leavin, he came in the door. He must've been there to meet them two youngfellas. I didn't cop he had annythin to do with them until after.

There was a pause.

—Did he say anything bout it tonigh?

—No.

Shane could tell that Griffo was annoyed, so he didn't mention that he'd confronted Lawless. To be fair, Lawless hadn't said anything about his mate, deflecting the conversation away from the issue.

Griffo exhaled thoughtfully in a low whistle.

—Righ nothin will probly come of it . . . But fuck it Shane, wha did I tell ye abou tha cunt? Ye don't wanna be startin bother with the likes of him. He fuckin knows ye – know me as well, he clocked us together tha first morning.

—How d'you know him?

—Never fuckin mind tha! spat Griffo.

Shane hadn't been on the receiving end of Griffo's anger before. It gave him a fright.

—Mind yer own fuckin business Shane, said Griffo. — And if ye want someone to sort this ou, ring Robbie fuckin Boyle, cause I won't be gettin involved. I told ye to stay away from the likes of Lawless. Dangerous cunts. I warned ye.

There was a longer pause, demonstrating Shane's shock at the way he'd been spoken to. He wondered how much money Griffo had stung Lawless for, and if he'd treat anyone like that or if he'd only done it cause Lawless was such a scumbag.

—Look, said Griffo. —I'm tellin ye these things for yer

own good. Yer better off avoidin trouble like tha. At the end of the day it's not gonna make ye any money. If ye get caught up in aggro, it throws the eye on ye. Next thing ye know the Old Bill are all over ye, ye can't move. That's all they give a fuck about, shit that'll get in the papers.

—Righ, righ, said Shane, seeking conciliation.

The mentoring attitude comforted him. In spite of Griffo's protestations that he didn't wish to assist or get involved, Shane allowed Griffo continue talking him through the situation.

—The thing is though, said Shane. —It's after comin ou tha . . . don't say this to anyone now?

—Wha? I won't, go on, Griffo said impatiently.

—It's after comin ou tha Elizabeth used to be with him.

—Elizabeth? *Your* bird? With Lawless?

—Elizabeth yeah, said Shane.

—Ah get away from her. It's not worth the trouble, said Griffo briskly, annoyed again.

Silence.

—Get away from her Shane I'm tellin ye! Lethal they are, mots like tha, it's gonna end in *fuckin disaster*! I would of never started doin business with ye if I knew this shit was gonna come up. Ye wanna get rid of her. Someone tha'd be with the likes of Lawless? Don't be sayin I said it now, but get rid of her.

—She's a deadly mot though.

—There's plenty of deadly mots out there! They're all deadly sure! I'm bein serious now Shane, ye don't know wha tha Lawless fella is capable of. A bird tha'd be mixed up with him is nothin but trouble. Give her the bullet and let tha be an end to it.

178

—She's sound though.

—They're all fuckin sound at the start.

—Ah, I dunno if I can finish it.

—Well look, it's up to yourself – an don't fuckin say I said annythin I'm warnin ye – but if I was you I'd get away from her like a hot snot. It's not fuckin worth it. Are ye ballyin up when you're ridin her?

—She's on the pill.

—They all say *that* as well! Wha'll happen if ye end up polin her? Then she's back with tha Lawless fella an you've a little youngfella or youngone an *can't* get away. Be fuckin careful Shane, this is serious shit. Aw for fuck sake, I shouldn't even be talkin to ye abou this on the phone! Say nothin abou me to her. Have ye said anythin already?

—No man, she doesn't even know ye.

—How do ye know she doesn't know me?

—Ah me phone was ringin one day and yer name came up and she asked me who ye were.

—An did ye tell her?

—No I just said ye were a customer, Shane lied. —She didn't know who ye were.

—Well fuckin keep it tha way. It's up to you wha ye do Shane, but *do not* fuckin get me involved in this – I'm warnin ye. We're mates an all, but this is business, and it's a risky business. I've me own problems to look after, an I don't need you gettin in me way, are ye wide? said Griffo.

—Yeah.

Shane was hurt and afraid. He loved Elizabeth. Even though he berated her himself, he'd never have said a bad word about her to anyone. Ever. Hearing Griffo put her down stung like a slap. His urge was to defend her further but he couldn't.

—Righ well, just don't mention my fuckin name, to yer mot *or* to Robbie Boyle, said Griffo. —And stay well the fuck away from Lawless if ye've any sense at all. Righ?

—Righ.

—Righ, go on . . . I'll talk to ye durin the week, said a still-surly Griffo.

The phone call had disturbed Shane further. Griffo usually played a friendly amiable character. The jovial giant had been replaced by a ruthless titan. This was a side Shane hadn't seen before. The undertone of violence shocked him. He felt sober – agitated, even though he had been drinking like a fish all day. The coke and alcohol mingled to strange effect, bouncing around in his system.

Shane reminded himself again that he still needed to change his drug phone number, since the Gard had taken it, the thought of which unsettled him even more. He took a Valium to ease the transition from tired wiredness to sleep. He'd heard that benzos were what the hospital gave you if you overdosed on coke. The thought that he'd taken the proper antidote already, and so he was unlikely to suffer Chalkie's fate this night, comforted him.

Shane was startled and bolted upright in the bed when he heard the noise of Chops's drunken entrance. Zonked on the Valium, he remained somewhere between consciousness and sleep for the next half hour or so – until a tap on the apartment door whipped him from rest again. He listened, wondering if it had been a strange dream. There was a louder knocking, more persistent. A seeping terror flowed through Shane, rising through the Valium and vestiges of alcohol. There was no reason for anyone to knock at the door. People had to be buzzed in through the security gate, and they'd always ring him first if they were coming. Why would anyone be at the apartment door? They must have been let into the complex first. There was a steel gate, an exterior door, two flights of stairs and another interior security door between the street and the apartment itself.

As the knocking grew yet louder, a single overwhelming belief pervaded Shane's thoughts, maybe borne of drug-induced paranoia: there was someone on the other side of the door who had arrived to kill him. Yet, despite this unshakeable conviction, he found himself a slave to the insistence of the knocking – banging now. In a weird daze, he stood up out of the bed and walked to the door, unable to believe what he was doing. As terror seared through his flesh, multiplying with each repeated bang, Shane walked toward the door. The thumping penetrated from the other side, seeping into his body and wrenching him from the depths of himself into stark awareness of the terrifying moment he was in. Incredulously, he saw his own hand twist the latch. He was flooded with the most intense panic he'd ever experienced as he opened the door.

And saw Chubbygirl standing there, drunk.

Her handbag hung limply from one arm, her other hand pressing a phone to her cheek.

—Hi Shane . . . really sorry, she slurred, stinking of beer. —Chops asked me over but I can't get through to him.

—Howye, said Shane, stunned.

The wave of emotion that had swept over him dissipated almost pleasantly. It left only shock that he had actually opened the door at the demand of the unknown.

—Go on into him there. I'd say he's asleep, Shane managed. —We were on the gargle all day.

She walked in past Shane and he shut the door.

—Thanks Shane. Sorry to hear about your friend.

—No bother, talk to ye later.

—Goodnight.

—Nigh.

Sleep didn't come for Shane after that. He couldn't stay awake either though, and wished he hadn't taken the Valium. His head would dip and he'd nod off, just to wake again with a start. The only remedy he could imagine was Elizabeth's company. But she wasn't answering her phone. The impulse to call had been too strong to resist, despite Griffo's admonition. He reminisced of her tenderly, missing her. Regretting calling her names. His watch read '3 AM'. He thought there was still a slight chance she could be persuaded to come over and soothe his troubles with her touch. To this end he composed a text.

> Howye, just awake here thinkin about you. Sorry for goin ballistic the other day, I was just freaked over Chalkie and everything. Head's wrecked over everything, want to talk to you. Ring me when u get this please x

No reply came, and ringing again there was still no answer. He went into the sitting room. Television provided some replacement company, but it was a poor cure for his troubles. Regrets and embarrassments tormented him. He scolded himself. A weak fool. Eventually, he passed into sleep as it was getting bright. After another jolt, he got up and shuffled to his bedroom. Chubbygirl's sweet snores and Chops's raucous sawing made a reassuring duet in the hallway. It was too late for Elizabeth to come now, so Shane put both his phones on silent before returning to a welcome oblivion.

The next day, the impulse to berate himself transformed into resolve to be smarter in future. The yearning for Elizabeth stiffened into fortitude. Stirred into action by outside events, he bucked his usual habit of spending days recuperating in bed. While normally he'd just ride out the comedown through inactivity, this time anxiety gave him energy. He cleaned the apartment and then went shopping.

Chops was saying goodbye to Chubbygirl at the door when he returned. Inside, they discussed Shane's predicament. Chops softly counselled caution, but wasn't in a position to provide real assistance. He was more delicate than Griffo, but his allegiance and concern were for Shane, not Elizabeth.

—Look man, she's a lovely bird. Ye know I've a lot of time for her. An I don't know this Lawless fella, but he sounds like a scumbag. Ye'd just wanna watch wha yer gettin yerself wrapped up in Shane that's all.

—Aw I know Chops, seriously. If she had of just fuckin told me who them fellas were none of this would have happened!

—Yeah, well, don't forget Shane, it was her tha warned ye bou them in the first place. Like, she migh have saved yer skin there ye know.

—If she hadn't known them they probly never would of came over at all though, Shane countered.

—She's from town, she's bound to know an awful lot of people.

—She knows a lot of awful people more like! said Shane.

—Ah I don't know man . . . D'ye love her?

—Yeah I do love her Chops, yeah. I'm mad abou her, bein honest.

—Well it's up to yourself Shane, nobody can tell ye wha to do.

Shane hadn't told any of the lads apart from Chops about any of this. Growing up, all the lads had learned quickly to keep their business to themselves when drugs, money or mots were concerned. He wouldn't have enlisted their help anyway – the likes of Griffo and Boyle were way above his mates. Older, stronger, better-connected. It was them he'd hoped would back him up. But he was glad to have Chops, even if advice was all he could offer.

—Fuck it man, I wish I could just get tha fuck ou a here an move away or somethin, said Shane. —Just me and her. This is gonna be hangin over me fuckin head now, it's a fuckin melt.

—Shit happens man. Just think abou it. Ye could of ended up brown bread – like Chalkie. Nothin migh come of this thing now, but *he's* gone forever. Just be wise man.

—It's out of my control though Chops.

—Thing is too man, a lot of shit happened this week. You're probly still comin down off the charlie a bit as well. Ye'd wanna just sort yer head ou an get on with things. Wait for a few days an ye'll feel better. We all get paro after bein out.

—I dunno. Maybe you're righ. Just don't say annythin to the lads abou any of it, ye know yerself.

—Course not pal. Me mouth is zipped.

Perfunctory texts had passed between Shane and Elizabeth during the day, but Shane was annoyed that she hadn't answered his call. He more than half suspected her of being unfaithful. He couldn't escape the thought that she might even have been with Paddy Lawless. He imagined her bumping into him at a party or a club and sneaking off with him to his lair. Some flat or apartment in the North Inner City. She rang him after she was finished work, as usual, and despite it all he was relieved to see her name flash up.

—Hello? said Shane.

Her response was lacklustre.

—Heye.

—What's up? he asked

—Nothin much, just finished work. Said I'd give ye a ring. Are ye alrigh?

—Grand yeah . . . What happened ye last nigh? asked Shane.

—At home. I was wrecked I'd me phone on silent.

—I was ringin like mad lookin for ye.

—I know, I saw the missed calls, she said snottily.

—Nice one Elizabeth. Like me mate dies, I migh be in a load of shit with them lads, an then I find ou you were with the leader of the pack. Then I can't even get hold of ye!

—Sorry Shane, I didn't think you'd be ringin! Sure I asked ye to meet up with me loads durin the week an all an ye didn't want to.

The 'sorry' was an accusation, not an apology.

—If ye didn't think I'd be ringin, why did ye have yer phone on silent then? he asked.

—Wha?

—If ye didn't think I was gonna be ringin ye, why did ye need to put yer phone on silent for?

—I was wrecked. I just wanted to go asleep, she said defensively.

—Who did ye think would be ringin ye then?

—Wha?

—Ye heard me. Does there be other fellas ringin ye at all hours?

—No Shane, I just put it on silent, Jesus Christ!

—Does Paddy Lawless be ringin ye?

—No Shane, he doesn't even have me number! I changed it an all after we broke up!

This aggravated him. That tiny piece of phrasing was so important – 'after we broke up'. Not 'after I broke up with him'. Lawless had finished it with *her*. She'd never rejected him. *She'd still be with Lawless if she could*, thought Shane.

—Aw righ so he *would* be ringin ye if ye hadn't changed yer number?

—For fuck sake Shane why are ye bein such a prick?

—Why d'ye think? Me head's fuckin wrecked over everything! Sure why the fuck were you with Paddy fuckin Lawless?

—I was young, I was stupeh – I don't know!

—It was only a couple of fuckin years ago. Ye couldn't a been tha young. You're only twenty now for fuck sake.

—I was still in school an all when I started goin ou with him Shane.

—Was it the money? Is tha why you're with me as well?

—Fuck off Shane I never asked you for annythin. An do ye know wha? I don't need this shite, I'm goin ou with the girls tonigh. An don't worry I've me own money to pay for it.

—Ah yeah – off ou chasin fellas.

—Well wha the fuck do you care? You're not even bothered with me!

—I have enough on me fuckin plate! An you didn't fuckin help either, fuckin addin to it. It's your fault I'm in the shit with them fellas!

—Yeah Shane everything's my fault.

—Me mate fuckin dies, and now all this, an you're givin me shit on top of it! Yer bein a bitch Elizabeth.

—Fuck ye Shane, I'm not lettin ye call me names again, you're a fuckin prick. I'm goin ou with the girls. Ye can ring me tomorrow an apologise.

—I won't be fuckin ringin ye tomorrow – if yer not gonna sort sort this ou now that's it, I'm not havin it hangin over me head when you're goin off out!

—I'm goin ou. Goodbye Shane.

—I'm warnin ye Elizabeth, if ye hang up on me, I'm fuckin finishin it!

—Do wha ye fuckin want! C'mere there's plenty of fellas want me Shane. Plenty! There's a party on in Harold's Cross tonigh one of the girls asked me to go to, there'll be a load of fellas there. I said no to her cause of you – but d'ye know wha? I'm fuckin goin!

—Tauntin me with it now! After the shit tha I've been through this week! Fuck ye Elizabeth, It's over!

—Fuck off Shane you're a selfish prick anyway. Fuckin *spa*! she said, hanging up.

Breathing heavily after the battle, Shane looked at the phone. He tried to ring her back, but her phone was switched off.

A NEWSPAPER ARTICLE

IT'S WAR

We reveal the cause of the fresh turf war that's brewing among Dublin's drug dealers

A NEW WAVE of violence looks set to spread across Dublin's North Inner City as rival gangs line up to do battle. Garda sources say that they are preparing to increase their operations in order to protect the public from the fallout from this potentially vicious feud.

After the arrest of minor-league dealers Dermot 'Delboy' Campbell (22) and Patrick Lawless (21) on drugs charges, allegations of informing have been made by their cohorts against a top Northside drug dealer. Campbell and Lawless were arrested in possession of €10,000 worth of cocaine earlier this year, and are currently serving their sentences in Mountjoy Prison. Both men are well known to Gardaí.

Gardaí believe that the accusations have been invented by an up-and-coming player in the Dublin underworld. The rumours have been spread by this wannabe godfather in a bid to oust a Northside rival from his position at the top of the roost. A source said that the young pretender is determined to rise to the top of the gangland food chain, and will use any means to do so. Although a major player in the drugs trade and organised crime, the Northside drug lord is now said to be running scared under the heat from his inner-city counterparts.

While there have as yet been no fatalities related to the dispute among Dublin's mobsters, a number of incidents of minor violence and vandalism have sparked fears that the situation may yet spiral out of control.

5

ELIZABETH BYRNE -v- SHANE LAOCHRA

Initially, both parties refused to give way, but eventually Shane appealed for clemency. It was a trial for him. Despite wanting Elizabeth back, he still smarted from the injuries she'd delivered. Plaintively, he petitioned his case, wavering between anger and sorrow, but Elizabeth maintained a rigid defence, accusing him of negligence and slander.

She told Shane that as far as she was concerned, there was no need for deliberation, the verdict had already been pronounced – by himself, in the first instance. She couldn't distinguish lack of care from malice. Her own judgement on the matter was to be final. For his inattention, justice was meted out quid pro quo. Elizabeth went out partying as much as possible. She made sure Shane knew this by posting rambunctious photos of herself and her friends on Bebo. For the insult, the sentence was silence in the face of Shane's appeals. This furthered his anger.

Spurred on by the prospect of Elizabeth conducting affairs with a third party, Shane made a contract with himself not to chase after her.

Other matters laid claim to his attention. These distractions, though often unwelcome, prevented him slipping into depression. His customer base expanded, largely built upon that one connection he'd made through Cynthia with the wealthy young Southsider. Rory worked in finance. Shane didn't really understand what he did, he just had a vague idea that he worked with computers. It was irrelevant anyway, so long as the money kept rolling in. And it did.

Shane started referring to Rory as 'the Golden Goose'. Rory was paying well over the odds for a quarter of unmixed coke every week. Shane guessed he was doing some dealing with this himself – probably just to cover the cost of his own habit, maybe to earn a bit of street cred from his mates. He also gave Shane's number to others though, providing a reliable, solvent and safe customer base. These upmarket vendees always called in advance, always paid cash, and would usually have Shane call to their houses. Much safer. Most of the lads from Shane's area still lived at home with their parents.

Although they had been business partners, Chops and Shane each sold different amounts to different customers. Shane soon overtook Chops to the extent it no longer made sense to work together. They still made little reciprocal drops for each other, or covered each other's business if otherwise engaged. But this was friendly and organic. The formal arrangement was wound up.

IGNORANTIA JURIS NON EXCUSAT
Ignorance Is No Defence

Shane still hadn't got around to changing his drug phone, even though the Gard had taken the number. He'd have to get another handset, then write down all the numbers from his phone, then manually transfer them into the new one, then activate a new unregistered SIM, then call his customers and ask them to delete the old number. If they still had the old one, Shane knew they would ring it too any time they couldn't get through to him – and this could reveal his new number to the Gardaí if they were monitoring the old one. He was reluctant to undertake this process and risk losing customers, despite the risk. His paranoia had been mounting since his brush with the Gards though.

Robbie Boyle battering the youngfella, Chalkie's death, bumping into Lawless and his mates again, and then losing Elizabeth on top of it all hadn't helped his mindset either.

POST MORTEM
After Death

Chalkie's post-mortem stated that he had died due to a heart attack resulting from cocaine toxicity. There were no surprises there. It made it into the newspaper – a tiny article buried near the sports pages, citing a warning from the coroner about ingesting damp cocaine. 'Death by misadventure.' The article made Shane shudder, as he thought of the times drink had splashed on coke at sessions and he'd done it anyway. He thought about lying cold in the bed. Being found a day or two later by his mother.

Chalkie's situation puzzled him. What was it like being dead? Black? Nothing? What was nothing like? It seemed too bleak. He'd often felt close to a sense – at the best times, when he was high – that being dead was some sort of bliss. The good times were becoming less frequent though. He was more likely to be sketchy than euphoric after taking drugs now, worries ricocheting through his skull. Still though, maybe that's what death was. Bliss.

The concept of his own mortality nagged him, but ultimately remained an unreal prospect. Like all his friends, Shane just did not truly believe that some day he would cease to exist. While he had a healthy disdain for the church, and no interest in obeying its laws, he did retain an *à la carte* Catholic belief in some 'grand explanation'. It was unarticulated. He didn't *have* the words to express it. But he thought existence was some sort of benign mystery. All would be revealed after death. Some cosmic force was looking after his life. Everything was destined to work out for the best. But this belief couldn't stem his growing anxiety.

ALIBI

Elsewhere

He remained cautious in his dealings, making sure always to stash the coke in his underwear, never to have revealing text messages on his phones – and always to have a bogus story ready about his destination if stopped by Gardaí. This was fine for checkpoints or random searches, but what if the

Gards made you a target? This became an issue sooner than he had hoped.

Driving up the quays one afternoon, Shane noticed a car behind him manoeuvre out into traffic. He took the next left to make sure he wasn't being followed, but the car zipped out again, taking the same turn. A Mazda 323, it didn't look like an unmarked cop car. Still unsure, Shane took a right onto Benburb Street then a left onto Blackhall Place. The car followed suit. It was definitely following him. His heart dropped.

Then he noticed the car had no insurance or NCT discs. Gards. He nearly relaxed – for a second he'd thought the pursuit might have a more sinister end. But he had a oner bag in his jocks and about €500 in cash on him, so arrest was now the threat. At the lights, he calmed his breathing and switched both his phones off. The car edged out of traffic to get alongside his. The occupants leaned over in their seats to get a good look at him. Shane braced himself for flashing lights and a signal to pull over. Adrenaline flowed into his system. He experienced a strange wave of calm anticipation. Flow. But when the light turned green, the car sped off toward Manor Street.

Shane took a circuitous route back to the apartment, suspicious of every car around him. Only eliminating vehicles that held old women, or children – or black people – from his paranoid gaze. Once home, he considered removing any illicit items from the house. The coke was well hidden, but the scales were more difficult to secrete.

RES NULLIUS

Nobody's Property

Everything dodgy was kept in shared areas of the apartment. He wondered what way it would turn out in court if both he and Chops denied all knowledge. He wasn't too optimistic about getting a favourable result in such an eventuality.

—Are ye sure they were Old Bill? asked Chops.

—Ah yeah man, they were *defo* followin me Chops, serious.

—I dunno man . . . In a Mazda?

—Yeah I was surprised at tha meself, but it only had the tax disc.

—Was it a Northie car? They oney have the one disc too.

—Ah no Chops it was a D-reg. Wha would Northies be doin followin me? They were five-o, definitely.

—I dunno. Sounds a bit paro to me man.

—I'm fuckin tellin ye. I oney hope I just happened to catch their eye or somethin, tha they weren't followin me. Good job I have the motor registered to me ma's gaff so they don't have this address now.

—Suppose.

The incident prompted Shane to shun most of his customers that weekend. He only met some posh girl and Rory, the Golden Goose. The business he turned down he gave to Aido and Dotsy, who were selling bag as well now. The only caveat Shane stipulated was that they weren't to exchange numbers with his customers. He organised the meets over his own phone, without giving Aido or Dotsy's numbers to the customers either. He just about trusted the lads, but not the same way he trusted Chops.

N.B.

Remember Well

Breaking from routine, Shane decided not to go out clubbing that Sunday. He was disconcerted about the situation with Paddy Lawless. Instead, he agreed to his da's request to meet for a few quiet pints. It was as well to get it out of the way on a weekend that he didn't even want to go on a mad one.

It meant that he had to cancel a planned rendezvous with Griffo though, who was irritated by the change of plan. He refused to rearrange, telling Shane he'd have to call him again the next day and see. He'd pushed Shane to meet him as planned, asking him where he was going to be instead, what he was doing. Griffo was overstepping the mark, but Shane explained where and when he was meeting his da to prove he couldn't make it, that he wasn't just being lazy.

Griffo had become more guarded recently – wary of him, despite the increased profits realised as a result of the surge in Shane's enterprise. He'd also changed his number again, and now he insisted Shane use a payphone to contact him rather than a mobile. The rigmarole of finding a pay-phone, then hoping to get through just to organise a routine meet annoyed Shane. Excessive, he thought. Subconsciously it exacerbated his own paranoia.

Having arranged to meet his oulfella at nine o'clock, Shane ambled down toward the pub. It was one his da drank in the odd time, down toward Ballybough. Shane had stopped going to that locale when he'd stopped going to Dubs matches, and he was a bit uncomfortable in the area – Paddy Lawless was from nearby. Drugs, feuds and aggro had the place riddled with Old Bill too, but he was more scared of being copped by Paddy or one of his mates. This was their territory. In fact, it was the last place in the whole of Dublin city that Shane wanted to be.

He felt he was being watched, like he was walking into a lion's den. He'd wanted to object to the choice of venue – but that would have confirmed his da's suspicions that he was up to something dodgy. Returned stares from passers-by and motorists spooked him. Were they just looking because he was looking, or were they looking at him? The area was busy, making it difficult to discount the notion that he was being followed. As always, he made a mental note of the cars that passed. He clocked a Primera going by twice in the same direction. This freaked him, and everyone on the streets became a potential Gard or Lawless ally.

Cap on, he kept his head down and eyes peeled – for Gardaí, for Lawless, but for Elizabeth too. The flats where she lived were nearby, and she had lots of friends around the area. He was still angry with her. All the more since she'd been so flagrantly trying to upset him via social media. But he still yearned for her like nothing else. All the time. He had to force himself to think of other things when his thoughts flickered toward her. It wrecked his head that just when he needed someone the most she wasn't there. Even worse, she was embroiled in all the shit that had come into his life. These thoughts preoccupied him as he made his way along the small side alley that led toward the pub's car park, and then to the secluded entrance. From the corner of his eye, he became aware of men walking close behind him.

It was the type of area where you didn't want to make eye contact with strangers, so Shane kept staring straight ahead. Anticipating the relief of their passing him by, Shane felt them quicken. They were nearly alongside him now. Then he felt the shock of being grabbed forcefully, by immensely strong hands.

SUBPOENA

Summons

He tried to whirl around but, clamped in the arms of a stranger, only his head whipped back. He saw a blur of arms and faces. Before he'd even had a chance to speak, cloth was roughly pulled over him so that the words that came were muffled.

—Wha!? Let go! Let go! Wha!? he gasped.

His lungs made deep, involuntary inhalations, as if he was drowning. There was no reply, but he heard purposeful voices speak urgently.

—Open it there.

—Have ye a hold of him?

—Yeah, yeah go on.

Wild with terror, Shane couldn't understand what was going on. A cold numbness spread across his body, like the shock of falling underwater. He felt frozen as the wet sensation oozed over him, weakening his legs and making him gasp again for breath in the darkness of his hood.

DE LEGE FERENDA

What the Law Should Be

—Please! please! he shouted.

He felt himself being pushed against a car, which shook a little.

—Go on quick, he heard.

He realised they were trying to get him into the boot of a car

—No! Shane shouted, as the men pushed him harshly into the boot. —NOOOO!!!!! NOOOOO!!!! he roared involuntarily, shocked at the noise that was coming from the depths of his being.

DE LEGE LATA

What the Law Is

BOOM! One fella hit him with an incredibly strong solid into the head. The blow stunned Shane, stopping his roaring dead.

—Get fucking in, the man said firmly.

—Please, please! Shane whimpered, trembling now.

BOOM! Another blow, the violence of the impact terrifying Shane, crystallising his course of action. This was all the duress required. He ceased resisting. The men pulled the bag tighter over him, over his shoulders down to his waist nearly. Then they bundled him into the boot before slamming it closed, plunging him into utter darkness. Through the cloth he'd been able to see specks of light, but now there was just black. Over the rhythm of his rapid breathing, he heard crunching gravel.

—His phone.

The voice was muffled, but Shane could still understand the words clearly.

—Get his phone there.

The lid opened to the welcome light of dusk. It pierced

through little holes in his hood once more, seeming beautifully bright in comparison to the entrapped darkness of the boot.

—Give us yer phone, said the first fella.

Shane knew better than to plead, after the terrifying strength of the blows. He struggled to remove his phone from his pocket. His arm was restrained by the hood, and the fella pulled it up roughly to allow Shane move. As he reached, the cloth rode further up again, and he could see that he was lying on top of empty plastic peat sacks that lined the boot. Too scared to look at the man, Shane gave him the phone and the fella tossed the boot closed again.

Pitch dark. His face stung from the punches. Three clunks, then a gentle rocking as car doors shut. The familiar noise of the ignition starting. He'd never felt so lonely in his entire life. An earthy smell and the sound of his own breathing.

Shane felt the car move, and he tracked it in his mind – right turn pulling out, then the indicator clicking, followed by a left turn onto the road. After two more turns he was lost. From then on it was just meaningless motion. He was pushed around in the boot, wriggling out of the hot sack to rustle over the empty plastic peat bags, but forced to maintain the same foetal position.

Panicked thoughts surged through his mind. Was it to do with that youngfella and Paddy Lawless? But they wouldn't go to the trouble of kidnapping him. It would even have been easier to just blast him? Unless they wanted to torture him . . .

Vidjos maybe? The 'RA?

They did things like this to drug dealers. Did the IRA

still even exist though? They wouldn't be bothered with a small-time dealer like him if they did, would they? It wasn't like he was shifting kilos of smack.

Was it the fuckin Gards? He'd properly pissed off that blondey one – he had it in for Shane. And Gards had brought the General up the mountains to teach him a lesson . . . No, not with those accents. They were proper Dubs. Couldn't be cops.

Elizabeth's oulfella? He was a bogey. Maybe it had got back to him about the drug dealing, calling her names . . . Unlikely.

Griffo? He almost seemed to hate Shane since he'd heard about the trouble with the Paddy Lawless crowd. Why would he do this though? Paranoia maybe, out of it on that coke. He could have got anything into his head. He'd been acting mad strange lately.

The INLA? For . . . some reason?

Shane's body became a mere conduit, just a receptacle for soaring terror, exponentially worse than anything he'd ever felt. Being in the dark just left a gaping black hole where hope used to be.

He knew that 'up the mountains' was where he was going, whoever it was taking him there. Each option was equally terrifying. Despite the fact that no conceivable explanation offered any solace, Shane felt the not-knowing as the source of his terror. The different possibilities flitted through his mind. There was no realistic scenario that he could imagine that didn't mean he was facing torture and/or death.

He cursed the fact that there was no light on his watch, and wished he'd replaced the cheap old thing as he'd intended. It would have been a comfort to know the time, but being able to illuminate the cramped space, if only with the little glow of a watch light would have given him greater succour. Then he remembered the drug phone in his back pocket.

It was an awkward manoeuvre, but he managed to slither his hand around to reach it. It lit up at his touch, offering a comforting ethereal glow, which reflected off the white peat bags.

Should he dial 911 or 999? He'd never called the emergency services before. Just try it quick – 999. The car pitched and yawed as Shane dialled, transfixed by the screen. As soon as he pressed the green button, a little icon appeared. A picture of a mobile phone with arrows shooting out urgently toward the three nines at the top. It struggled to connect with only one bar of signal.

Briskly, Shane concocted a mental construction of what he was going to say to the emergency people. 'I've been kidnapped. I don't know where I am. I've been trapped in the boot of a car by two men, maybe more.' They could probably trace the call and get his location. That's why Griffo was so paro about mobiles – 'triangulation' or something, he called it.

But then the phone flashed and emitted a crushing series of rapid bleeps. Shane was in total darkness again. The battery was dead. He hadn't bothered charging it, he hadn't planned on dealing that night. He managed to turn it on three more times though. The first time it allowed him to dial before switching off. The second time he managed to key in two nines before it went dark. The third time he couldn't even enter his pin code before it expired. After that, it only flashed tantalisingly when he held the power button.

Moving faster now, the car threw Shane about violently in the cramped boot. His foetal form hit the lid every time they went over a bump on the road. His head was pushed down into his body whenever the car made a right turn, cramping his neck. There was only noise, movement, and the smell of soil mixed with a nauseating tinge of petrol. The rest was utter darkness. A deep, heavy, bottomless black.

Shane pressed up against the lid as hard as possible. He scrabbled furiously in the darkness, hoping to find some tool or implement to aid his escape. All he could touch was the slickness of the thick plastic bags, the brush of the carpet that lined the boot underneath and the vault of shiny steel close above.

Ignorance of his situation had been the spur of his anguish, and now inability to further his cause added to his terror. The sensation of utter powerlessness was not one he'd ever felt before. He'd been in arguments and fights, been arrested as a boy. But in those instances he had had some ability to influence the outcome. Now he found himself at the absolute mercy of persons unknown.

Powerless, he prayed. It was the only thing he could do to try and effect change. He mouthed 'Our Father' hurriedly, rushing through the prayer again and again. 'Ár nAthair, atá ar neamh . . . ' He clenched his eyes shut, pleading, bargaining with God. Promising he'd be good in future if he could be acquitted from this situation.

His image of God was a grey-bearded man in the darkness, light years away. A spectre in a sea of black nothingness. He continued mumbling his prayers to this insubstantial image. Unbeknownst to him, the words coming out of his mouth morphed into a desperate cry of 'Mammy!' as tears fled his eyes, and he started to convulse.

Desperately mouthing the solemn intonation of the 'Our Father' again, his teeth clamped down on his tongue sharply, the pain mingling with the stinging remnant of the punches to his head. This added a remote cause to his despair. Angrily, he railed against God, cursing him, abandoning all hope of being saved. A vicious mantra of 'FUCK! FUCK! FUCK!' sprang from his lips, his still-tender tongue lashing out the word.

Although now resigned to his fate, he violently mourned the deprivation that death implied. He was tormented by images of the earthly pleasures he would now be forever denied. *This is it. I'm going to die,* he thought, each word pronounced boldly in his mind. *I'm going to be dead. There will be no more time and I will be dead.* Suddenly, oblivion was real to him.

The drive continued, and he felt the car gradually ascending. He pictured it from above – as a dinkie on a track making its way up to the mountains. He hoped the end would be quick. And that afterwards there would be no more pain.

Still taunted by vivid pictures – of life, food, drink, friends, women – Shane craved oblivion, if only to stop the parade of images. But although he had lost faith in the Lord's power to save, he still feared his judgement. This invigorated his dismay as he felt the car slow, then tremble over rough ground for some minutes before drawing to a halt. Now he heard only one word, repeating rapidly through his mind. *Please, please, please, please, please.*

IN SITU

In Its Place

The car stopped and the driver turned the engine off, leaving a moment of silence. The quiet stillness felt strange. Shane pushed the useless phone to the back of the boot, not wishing to aggravate the men any further by revealing that he had tried to escape. Clicks signalled doors opening, then the car rocked as the men got out heavily.

The lid of the boot was opened. It was dark outside by this time, but Shane was amazed at how vivid the star-speckled deep navy of the night sky was. It was bright in comparison to the swallowing nothingness of his compartment. A fella had opened the boot, and he was flanked by another two. They wore hats and caps. In the light, Shane couldn't make out many of their features, only that they were big.

—Righ, the fella said to Shane. —You, get ou.

He was the leader – it was his voice that had told one of the others to get the phone. Shane complied eagerly, speaking as he clambered out.

—Lads, wha did I do? Please, just tell us, please?

Uncontrived, his voice was pleading and desperate as he stepped onto the little boreen. It wasn't a road, just a rutted tyre track with a strip of grass running the length of its middle. The track was flanked by thick hedges on one side and an overgrown field on the other.

—I don't know wha I did, please . . .

—Shut up fer a minute will ye, said the leader. —Bring him over there.

Shane heard the leader open a car door again, while

another fella marched him off the boreen through long, damp grass, toward the shelter of a row of bushes.

—Aw what's goin on man, please? Shane appealed.

—Wait now, the man said firmly.

—Have ye ties? the leader called from the car to the second man.

—I have one yeah! Righ, stop here, he said to Shane.

CUIUS REGIO, EIUS RELIGIO

Whose Realm, His Doctrine

Again, Shane complied obediently, respecting the authority of the assembly. The two others made their way through the grass toward him, while the man holding his arm kneeled at Shane's feet. He fumbled around his shins and then, with a shrill ripping noise, Shane felt something tighten around his calves. He looked down to see a thick white cable tie binding him. His hands were bound together next, in front of him, not behind his back. As if in prayer or supplication.

—Sit down there, said the second fella, lifting him from standing position onto the ground, firm but gentle.

Shane marvelled at the range of white pinpricks flung across the sky above him. A reply to the city lights. The heavens had a form out here, a solidity that justified the term 'firmament'. Enclosed in this star chamber, he looked back to the two men as they tramped their way toward him. Each was carrying a long instrument by his side. Shane reeled a little as he realised that they were hurley sticks. He looked to the man who – through that one act of placing him mildly on the ground – had established himself as a protector in Shane's mind.

—Aw please man, don't let them do tha to me, c'mon man please.

—Be quiet, said the man with a hint of annoyance.

—Relax you, said the leader. —We're only gonna have a talk with ye now.

IPSO FACTO

By the Fact Itself

The hurley sticks solidified Shane's darkest fears, and he was impelled to rock back and forth on the ground. He wanted to plead, but he didn't want to disobey orders. The instinct to speak was diverted into this desperate motion of a frightened child. The rocking was accompanied by an involuntary low moan, which he tried to stifle.

He glanced at the hurls – he could imagine the intensity of being struck with the sharp sides. There was no relief that it wasn't a gun. Being shot dead was an inconceivable threat. The consequences were metaphysical, Shane couldn't comprehend them. But he had been hit by a hurl before, he knew what it felt like: intense pain, grievous bodily harm. Faced with the prospect of being purposefully beaten, with no hope of escape, he was terrified.

For a while, the resignation of despair had let him succumb to his fate. This was disrupted by the reality that now presented itself. He felt his blood drain, and a white, relaxed lightness in his stomach. This was followed by a pleasant sensation of warmth on his leg. He'd pissed himself. Suddenly drained, he slumped forward. He tried to say something before he fainted, open-mouthed.

★

Tumbling through a swirling churning blackness with incredible speed, Shane wondered what was happening. The rhythmic whirling grew in intensity, like a train in a tunnel. *This has to stop soon,* he thought. When he suddenly awoke, it was like breaking the surface after being underwater. After a cold sensation of dew-kissed grass against his face he was pulled upright, confused. Disorientation melted into renewed panic. His wet crotch started to feel cold.

—Are ye awake?

The leader leaned over him, slapping him limply on the face.

—Yeah, yeah, said Shane, hyperventilating.

—Righ . . . D'ye know why yer here?

His voice was a little less aggressive than before.

—No . . . Please.

AFFIDAVIT

Sworn Testimony

—I think ye *do* know why yer here, Shane.

—I don't man, I swear to God.

—Think abour it. C'mon. Why d'ye think yer after bein brough up here?

—I don't know man, I swear to Jaysis.

The other two men stood over him, shifting on their feet

every now and again, while the first fella crouched interrogating him.

—Now Shane, I'm sure ye can think of a few things. I'm gonna tell ye all abour it, but I want you to say it first.

—I don't know man I swear.

—What might it be? Think.

DUBITANTE

Doubt

Shane thought. There were loads of ideas going through his mind, but none appealed to him as an explanation which might appease the man. If they were the 'RA or vidjos, maybe it was just the general drug dealing. If they were doing this for the youngfella he'd battered with Robbie Boyle, it was self-explanatory. If it was Paddy Lawless behind it, it could be over the youngfella *or* Elizabeth *or* whatever shit had happened between him and Griffo. If it was Griffo, the trouble with Paddy Lawless might have started feeding into some paranoid fantasy. If it was Elizabeth's da, it could be the fact that he was a drug dealer who'd been riding his daughter. If it was the INLA . . . Shane couldn't think of a reason. He didn't know what the INLA did or didn't do – only what the papers said about them. He couldn't make any sense of that either.

Revealing any of these thoughts seemed likely to further anger the men. Shane didn't know what *they* knew or didn't know. Telling them something they weren't already aware of might throw fuel on the fire.

—I don't know man seriously. Would yis not just tell me? Maybe yis have it wrong or yis have me mixed up with someone else.

—Don't think so Shane, said the first man.

—Ye migh as well tell him wha he wants to hear, said the third man, speaking for the first time, as he clubbed the leader shoots of grass with his hurl.

There was silence as they waited, pressure mounting on Shane to tell them something.

—He's not talkin lads, said the leader. —Give us his phone ou there till we have a look.

Shane was surprised they hadn't tossed his personal phone away immediately. He'd presumed anyone else involved in illegal activity shared the deep paranoia about mobile phone tracing that Griffo had instilled in him. The leader started reading his texts. Shane was worried, in case Elizabeth's da was behind this, because the angry texts to and from Elizabeth were still there. There was nothing else to worry about, just messages from mates. Nothing incriminating.

—Shane, said the first man absentmindedly as he scrolled on through the texts. —I migh as well tell ye now, ye'd be better off to start talkin. If ye tell us the truth now, we'll go easy on ye. Well . . . *easier* on ye. We know anyway, we just wanna hear it from *you.*

—Seriously, replied Shane. —I don't know wha I'm after doin on yis but I swear to God if ye tell me I'll try and sort it wha'ever it is, wha'ever yis want.

—It's not us you have to be makin things up to. Now c'mon. Just go through the reasons ye migh have been brought out here and tell me the first tha springs to mind, we haven't all nigh.

Shane waited a few beats while he thought about it, and then finally felt compelled to say something. He didn't make a conscious decision, it just came out – his mouth seemed to be on autopilot.

—Drugs?

—Wha drugs? said the man, in a tone which Shane took to indicate that this was what he had wanted to hear.

—Coke?

—Wha about coke?

ACTUS REUS

Guilty Act

—Tha I'm sellin it?

—So yer sellin it an all are ye? Yer a drug dealer, is tha wha yer tellin me Shane?

—Oney coke.

—Oney coke. Wha abou Es?

—I do take the Es, but I oney sell coke.

—Is tha righ? D'ye not sell hash?

—No.

—Why not?

Shane wanted to appease the man, so he plumped for honesty.

MODUS OPERANDI

Method of Operation

—There's more profit in coke. I don't smoke hash meself. An the hash is too big to hide properly.

—Is tha righ? . . . An c'mere then tell me this now – have ye ever sold gear?

—No way man! I wouldn't do tha.

—Who d'ye sell the coke for then?

—Wha d'ye mean

—Who are ye workin for sellin drugs?

This confused Shane.

—No one like . . . eh . . . meself.

—Ye just took it upon yourself to start sellin drugs did yeh?

—Eh . . . mm . . . yeah.

—An how the fuck did tha come abou?

—I was takin Es and doin coke meself anyway. So I just started gettin a bit more for mates and then sellin a bit to get some for meself, Shane lied.

Talking to someone, even his captors, eased the panic. Having to think of what to say distracted his mind from the prospect of imminent and terrible pain.

—An where d'ye get it then if yer not workin for anyone?

—I just buy it off a fella.

—Who?

IMPRIMATUR

Sanction

This was the danger zone. If this was the 'RA or vidjos, they might want the names of other dealers before they battered him. If it was something to do with Griffo, it could be a test to see if Shane would rat him out. If it was something to do with Paddy Lawless and his crowd, they could be trying to get info about what was going on between him and Griffo. He still didn't know what the fuck was going on.

—Who do ye buy the coke off Shane?

—Just this fella I met in a club.

—What's his name?

—He calls himself James, but I don't think that's his real name, Shane lied again.

He spoke only when spoken to, allowing the men continue to direct the cross-examination. But they seemed unsure of his testimony, despite their claims to knowledge.

—And where's this 'James' fella from?

—Tallaght.

—Is his number in here, said the first man, nodding toward the phone he still held in his hand.

—No, I just have it written down cause he gets me to ring him from a payphone.

—Check his phone there, said the first man, handing the phone to the second fella.

He scrolled through it.

—There's a James Cleary here, said the second man.

—That's not him, that's me sister's fella, said Shane.

—Lydia's fella? said the first man. —Are ye sure?

—Yeah.

IN LOCO PARENTIS

In the Place of a Parent

Shane thought about this. He realised it was his da who had organised the whole thing. Instantly, the terror dissipated, and the flurry of confused thoughts clarified. There was still adrenalin, but it was beneficial, allowing him to think fast and assess the situation. There was no joy or relief, just a sudden absence of anxiety. As if it had never been there.

—No Jimmies in the phone either? said the leader to the second man.

—No, said the second man.

—I don't ring him off tha phone, I oney ring him off a payphone, said Shane again.

He was galvanised by his enlightenment.

—An then ye go up to Tallaght to meet him?

—Yeah.

—Are ye sure yer tellin us the truth there? Are ye not gettin it off a fella from town?

—No.

—Is Robbie Boyle not gettin ye to sell it for him?

—No! Jaysis I was oney drinkin with him once or twice, I hardly know the chap.

—That's not wha we heard, said the leader. —An ye don't want to be lyin to us now. It's Robbie Boyle yer sellin the coke for isn't it?

—I'm not sellin coke for him. Look lads, ye can do wha yis want to me, but seriously I'm not sellin it for anyone. I was drinkin with Robbie Boyle once in the Mercury and once in a club in town. That's the only times I ever met the chap.

—Check is Boyle's number in there, said the leader to the second man.

Thankfully, it was the drug phone Shane had Boyle's number saved on.

—Are ye sure now you're tellin the truth? Remember Shane, we might have talked to Robbie ourselves.

SUB JUDICE

Under Judgement

It wasn't a very advanced inquisition, Shane could tell the man was bluffing. If it was true, Boyle would only have confirmed Shane's story. He wondered what sort of summary justice this special court intended to mete out. Three judges, no jury. He knew it wouldn't be anything too serious – his da was rough, but there'd be no actual bodily harm. Just a show trial to scare him. He wasn't going to be killed. He felt contempt for his da. Fucking eejit.

So it went on, the fella acting the hard man and asking Shane questions. He could tell they'd done this before. They'd probably been involved in the anti-drugs movement with his oulfella, or done the doors with him, or actually were 'RA heads doin him a favour. He also knew that the other times they'd done this they'd probably carried out the threats. He no longer felt fear, but there were going to be serious consequences. There was no way he'd ever be on talking terms with his da again.

The questioning quickly turned into an anti-drugs lecture, much like ones he'd received from his father on countless occasions. He was told of the dangers of overdose, addiction, arrest, vendetta. There was an addendum on the morality of dealing. Shane nodded along cheerfully.

—Righ. We're gonna let ye go this time, but if we have to take ye up here again ye won't make it back down, d'ye hear me?

—I hear ye.

Once he'd realised his da was behind it all, he'd known he was just going to be let go. They weren't gonna do anything. Then the first man stood up suddenly and swung back his hurl, grimacing with intent, holding it so it would come down on the sharp side.

—Just make sure ye remember! he shouted.

LEX TALIONIS

Punishment

Reeling in the muck, legs still clasped by the cable tie, Shane put his arms up to shield himself and turned his face away from the coming blow . . . before he felt a swift smack on his side.

IN TERROREM

In Fear

The fella had hit him with the flat of the hurl on the flank of his arse, hard enough to hurt, but nowhere near enough to do damage. Shane felt humiliated after flinching so dramatically when the fella was only toying with him.

—Yer lucky that's all yer gettin. Up, said the first man. —Cut the ties off him, he said to the third man.

The second fella pulled Shane off the ground.

ADJOURNMENT SINE DIE

Indefinite Adjournment

The men tramped back through the grass toward the car and Shane followed. He stood by the rear passenger door.

—I don't think so son, said the leader.

—Ah! started Shane.

—Me bollix. Ye may go back the way ye came. Go on. In the boot, he chuckled.

The other two men laughed too, as Shane stumbled around to the back of the car. The leader opened it via a latch from the driver's seat and Shane had to climb in himself before the second man walked round to close it.

—Toughen ye up, he said as he brought the lid down gently.

This time Shane's immersion in darkness wasn't fraught. He nestled into the compartment almost snugly. He remembered that the drug phone was in the boot. This gave him a welcome chance to retrieve it without drawing attention.

On the journey down, there was no surge of relief, no newfound joy in being alive. Only a pressing desire for a hot shower and bed – and an outrage verging on disbelief that his father would perpetrate this crime against him.

He didn't countenance the notion that his father had organised the whole thing out of concern – that it was an effort to preserve Shane's *life*, to save him from ending up like Chalkie. He just resolved never to trust him again. And, if possible, never to talk to him again either.

When the car stopped and the lid of the boot was opened the first man drew back his face in disgust.

—There's a bit of a bang off ye there son, he said.

—Ah Jaysis . . . Are ye after pissin yourself or somethin? the leader said. —We were gonna ask ye in for a pint an all!

IBID.

The Same Place

Shane found himself back in the pub car park where he'd started. The men were in a boisterous mood, chuckling and joking as they bustled outside the car.

Shane remained quiet and crawled out of the boot. A wizened and swaying solitary drunkard stood near the pub door smoking. He eyed Shane with mild concern, then looked at the men.

—Alrigh Dave, said the leader.

—Grand, said Dave definitively.

IDEM

The Same Person

Ignoring the young man who had just climbed out of a car boot, the oulfella stamped out his cigarette and retreated into the warmth of the pub. He looked like he had his own troubles to worry about.

Shane didn't know how to behave. Standing at the back of the car, he brushed himself down roughly. He was embarrassed at the smell of piss off himself. He didn't know whether to just walk off, or if he should say goodbye to the men or just give them a wave or what to do.

—Righ, said the first man. —Here's yer phone back. An remember – ye don't want to go back up there with us again, righ?

—Righ, said Shane taking the personal phone.

—See ye now, said the fella, jubilantly slamming the boot.

The three men walked into the pub, and Shane was left in the car park alone. He wandered out onto the main road then looked around. It felt good to be free. He wondered if his da was actually in the pub, or would the men just ring him and tell him what had happened.

Three taxis went by, but Shane was waiting until he saw one with a black fella driving – he wanted to be sure it wouldn't be someone who knew him. Usually he sat in the front and chatted with the driver, but today he got into the back, hoping the driver wouldn't notice the smell. The black fella glanced at him in the rear view mirror as Shane told him the destination. A few moments after they set off, the driver looked in the mirror again.

—You piss yourself or somethin? he said, his accent mingling Dublin with West Africa.

When the taxi pulled up outside the apartment, Shane gave the black fella a €50 note without asking for change. Compensation for the smell. The car wouldn't have been properly soiled, it had leather seats.

—Thank you brother, said the black fella without conviction.

HABEAS CORPUS

You Shall Have Your Body

Inside, Shane got naked and straight underneath the hot, powerful electric shower. He soaped and scrubbed himself assiduously, enjoying the sensation of the water on his skin. Chops was playing a gig. Shane knew he'd be going out afterwards, maybe not returning until late the next day.

Shane padded naked out of the bathroom toward his

leaba. The bedclothes were clean and cosy. He put on a pair of fresh boxers before sliding under the clean sheets. His watch said 12:45. Needing someone to talk to, he rang Elizabeth. She cancelled the call. He sent her a text:

Need to talk to u ring me

The reply came swiftly:

Nothing to talk about

She was probably out with the girls. Or some fella even. He constructed and fired another message off rapidly.

Somethins after happening Elizabeth, serious. Need to talk to someone.

EX GRATIA

By Grace

Moments later, the phone flashed 'Elizabeth', to his enormous, overwhelming relief.

—Wha? she said in a bothered tone.

The sound of her voice and the lack of background noise told him she was just at home. In bed.

—Aw look Elizabeth . . . seriously somethin *mad* is after happenin an I just need ye to listen to me and be there for me righ? I'm no askin ye to get back with me or annythin, but you're the oney person I can talk to.

—Wha is it?

—Will ye promise not to tell anyone? This is serious now.

—I won't.

—Swear?

—Yeah, I swear. Go on Shane just tell us . . . Ye have me worried now, she said.

Whether her tone now betrayed annoyance or concern Shane couldn't tell.

—C'mere ye can't tell *anyone* abou this – not even *mention* it to anyone else. Nobody.

—I won't Shane, what's after happenin?

He told her the story, waiting until the near the end to reveal that it had been his da behind the whole thing.

—Jaysis Shane, wha're ye gonna do? she gasped.

—I don't fuckin know, I'm freaked.

—Oh my God! Aw Jaysis, Shane. I'm sorry for sendin ye tha snotty message, I didn't realise.

—It's alrigh. I'm glad I had ye there to ring, there's no one else I can talk to ye know.

—Are ye alrigh? she asked, voice trembling.

She avoided commenting on the actions of his father, not wanting to put down one of Shane's parents.

—Aw I dunno missus . . . me head's wrecked like. I though I was gonna die an all.

—Do ye want me to come over to ye?

—I don't know . . . I don't want ye to feel obliged like.

—I want to, she said sweetly. —I don't want ye to be on yer own after somethin like tha.

—Are ye sure?

—Yeah, Jesus, ye poor thing like. I'd probly be in the hospital havin a breakdown if it was me.

Shane laughed.

—I'm serious Shane! I don't know how you're bein so cool about it like, I would of been shittin meself.

—Yeah.

He didn't mention the fact that he'd literally pissed himself.

—Well will I come over?

—Ye know I want ye to. But only if *you* want to . . .

—Righ well I'll order a taxi now righ?

—Righ.

She rang him back a few seconds later and they chatted again while she waited for the taxi. Twenty minutes later she was buzzing the apartment door.

She hugged him tenderly when she came in, then held him tighter, squeezing him. Shane clasped her in return, savouring her presence against him, her sweet fragrance. They stood in the hall hugging like this for ages. It felt *so* good. The familiar feel of her body, her unique smell. It was better than a drug hit. He was more addicted to her than any substance. He didn't get withdrawal from cocaine or ecstasy. But being deprived of her presence was physical and emotional torture. Nothing less.

IN FLAGRANTE DELICTO

Caught Rapid

She pressed closer against him, and he felt an arousal. Tender affection turned sexual. They kissed deeply before moving to the bedroom and making love. Afterwards, she hugged him close again.

BONA FIDES

Good Faith

—Aw I got such a frigh when ye told me tha Shane, thinkin abou wha could of happened. I dunno wha I'd do if you were gone for good, she said, tears welling in her eyes.

—That's not gonna happen, he said.

Now came relief. Reunited with Elizabeth, having her treat him so tenderly and with such genuine concern convinced him that at least one of his problems had been solved. And maybe his other difficulties could be conquered or would sort themselves out. His fears could be vanquished. It was possible. He'd found hope again.

—Wha're ye gonna do? Are ye gonna say it to yer da?

—I don't wanna talk to him ever again, said Shane. —But I don't want him to think I didn't cop it was him behind it either. Even if they hadn't of given it away, I probly would have realised it afterwards. It happened righ where I was meetin him. Too much of a coincidence.

—Fuckin hell Shane.

—I know.

—Are ye gonna say it to yer sister? asked Elizabeth. —Or yer ma?

He'd been considering it. He wanted to prevent his oulfella interfering in his affairs – he'd no intention of giving up selling, and he wanted to continue unmolested. Only the prospect of alienating or angering the rest of the family would deter his da from interfering.

Shane suspected that his da had played his last card anyway. What was he gonna do next, have him kneecapped? No. He'd tried to put the shits up him, it had worked for a while, but it had just made Shane lose any connection he felt with him. Since his da had punched him that first time, Shane had been losing respect for him. This was the nail in the coffin.

Elizabeth stayed with him all the next day. She cooked dinner and they cuddled on the couch, wrapping themselves eagerly around each other. His da rang him in the early afternoon. Shane just put the phone on silent.

—So what's the story now? Shane asked as they lay curled up together.

—Wha d'ye mean?

—With me an you like.

—Well wha d'you want to happen? Elizabeth asked.

She looked up into his eyes.

DE NOVO

Anew

—I wanna get back with ye.

—I wanna get back with you too . . . I never wanted it to finish Shane, I was just pissed off. Me head was wrecked an I couldn't stop thinkin about ye the whole time we were broke up.

—So is tha it then? We're back together?

—I suppose so, she laughed.

CONSENSUS AD IDEM

Consent of Both Parties

The two of them looked at each other and giggled. Shane felt euphoria – for the first time in a long time, even on E.

—If ye really do want to? she added. —You're not just sayin tha cause I came over to ye last nigh an all? Cause I would of comin over an'annyway.

—Not at all! Sure ye know I wanted ye back the whole time as well Elizabeth.

She hugged him and they kissed emotionally. Then the door burst open.

—What's the story? said Chops, as he bustled in. —Ooh sorry. Ah Jaysis look who it is!

He broke into a grin.

—What's goin on here then?

—Heye, Elizabeth said coyly, a big smile on her face.

—What's the story man? Shane smiled.

—I won't ask, said Chops. —C'mere I'll leave you two lovebirds at it.

He made to turn around and close the door.

—No man yer grand, c'mon in, we're just chillin out.

—Yeah c'mon an have a cup of tea with me, said Elizabeth. —This fella here won't make me one.

She smiled at Shane.

—Alrigh, said Chops. —Jaysis I go away for one nigh an look wha happens!

Chops was happy to have Elizabeth back around – he liked her, and he enjoyed a bit of female company. The hint of perfume about the place. Shane was glad at his reaction. The approval of his trusted friend meant a lot to him.

They were happy, the three of them.

After Elizabeth went to work the next morning Shane rang his sister on her mobile.

—Lydia?

—Howye Shane, c'mere I'm in work can I ring ye back in a while?

—Yeah no bother.

A few minutes later she called back.

—Listen Lydia I have somethin to tell ye righ. Now promise me yer not gonna go mad?

—Wha're ye after doin?

—It's nothin I'm after doin, it's just a bit mad, an I need yer advice.

— Is everything alrigh?

She wasn't used to Shane confiding in her. Sometimes they'd discuss personal things together, although not so much since he'd moved out. But he'd never called her specifically to ask advice before.

—Yeah it's grand now, just somethin a bit mad happened the other nigh, an I wanted to talk to you before sayin anthin to Ma.

—Righ . . . Does this have anythin to do with you sellin coke?

—How did *you* know?

—Ah it's fuckin obvious Shane! All tha money yer spendin. An sure I know well Chops is sellin stuff. And Dotsy and Aido now too. Sure yis are all at it.

—Does Ma know?

—No, sure she hasn't a clue, ye know yerself . . . Well I don't think so. She might know you're up to something, but I'd say she doesn't even want to know. Anyway wha happened – ye got arrested did ye?

—Jaysis no, thank God. Well sort of I did . . . but not by the Gards.

—Wha?

ET CETERA

And Such

He told her the story, but he toned down the tale for her ears – unlike when he had related it to Elizabeth. Still, Lydia was outraged.

AD HOMINEM

To the Man

—I can't fuckin believe it Shane. The fuckin prick. Where was he when we were kids? Takin us out for an hour once a month, then leavin us in Nanny's. Now he thinks he has a righ to do somethin like this?

—I'll ring Childline on him.

—It's not funny Shane, it's fuckin serious. I'm gonna ring him now when I get off this phone, I swear to God.

—Don't Lydia.

She seethed silently down the phone, but Shane could tell she'd accede to his demand. The two of them were in it together.

—Will you tell Ma? Shane asked her.

—Yeah if ye want. Someone's gonna have to tell her somethin anyway, cause I've had enough of him now honest to God. I can't believe it.

They agreed on a version to tell their ma. Lydia promised to call over to the house in person. Shane was taken aback by how supportive she was. He felt better knowing she was behind him. Now that he had Elizabeth back too, he felt stronger. Some of the gnawing anxiety that had been plaguing him dissipated.

His ma rang his da that night and lambasted him, denigrating him for all his neglect and lack of concern down the years, and for using violence against his own son – her child – after she had warned him not to. Shane's da was shocked that she knew everything. He'd realised Shane would probably twig it eventually, but had been prepared to flatly deny it.

She informed him of Lydia's opinion on the matter too. It stung him badly. He loved Lydia. Respected her. He felt guilty when he thought of her. Despite his inattention, she'd turned out to be a smart capable, hard-working young woman. Now it was three against one. He tried to counter the criticism by attacking Shane, throwing in the revelation that he was selling drugs. Shane's ma was unfazed.

—It doesn't matter, even if he *is*! That doesn't give you the righ to go an do the likes of that. He's not an animal!

She didn't let herself believe it fully, choosing to focus on the matter at hand.

—Somethin had to be done, it was for his own good.

—Look, I reared those children, you've no righ to come along now an start layin down the law.

—C'mon, ye didn't rear them on your own.

—You left before Lydia started school.

—I didn't leave ye to do it all by yourself.

—No you're righ. I had help. Your mother, God rest her

soul, helped me when she was alive. Even your poor aul father did more than you ever done.

—That's not true now, I paid my way.

—It takes more than money to rare a child, an wha you paid me barely kept them in britches. Well ye can just stay away now. If they want to talk to ye that's up to them, but I'm warnin ye, if you get anyone else to go near tha youngfella again I'll be goin straight to the Gards. An I'll get a barrin order on ye as well.

—Ah c'mon, there's no need for this. I oney wanted to scare some sense into the youngfella! D'ye want him to end up like his mate? Dead in the bed?

—I'd rather tha than he ended up like you!

She shocked herself. She didn't mean it. It would kill her if anything happened to Shane. But she stuck to her guns and told his da where they all stood, that he was to leave Lydia and Shane alone. They'd contact him if they wanted.

—An are you not gonna talk to me now either? he said, self-pityingly.

—The only reason I've talked to you for the past twenty years is for those children. You made your choices when you left this house, so there's no use complainin to me now.

Even though she was infuriated by his methods, she was anti-drugs herself. But there was a difference between her policy *de jure* and *de facto*. She saw that Shane was happier than he had been, that he had money. As far as she was concerned, it was better to let sleeping dogs lie. To hell with Shane's da. She felt liberated by Lydia and Shane's attitude, her anger and frustration released. When they were younger, she'd held her tongue, reasoning that the children should form their own opinions of their da. Now that their

Nanny was gone, there was little reason left to try and maintain good relations.

—I used to be angry with you for leavin, she said, —but I'm better off without ye, and the truth is the children are better off as well.

She hung up the phone and felt a powerful glow of satisfaction.

MUTATIS MUTANDIS

With Due Alterations

Even though he hadn't felt too upset, the event did have an impact on Shane. He suspected he would feel it even more down the line. Somehow, the shock carried him through though – he felt spurred to action, not stuck in a rut like before.

A month or so later, Elizabeth and Shane went out on the town for a Saturday night together. After a meal, they ended up in a new-ish nightclub, on Essex Street in Temple Bar. A typical Celtic Tiger super-pub, the decor was palatial, the place was overcrowded, the service was poor and the music was utter shite.

After one drink, they decided to go off and meet Elizabeth's mates in the George. Shane stood beside the entrance while she collected her jacket from the cloakroom. He could overhear the bouncers talking on the other side of the door.

—Wha're they like?

—Ah they're fuckin deadly. I take one if I'm watchin a bluey. Abou five wanks in a row I had.

Shane recognised the voice.

—Would ye be bothered takin Viagra just to watch a dirty fillum though? said another doorman. —A bluey watchin a bluey wha?

—Closest I get to gettin me hole these days.

Elizabeth returned with the jackets.

—D'ye know who's on the door there? Shane asked her smiling.

—Who? she asked, putting on her jacket.

—Me oulfella, Shane laughed.

—Are ye serious? said Elizabeth, concerned. —Fuck. D'ye wanna go out the back way?

—No it's grand. C'mon . . . I'm goin out the front door like a free man, he said, opening the door for her.

CORAM NON JUDICE

Before One Without Authority

His oulfella, still engrossed in banter with the lads, turned around and glanced at the couple before doing a double take, his eyes settling on Shane.

—Howye, he said, staring into his son's face.

RESTITUTIO IN INTEGRUM

Restoration of What Is Right

—See ye after, said Shane to his father, buttoning his jacket as he fixed his stare into his father's eyes.

Elizabeth took Shane's hand and they walked out into the crowded street.

A JUDGEMENT

Judgement Title: DPP -v- Patrick Lawless
Court: Court of Criminal Appeal
Composition of Court: Higgins J., Taylor J., Doherty J.
Judgement by: Higgins J.
Status of Judgement: Approved

Along with a co-accused, the applicant pleaded guilty in the Dublin Circuit (Criminal) Court to possession of approximately €11,000 worth of cocaine in a motor vehicle at Blackhorse Avenue on 12 December 2002. His Honour Judge Hendry imposed a sentence of five years with immediate effect.

At the sentencing hearing, the principal issue was whether these drugs were the property of Mr Lawless and his co-accused, or whether they were acting on behalf of a third party in transporting the drugs. Although there was no doubt over the issue of possession, the matter of whether or not Mr Lawless and his co-accused stood to profit significantly from the sale of the drugs did constitute some grounds for mitigation.

It was the contention of counsel for the applicant, Mr Davis, that the co-accused were merely transporting the drugs, as payment for which they would receive a small amount of cocaine for personal consumption. Before sentencing, Judge Hendry solicited evidence from Garda Jerome Troy in relation to Mr Lawless, and the following exchange took place:

Judge: Do you believe this man to be organising the sale and distribution of drugs himself?

A. I do.

Judge: Based upon what evidence?

A. Basically, his association with high-level drug dealers in the North Inner City.

Judge: They would be known to you?

A. They would.

Judge: And what reason have you to believe he is not merely indebted to drug dealers, and forced to carry out their orders to feed his own habit?

A. Basically, having observed him personally on numerous occasions associating with the higher level of criminals.

Judge: And you're satisfied he stood to profit significantly from the sale of the drugs in question?

A. I am.

Judge: I'm obliged. Thank you.

A. No bother.

On appeal to this court, the principal argument was that Judge Hendry had fallen into error by soliciting the opinion of the Garda in relation to extraneous relationships to the offence to which the applicant had pleaded guilty. We agree that the learned judge fell into error in the manner submitted, but since we would in any event have imposed a not dissimilar sentence, we nonetheless affirmed the sentence in question.

In this circumstance, we cannot say that the learned sentencing judge erred in imposing a sentence of five years imprisonment, even if he did have recourse to inadmissible hearsay evidence during the sentencing process itself. It was for these reasons that the Court dismissed the applicant's appeal against the severity of sentence.

6

It had been months since the incident up in the mountains. Lydia hadn't spoken to her da since. Via text, she asked him to stop ringing. Shane just ignored the phone any time he saw 'Da' flash up. And he'd stopped answering private numbers long ago. The calls dwindled to a halt.

Although deeply upset by this turn of events, their da didn't make any other attempts at reconciliation aside from the calls. He'd no idea how to even send a text message, the written word wasn't for him. His absence didn't impose much on Lydia or Shane. They didn't think of him at all – until Shane got some disturbing news. He received a phone call from his ma telling him that his granda – his da's da – was dying.

Their granda had been in and out of hospital since his wife had passed away. After her death, he'd deteriorated

235

rapidly, forgetting to wash, turning to drink. Since he'd been unable to look after himself, the family had chipped in to make sure he was clean and healthy. There was a meals-on-wheels service too – though sometimes he declined to answer the door to them and the silver-foil trays would be left outside to sit on his windowsill. He refused to partake in the events at the associated day centre. Despite the best efforts of all concerned, he slipped into senility and, after numerous disturbing incidents, his care had to be handed over to the Eastern Health Board.

While medication had stabilised the dementia, he'd now developed an aggressive form of lung cancer. Shane's immediate emotion on learning this was guilt. He hadn't been to see his granda in the home at all. His ma said she'd ring Lydia after work to tell her, but Shane decided to call his sister himself.

—Howye Lydia.

—What's up?

—Did ye hear abou Granda?

—No, what? she said.

—He's not well.

—Is he on the way out like? she asked in a whisper.

—Yeah, cancer. He only has a few months.

—Who told ye?

—Ma just rang me there.

—Jaysis.

—I know. I feel bad not goin up to see him, said Shane. Lydia had been a few times.

—Does he know he's dyin? she hushed.

—I dunno.

—He mightn't understand anyway.

—Wha is he like, is he just ou of it? asked Shane.

—They have him just sittin there all day. He just sits there starin.

—Does he recognise ye an all? Shane asked.

—Ah yeah, he's not tha bad yet! said Lydia. —Some days, like, he might get confused an all, but he still knows who everyone is. Aw it was gas righ! The last time we went up, we were sittin there with him and the nurse was pushin this trolley righ, an the wheels made a big creakin noise an he jumps up in the chair an goes, 'Who has tha parrot? Who has a parrot in here?'

—No way.

—Yeah it was mad. He was convinced there was a parrot in the ward!

—Will ye go up with me? Shane asked her.

—Yeah I'll go with ye. When d'ye wanna go up?

—Tonigh?

—I've no car with me, said Lydia.

—I'll pick ye up, said Shane.

—Righ no bother. I'll see ye outside around six then?

—Sound.

When Shane collected her, she was in good humour, giddy after finishing work. They joked and had the craic, avoiding the news of their granda's illness.

—How's Elizabeth? she asked as they neared the hospital.

—Grand.

—How're the two of yis gettin on?

—Grand.

—Is tha all ye can say – grand? How's things goin with the two of yis?

—Graand!

—Jaysis Shane, you're so in touch with your emotions. You're a real 'new man' type aren't ye?

—Fuck off.

—So eloquent as well.

—Ask me bollix.

She laughed as they pulled into the hospital car park. Inside the building, they passed the reception desk without stopping. Lydia knew the right ward. She paused before going in and squirted some hand sanitiser from a dispenser on the wall. Shane copied her, rubbing the liquid in vigorously.

The ward nurse smiled at them, and they made their way over to their granda. He was sitting by the window, staring ahead, just as Lydia had described. But, facing the wall, he was ignoring the view. There was also a TV switched on in a far corner. The sound was on mute.

—Heye Granda! said Lydia.

He turned his head and stared at her for a few moments.

—Ah howye daughter, he said in a husky treble. —Lydia . . . How are ye doin?

—I brought someone to see ye, she smiled.

He turned his attention to Shane, and he stared for a long time as Shane fidgeted, not knowing what to say.

—Howye Granda, he managed.

—Ah Janet! Sorry I didn't recognise ye there Janet. How're ye doin? he said to Shane.

Lydia snorted, and looked at Shane.

—No. Granda, this is Shane. Yer grandson. My *bro-ther*! *Shay-ene*!

She couldn't keep the giggles out of her voice and had to look away after she got the words out. Shane smiled at the extra syllable she gave his name.

—Oh that's right, said their granda, unfazed. —Hello Shane. Bejaney. You're gettin big.

He shifted around in his chair to get more upright.

—And how's your father? he asked the pair.

—Grand, said Lydia, hoping to avoid the subject.

—He hasn't been in to see me this week. Busy I suppose.

—Yeah, said Lydia. —Here, Shane brought ye in some chocolates.

This wasn't true. On her lunch break she'd bought a box of Dairy Milk, but since she'd been in to the hospital a few times already, she attributed the gift to Shane.

—Oh thanks very much, good lad. Not like your father, he chuckled. —How's school?

—I'm finished school now, Granda, said Shane.

Lydia pulled over two seats and they sat down around their granda's chair.

—Bejapers, the time flies . . . An what are ye doin with yourself now?

Shane gave Lydia a quick glance, embarrassed.

—I'm doin DJ, Shane lied.

—Oh very good. On the wireless?

—No, in clubs.

—Discos, put in Lydia.

—Oh very good, said their granda. —I'd say that pays well.

—Ye'd be surprised, Lydia said, raisin her eyebrows.

—How are you an'annyway? said Shane quickly.

—Oh I'm grand, can't complain. They keep feedin me annyway . . . They haven't forgot about me . . . Not yet annyway.

—That's good.

—An are the nurses nice? asked Lydia, lowering her voice.

—Oh they're not too bad . . . Could be worse, he chuckled.

—What's the food like, Jopa? asked Shane, using the name they had called him when they were babies.

Their granda's name was Patrick Joseph, and his friends had called him 'Pajo'. As a toddler, Lydia had jumbled it, mixing up Granda with Pajo and coming up with Jopa. Shane had followed her, and it had stuck. Even their da called him Jopa now. Memories of time spent in Nanny and Jopa's house flickered in Shane's mind. Nanny giving him jam sandwiches, and tea in his bottle instead of milk. Jopa patiently teaching him how to play hurling. Their da collecting them and driving them back to their ma's after he finished work in the garage.

—The food's all right. It does the job, said Jopa.

—What did ye have today? asked Lydia.

—Ryan Tubridy.

—Wha? said Shane, beginning to laugh, himself.

—What did ye have for dinner? Lydia asked. —Today?

Jopa frowned and shook his head.

—Oh. Fish or somethin it was! It wasn't very nice.

—An how are you feelin in yourself? said Lydia.

—Grand. I'm supposed to be havin an operation next week. The head honcho came in yesterday, in his suit. He had all his students examinin me. I told him he looked like a second-hand furniture salesman. From Limerick.

Lydia and Shane exchanged glances of nervous amusement.

—They're doin a special study on me.

They looked at each other sceptically. They didn't know what to say.

—I think they want to put me in a museum or somethin.

240

Not until after I die though, Jopa added. —Do you know when that is?

This disturbed Shane. It was shocking, like something out of a horror film.

—They don't tell me an'thin of course, continued Jopa. —I don't know how it's organised at all.

—Don't be worryin yourself Jopa! said Lydia. —You've plenty of life left in ye.

—I do in my eye! said Jopa firmly. —It'll be like poor Mary.

Mary was their nanny's name. She'd died slowly of cancer, lying in pain for months, sinking into a hospital bed.

—Don't say that now, Jopa, Lydia patronised him. —You don't know what's around the corner, isn't tha righ Shane?

At the end of the visit, Shane awkwardly put his hand on Jopa's arm. Jopa reached out and grasped his hand, shook it, then clung onto it firmly. Shane was surprised at the strength that still resided in him, and touched by the emotion in the gesture. Lydia leaned over Jopa and kissed him on the cheek, hugged him. Jopa patted her back gently.

The visit provoked questioning for Shane. What was it going to be like for Jopa? A gradual retreat from yourself? Slowly losing your senses before ceasing to exist? Would it be painful? Was that worse than what happened to Chalkie – or what Shane had thought was going to happen him up in the mountains? Or was slipping away better, leaving time to think about things? Make your peace with everyone. With God and all.

Afterwards, Shane dropped Lydia off at her boyfriend's. He tried to pay her for the chocolates, but she pushed his hand away. As she got out of the car, Shane threw fifty quid into her open handbag without her noticing. The visit had shocked him. He wanted to do something to help, something to protect his loved ones, but there didn't seem to be any action to take. He'd felt a felt a strange surge of love, intermingled with guilt and foreboding, and wanted to act. But even this gesture felt futile, and only intensified the sense of impotence and guilty fear.

He tried to put it out of his mind. He had to find a payphone on the street to ring Griffo. Tedium. But he'd absorbed Griffo's warnings about the Special Branch's rapidly evolving technological capability. When Griffo changed his phone number, he used to just get a new SIM card, but he was adamant that the Garda could identify *individual handsets* now, as well as numbers. He explained to Shane that he now bought used ready-to-go handsets – with the SIM still inside – off random youngfellas he'd stop in the street. He'd throw them a oner in exchange. They could buy a fresh one for less than fifty quid, and Griffo would have no provable connection to the phone. If you bought the phone yourself in a shop, there was a record of when and where you'd bought it, and you'd be on CCTV making the purchase.

—Even then, it only half protects ye, Griffo told Shane, —cause the cunts can probly suss out who ye are from the *list* of numbers ye do be ringin an the numbers tha do be ringin you.

Shane put coins in the payphone and dialled Griffo's number.

—Hello?

—Hello?

—Yeah?

—It's the youngfella from the earlyhouse, said Shane.

This was the code they'd arrived at to avoid mentioning names.

—Ah . . . Howye doin?

—Not too bad. Are ye around?

—I'm just doin somethin here at the minute, I can meet ye at the place I met ye the last time, an hour after I met ye the time before last.

Shane worked this through in his head – the last time he'd met him it had been in the car park of their local, and the time before last he'd met him at nine o'clock – so Griffo wanted to meet him in the local at ten. Lately, Shane had grown comforted by this routine, which he previously had thought excessive. After the incident up in the mountains, and being followed by the Gards, he was as wary as a street cat. Now he had respect for Griffo's discernment, welcoming anything that had the potential to insulate him from getting arrested and convicted.

—The usual is it? said Griffo.

He was referring to the amount of cocaine Shane wanted to buy.

—The usual, yeah, said Shane.

—Sound kid, see ye then.

Griffo was moving back to his own friendly self of late, even though he knew Shane was back with Elizabeth.

Shane parked down the road from the local. That way if anyone was watching the car park, they wouldn't see him get out of his own car and then into Griffo's, which would have looked odd. The youngfella was in the front passenger seat of Griffo's car, as usual. He gave Shane the coke without saying anything. Griffo never carried anything himself anymore.

Shane had upped his order now, from an ounce to a half bar. This was more than four times the old amount. He had the funds to cover the whole lot squirreled away different places – more than enough – but he got it on tick now, for the sake of convenience. It meant having less cash lying around the apartment. He could just pay Griffo as he went along, instead of saving to buy the big order outright. He shoved the bulky bag down the front of his pants, just about getting away with it.

—You go on there, Griffo said to the youngfella.

The youngfella left the car, still without a word. Shane had met him loads of times now, but Griffo had never introduced them. *He's just a skivvy*, thought Shane, *probably carries the stuff cause he owes Griffo money he can't pay.*

—Righ man, I better head, said Shane.

—Hold on, I just wanna ask ye abou somethin, said Griffo, scanning the car park.

—Yeah?

—Not in the car though, we'll go in and get a 7 Up or somethin.

—Alrigh . . .

Shane noted that Griffo had waited until Shane was holding the drugs before going in for a chat. They walked into the pub casually.

—Wha d'ye want? Griffo asked Shane at the bar.

—Get us a ginger ale there, said Shane.

—Give us a diet 7 Up and a ginger ale, said Griffo to the barman.

—7 Up Free and a ginger ale, coming up, said the country barman. —I'll drop them over t'ye lads.

They sat at a table in a quiet corner, and Griffo flipped

beer mats, surveying the customers in the bar. They waited for the drinks without speaking.

—There ye go men, said the barman. —The shtrong shtuff.

Griffo handed him a tenner.

—That's grand Liam, he said, indicating that the barman should keep the change.

—Thankin you kindly sir.

The barman went off, down into the cellar. There were only a few couples in the lounge, and the usual oulfellas sitting at the bar. Griffo put his hand on his glass and huddled forward.

—Righ, he said to Shane. —I need to ask ye a bit of a favour.

—Fire away.

—Ye probly noticed I was a bit tense there for a while?

—Yeah.

—Sorry abou tha kid, just under pressure ye know, he said looking Shane in the eye. — Don't say an'thin but there's a bit of shit goin on at the minute . . . D'ye reckon the Old Bill know yer gaff?

—The apartment? No I don't think so, said Shane. — Why?

—It's not definite, but I migh need to use yer gaff for somethin.

—Wha like?

—It's only fer a few hours.

—Wha is it?

Griffo bent forward even further.

—I shouldn't be tellin ye this yet, but I know ye can be trusted. There's somethin goin down an a couple of lads need a clean gaff they can go back to for an hour or so, said Griffo in a whisper.

—Righ . . . , said Shane, not understanding.

—For a shower an all, d'ye get me? said Griffo, lowering his voice even further.

—Oh righ, yeah I get ye.

Shane's heart thumped a little, realising what Griffo was implying.

—I migh need you to do somethin as well . . . Nothin too bogey. Just a bit of tidyin up . . . So is tha cool? Griffo continued in a less conspiratorial tone. —We'll whack a few quid off wha ye owe me, he said, leaning back in his seat smiling.

—How much are we talkin?

—Jaysis yer a righ little businessman aren't ye? Shouldn't have taught ye so well. We'll knock a monkey off it righ?

That meant he'd cancel €500 of Shane's debt. The actual monetary cost to Griffo for that amount of cocaine would be around half of that.

—Sound, said Shane.

He was surprised to be offered money at all, Griffo was usually stingy.

—When is it? he asked.

—Don't know for definite, I'll let ye know a day or two before. But listen now, *do not* fuckin say annythin to anyone. I mean it. None of the lads, none of yer mates, nobody. Too many cunts end up locked up or even shot over loose talk. I shouldn't of even told ye what it's for, but I know I can trust ye – just don't say annythin to anyone else about it righ?

—Defo. No way man. I won't say a word.

Shane had been planning to tell Chops – it was his apartment as well – but he'd just have to make up some excuse and ask to have the place to himself for a day.

—Righ, well, I'll be in touch. I'll probly just buzz up to ye when I know wha the story is. Tryin to stay away from them phones. Bleedin lethal so they are!

—No bother.

Shane had noticed that Griffo no longer even took his phone out with him.

—Righ, I'll go on. Give us a minute there so the two of us aren't walkin ou together ye know.

—Sound.

—See ye after.

—Good luck.

The prospect of being involved in something like this excited Shane. He'd often wondered what went on with Griffo's business – but had always known better than to ask. The drive toward violence that marked the young was still in him, even if it had been tempered by his experiences over the previous year. The only prospect of security that he could imagine was being feared.

The next day, he went into Specsavers and bought a pair of glasses: just plain lenses, no prescription. He'd taken to wearing caps again, to hide his face, but worried that they made him look more dodgy. Counterproductive. Glasses would make him look less rough, less interesting to Gards. Since they'd taken his phone number, he had completely stopped having customers – even friends – up to the apartment. Because he met everyone outside now, he wanted to look as innocuous as possible on the street or in the car.

Even though the attention from the Gardaí had made

him edgy, Shane couldn't ignore his more profitable customers. Rory had put him on to a host of wealthy young professionals – arty, bohemian types. 'Hipsters', people were starting to call them now. They bought loads off him, always paying up front. They presented no threat of violence. He was reluctant to turn them down at any time. He feared they'd turn to other dealers. So he continued to ignore his instincts and kept the same number.

Although he had most of his customers' numbers saved, he knew that he would lose some business if he changed his own. He often got calls from people he didn't remember, people he'd met out, friends of friends – or friends of friend's friends – the wealthy posh types he'd no way of getting back in touch with otherwise. It gnawed at him, knowing that the Garda had his number, but he held onto the SIM card despite the anxiety it caused, telling himself he'd just keep his mouth shut if he was arrested, and they probably wouldn't go to the hassle of collecting the evidence from the phone company. Not for a youngfella just caught with a bit of coke. He convinced himself that, because the phone was unregistered, it would be difficult to prove in court that it had always been his. He imagined he could get away with saying he'd only just bought it. But really he was just letting his greed get the better of him.

Though he had more cash than ever, because of his paranoia, he avoided going out, even just for a walk around town. He preferred to sit in and watch a DVD rather than go to the cinema, eat ready meals rather than go out for dinner. Sometimes, to Elizabeth's delight, he even skipped his weekly Sunday session. She didn't like it when he went out, anxious that he'd cheat on her.

The earlyhouse and the Pink Pound had almost stopped – Shane thought it likely that he'd run into someone there who was close to Lawless and his crowd. He regretted getting Robbie Boyle to batter the youngfella now. If he hadn't been so drunk at the time, he would have realised that the fella hadn't recognised him, that he'd have been better off leaving it. Or getting someone to give the youngfella a hiding on the sly. He wouldn't have known where it was coming from then. Dish best served cold and all that.

The Saturday following Griffo's request, Shane was sitting in on his own in the apartment. Chops was playing a gig, and Elizabeth was out for a few drinks with her work crowd. Shane got uneasy when Elizabeth went out too. But in fairness she rarely got totally hammered the way other girls did. He got a phone call from her just after eleven.

—Hello, said Shane, surprised to hear from her.

—Heye.

He could hear she was in a car.

—Where are ye?

—I'm in a taxi on me way over to ye, she said. —Is tha alrigh?

She was a bit drunk.

—Yeah, course, sound. Are ye not stayin ou?

—No. I can't really talk I'll tell ye when I get over, she said.

—Is somethin up?

—I'll tell ye when I get over, she said.

Shane presumed she'd had a fight with one of the girls. He was glad she was coming over to keep him company, relieved she wasn't going be out for the night.

—Heye, she said, when she came in the door.

She looked rattled.

—What's up? asked Shane, as they settled on the couch.

—Aw I'm nervous tellin ye, she said.

—Why? Is somethin after happenin?

—Sort of.

—Go on.

—Aw I'm just nervous yer gonna go mad at me. After the last time an all like.

—The last time wha?

—The stuff we were arguin abou before.

—Paddy Lawless? said Shane.

His blood ran cold. Was Lawless after approachin her? He felt the old fear seep into him again.

—Not him, but it's sort of to do with him, she said anxiously.

—Just tell us Elizabeth, seriously, yer freakin me ou here.

—Aw . . . Well I was drinkin in Venus – ye know tha new place up on South William Street? – with the ones ou of work, an this bird comes up to me. This youngone from the flats.

—Your flats?

—No, the flats across the way, but I don't know her annyway, I oney know her to see. Anyway, she comes up to me in the club an says, 'Are you Betty Byrne?'

—Righ.

—So I says, 'Yeah,' an she goes, 'Is your fella Shane Lackey?'

—Shane Lackey?

—That's wha she said.

—Righ . . .

—So I says, 'Yeah,' an she says, 'Well he'd wanna fuckin

watch himself. Tha was my fella he got battered an if your fella is seen around town he's fuckin dead.' Now, she was fuckin locked righ, fallin over nearly. So I says, 'Excuse me, don't be threatenin my fella,' an she says, 'You'd wanna watch it as well ye little tramp.'

—Fuck . . .

—Now the girls were beside me an they heard all this. They were abou to get up an all, but I says, 'Leave it.' So I just said nothin to her an got up an walked ou. Dermo an all came ou after me, but I got in a taxi then an rang you, cause I wanted to tell ye straigh away.

—Righ . . .

Shane was tryin to process the information.

—Do ye know who she is? he asked.

—Ah she's just a little knacker Shane. She's a spa like.

—Is she connected?

—I don't know. I wouldn't think so. Well, she's from the flats like.

—D'ye know her name?

—No. I can find ou. I knew a few of the girls she was with. They must of told her I was with you.

Shane thought about the situation. If the youngfella's bird was coming up to Elizabeth in a club and threatening her, it was unlikely that there was anything planned. Anything serious anyway. Still, if he saw Shane in town, it sounded like he'd want to give him a hiding. And a good beating could leave you dead just as easy as getting shot. Or the fella might be the stabbing type, when he had few drinks on him. It'd be easy to grab a knife somewhere in the heat of the moment. But Shane had guessed that that was all the case anyway. And at least they didn't know his proper name, to trace him or whatever.

—An ye didn't say annythin else to her? asked Shane.

—No.

—Ye didn't correct her when she said 'Lackey'?

—No way! Sure I hardly know how to fuckin pronounce your second name annyway! Ye know me, I'm no good with tha bleedin leprechaun lingo.

—Alrigh. Fuck it, Shane laughed. —Just find ou who she is if ye can. But don't make it obvious yer askin abou her.

—Righ.

There was a pause. Elizabeth was glad it hadn't caused an argument to erupt, but still a little nervous.

—C'mere Elizabeth, can I ask ye somethin?

—Yeah?

—I don't wanna cause a row, I just wanna know, he said.

—Go on ahead, she said nervously.

—When was the last time ye were with Lawless?

—Years ago like. When we broke up like, she said straight away.

—An ye haven't been with him since?

—No!

—Who finished it with who?

—I finished it with him.

He was relieved.

—Wha happened? he said.

He wanted and didn't want to know what Lawless had done on her.

—Well, after he got locked up—

—When was tha?

—Ah a few years ago, three or four years ago probly.

—Wha did he get locked up for?

—Him an another fella got caugh with a load of coke.

252

—Righ.

—Well, after he got locked up, I was goin in to see him an all. An one of the days I was goin in to see him, there was this bird—

Elizabeth had gone red.

—I went up as a surprise, to the Joy to visit him like. An I was told I couldn't see him, there was someone else in with him already. So I waited, an then I seen her comin ou. I sort of knew he was with this bird when I was with him, but I was in denial about it. But tha day just rubbed me face in it.

—So ye finished it with him?

—Yeah, she said quietly.

—An how did ye know he was with yer one when he was with you?

—Ah I was a fuckin eejit. Everyone knew abou it. It was common knowledge like.

—An ye were still with him?

—He just denied it like, but I knew, at the back of it I knew. An then when I seen her, I knew for definite an tha was it.

—An did he try an get back with ye when he got ou?

—No.

—Did he get in touch with ye at all?

—No.

—So ye didn't see him until tha mornin in the early-house?

—Well he came up to me a few times in the local an tha . . . but I didn't want annythin to do with him Shane, honest to God.

Mulling it over, Shane couldn't decide how to feel. There was more to the story, he could sense it, but he didn't want to push it. He didn't want to know. He'd been relieved when Elizabeth said that it was her who had finished it. Even if she was lying, it was what he wanted to believe. The fact that it wasn't until after Lawless got sent down took away from it though. Would she have finished it with him if he hadn't got locked up? Would she finish it with Shane if he got locked up?

He dropped it, and did his best to put it all out of his head. He cuddled up to her. Shane loved her no matter what anyway – and that mattered more than anything else. Now that Griffo was back to his old self, he'd ask for advice about the problem with the youngfella. He'd wait until Griffo used the apartment. That way Griffo would owe him.

Shane needed to make sure that he had the apartment sorted for Griffo first. He broached that subject with Chops on the Monday, using the excuse that he wanted to cook Elizabeth a romantic dinner.

—Sound, no bother, just give us the nod an I'll make meself scarce, said Chops.

—D'ye mind?

—Not at all man! Anytime, just say the word. I migh get ye to return the favour soon enough actually.

—Oh yeah? Are ye gonna make dinner for Chubbygirl? It'd wanna be a big meal to satisfy her!

—Shut up you. Another bird actually.

—Go on ye sly dog ye! Wha little slut are ye lashin ou of it now?

—I wouldn't put it like tha, said Chops.

—Gerrup ou a tha, ye dirtbird! I know your style. You go through more holes than a rabbit. Every orifice, ye do be stickin it in. In their ears an up their nose, the whole fuckin lot.

—It's yer cousin, Chops blurted.

—Janet? said Shane.

—Yeah.

—Oh . . . Jaysis . . . congratulations . . . When did this happen? he asked, embarrassed.

—Aw look sorry man I was gonna tell ye . . . I kissed her one nigh in town after she helped us ou with the apartment. She was still with her fella an all then, so I said nothin. But she split up with him there a few weeks ago. It was her I was ou with Saturday nigh. She came back to the session an all. I didn't wanna say anythin to ye before cause I wasn't sure wha was happenin with it.

—Ah no bother man. She couldn't ask for a nicer bloke, said Shane.

He meant what he said. It didn't bother him that Chops was riding his cousin, but he was abashed at what he'd said before he knew it was her.

—D'ye like her? Shane asked.

Looking back, he remembered a bit of flirting between Janet and Chops when she'd been viewing apartments with them.

—Ah I do yeah, Chops said earnestly.

—Well then sure, she's a big girl, she can look after herself . . . Not as big as your last girl mind you.

—Ask me bollix.

—Ah I'm oney messin pal. I'd rather see her with you than with anyone else, said Shane.

—In tha case I have somethin else to tell ye.

—Go on? said Shane.

—I rode yer ma.

—Fuck off.

They laughed.

Shane went into the kitchen cheerfully and started to fill the kettle. It got to about halfway full before the water dwindled, and then dried up completely. He called Chops over to have a look.

—It migh just be cut off for a while or somethin, said Chops. —For repairs or tha. Knock into the neighbours there and see if they've water.

Shane hurried out and knocked on the door of the next apartment. A Polish couple lived there. The lads only knew them to say hello to. They'd complained about the noise from Chops playing his decks once, but politely. The girl answered the door.

—Yes? she said, with a startled, rising intonation.

—Sorry to bother ye there, said Shane. —It's just our water is after goin. Is yours still on?

—No water?

—No, it's after goin, he repeated.

—I check eh . . . wait moment plis, she said.

Shane heard her padding back down the hall, followed by the sound of running water.

—Here, water is fine, she said, smiling on her return.

—Alrigh cheers, said Shane.

He stood in the hall thinking, and then heard someone shuffling over carpet before Chops came through the fire door.

—Griffo's after buzzin up for ye there man, he said to go down to him.

—Sound, said Shane.

He bolted down the stairs and walked out into the sun, spotting Griffo through the bars of the steel gates.

—What's the story kid?

—Howye man.

—No bother.

Griffo lowered his voice to a whisper and got straight to business.

—Listen, tha thing I was talkin to ye abou, it's gonna be tomorrow mornin, sometime between eigh and nine.

Shane could tell Griffo was in a rush, so he interrupted.

—There's a problem there Griffo. The water's just after goin.

—Ah yer not serious?

—Straight up, it's only after goin this mornin.

Griffo eyed him a little sceptically.

—Is it just turned off or is it broke? he asked.

—The neighbours' is workin grand an all, so it must be broke.

—Can ye get it fixed today?

—I'll try.

—Bollix, said Griffo, wincing. —It's no use usin your gaff if there's no water. See if ye can get it fixed today, will ye? An ring me this evenin – from a payphone now – an just say, 'Are ye goin down to watch the match?' if it's fixed.

—An wha'll I say if I can't get it fixed?

—Ah do your best for me will ye? It'll fuck things up now if I've to try an organise somethin else at the last minute. But if it's not fixed just say . . . 'I heard yer auntie's not well,' righ?

—Sound, no bother.

—If ye get it sorted I'll drop back over to ye tonigh to sort things ou . . . Righ, fuck it, go on sure, I'll talk to ye later.

Shane went back in and rang their mate Mick, who was an apprentice plumber.

—Can ye come over now an take a look at it?

—Ah I can't Shane, I'm in the middle of a nixer here, said Mick.

—Ah please Mick, I'll sort ye ou, honest to God.

—Wha are ye in such a hurry for?

—I promised Elizabeth I'd make her dinner tonigh, said Shane.

Chops looked up from the couch, surprised.

—That's tonigh now is it?

—Yeah, sorry, said Shane.

—No bother, wha time d'ye want me out? asked Chops, still surprised.

—Ah this evenin. Sorry Mick, hold on, said Shane into the phone before turning back to Chops. —This evenin, around seven or somethin.

Shane thought about this. Chops was unlikely to come home from his ma's before Griffo's lads arrived in the morning, but he'd have to make sure.

—An I'm makin breakfast in bed for her an all tomorrow. She has a day off.

—Jaysis, you're pullin ou all the stops. Ye must have done somethin real bad on her this time! laughed Chops.

—Sorry Mick, said Shane returning to the phone conversation. —Please man, I'm beggin ye I'll pay ye wha'ever. An I'll owe ye a favour.

Mick reluctantly agreed, before hanging up. Shane was getting flustered, aware that what he was telling Mick was entangled with what he'd told Chops. He wondered if Chops was suspicious. He might think nothing of it. It might be all right. Once neither of them said anything to Elizabeth. No, he'd have to put Elizabeth wide and warn her not to contradict Chops if he mentioned it. What would he say to her was the reason he'd wanted Chops out though? *This shit turns you into a lying cunt,* he thought to himself.

Chops left before Mick arrived. Shane felt bad making him leave. Mick managed to fix the water on the spot though. The pump had just needed to be reset. Gratefully, Shane pressed two fifty-quid notes on him. Mick tried to refuse the money, but Shane insisted.

—Sure if you hadn't come up I would of had to get someone ou of the Golden Pages, an he would of told me a load of waffle an charged me at least double tha for fuck sake!

He was happy to give his friend the money. Apprentice wages were fuck all. A hundred euro would mean more to him than to Shane. Still, Shane mused, it was a pity that Mick didn't do coke. If he did, he could have just given him a oner bag, and the cost to Shane would have been less than €50. The same way Griffo cancelling €500 of Shane's debt for letting him use the gaff would actually cost him less than half that. But the money didn't mean anything to Shane really. He was earning well over a grand a week.

Once everything was sorted, Shane went straight out to ring Griffo. Extra cautious, he avoided the phone box that he usually used. Instead, he used the phone in a dreary city-centre pub, nervous a Gard might spot him on the street. Sure who else used street payphones now? Only junkies, drug dealers and gangsters. Everyone else used their mobiles.

Holding the clunky receiver in the pub, Shane pushed the spectacles he'd bought further up his nose, and listened anxiously to Griffo's phone ring. He noted the appealing smell of furniture polish that was mixed with the scent of stale Guinness rising from the freshly hoovered carpet. The signature aroma of an Irish pub in the morning.

—Hello?

—Howye, said Shane, suppressing the urge to use Griffo's name.

—Ah howye, Griffo replied expectantly.

—Are ye goin down to watch the match?

—I'll go down an watch the match with ye kiddo, no bother. See ye shortly.

★

Shane waited in the apartment. When Griffo turned up, he was carrying a bulging sports bag.

—Righ! This just has a change of clothes for the lads in it, said Griffo, gesturing toward the holdall. —An towels an all. I didn't know wha ye had here so I bough stuff just in case.

—Sound, said Shane, trying to appear au fait with the procedure.

—Ye can use it after for the clothes they'll be wearin, said Griffo. —You'll have to get rid of it all then. There's a place up near yer ma's you can burn it, no one'll see ye. I'll tell ye how to get there now.

—Alrigh, said Shane, nervous.

—Have ye a spare set of keys for the apartment? asked Griffo.

—No, said Shane.

—Bollix. I should of said it to ye. Not to worry, not to worry kid, you'll be here anyway?

—Yeah, course.

—They're probly gonna turn up between eigh and nine, but don't move until at least eleven just in case. Better say twelve, be on the safe side.

—I'll be here, no bother.

—Righ, sound. They're gonna leave somethin else here with ye. Ye know wha I'm talkin abou?

Shane could guess.

—Yeah.

—It'll be in a bag with a lock on it. Tha way, on the off chance you get nabbed with it, ye can say ye didn't know wha was in the bag. There'll be no dabs or anythin on it either.

—Dabs? asked Shane

—Prints, said Griffo.

—Wha do I do with it?

—Eh . . . , said Griffo, still processing the plan through his head. —Yeah, I'll be gettin someone else to call over an collect tha after them fellas leave. I'll give them an hour or two. Ye don't have to go annywhere annyway?

—No.

—Sound, righ. I'll get a youngfella to call over an you just give him the locked bag. —Then you take the sportsbag ou to tha place and torch the lot, righ?

—Sound.

Griffo explained to Shane where he should go to burn the stuff, and then ran through the whole scheme again.

—Righ, I have to shoot. So yer alrigh with everythin yeah?

—Yeah, sound.

—Now don't be sayin annythin to anyone now. Not yer

bird, not yer mates, an especially not when yer locked down the boozer. D'ye hear me?

—Yeah, no bother Griffo. I wouldn't annyway.

—I know, I know kid, but I have to say it, ye know? Righ, I better leg it. I'll call over to ye in a week or so. Don't ring me unless there's a problem. Actually definitely don't fuckin ring me if there is a problem either, Griffo laughed.

After Griffo left, Shane sat and thought about things. He wondered who was the nexus of this plan, and what had precipitated it. Unable to come to any conclusions, he marvelled at Griffo's ease in dealing with it. The experience, the organisational ability, the coolness. There was power there. A network of people Shane didn't know, each playing their part. It made Shane feel strong be part of it. He savoured the prospect of becoming more involved, imagining what the lads would think if they knew. He thought of how impressed Dotsy and Aido would be, and how Chalkie, especially, would have been in awe of this.

At six o'clock, the buzzer rang again. The intercom had a receiver like a phone, and when Shane lifted it he could hear the wind outside and cars passing by.

—Heye, it's me! said Elizabeth.

—Howye, said Shane, buzzing her in.

He hadn't figured out yet what he was going to say to her.

She clattered in the door with shopping bags full of new clothes.

—Surprise! she said jokily. —I was just in town shoppin an I thought I'd drop in to the aul love of me life an see how he is.

She smiled charmingly. The hairdressers was closed Monday. Shane cursed himself for forgetting that she always did her shopping that day. The apartment was so close to Henry Street that she often called in afterwards.

—Are ye not happy to see me no? she asked.

—I'm always happy to see you babe, he said stepping forward and holding her, kissing her on the cheek. —C'mon an I'll make ye a cup of tea.

—Ooh this is a treat. Chops is the oney fella around here tha makes tea for me usually, she slagged. —Where is he?

They walked through to the sitting room and she put her shopping bags down on the couch.

—He's up in his ma's for the nigh, said Shane. —I was gonna say to ye actually, I had to ask him to stay ou there tonigh.

—How come?

—Aw I'll explain it to ye . . . I needed the gaff to meself righ? So I told him I was makin you dinner. So if ye see him, ye have to pretend tha I did – an tha ye have tomorrow off work.

With a contemplative, displeased expression, Elizabeth looked Shane up and down.

—Wha did ye tell him tha for?

She stared at Shane with quizzical suspicion inscribed on her face. Shane sensed a storm coming.

—I had to tell him somethin cause I needed to get him ou of the gaff for the nigh.

—For wha?

—It's a long story . . .

—Well, ye better start quickly then. Wha is it?

—Aw ye can't tell anyone this babe, righ?

—Go on, wha? she said, sceptical.

—There's somethin goin down, said Shane, —an I need

to let a couple of fellas use the gaff. For a shower an all. D'ye get me?

—No.

—Somethin serious.

—Wha?

—I can't tell ye, honest to God. I'm oney tellin you because I trust ye. I shouldn't even be sayin an'thin.

—Tell me wha it fuckin is Shane, I'm not gonna say annything to annyone, said Elizabeth, perturbed.

—Look that's all I'm sayin. I can't say annymore. It's serious Elizabeth. Ye can stay for the evenin, but—

—Oh thanks very much! she said abruptly.

—Ah c'mon, don't be like tha! Look I'm under pressure here.

She stood there silently.

—What's wrong? asked Shane.

—Nothin.

—Wha?

—Nothin, she said.

—C'mon, I know there's somethin wrong.

—It's nothin Shane.

—Tell me.

—No, it's nothin.

—Look I can tell there's somethin wrong with ye.

—Never mind, forget about it.

—Aw c'mon just tell me.

—No, forget it. Doesn't matter.

She stood and stared impassive, her hands on her hips. He hated it when she got like this. There was a pause.

—It just sounds very suspicious. I call up an surprise ye, an then it turns ou yer after gettin rid of Chops so ye could have the place to yerself?

—Wha d'ye mean?

—Well are ye sure it wasn't tha ye had some girl comin up here to see ye?

—No! Jaysis, said Shane. —Sure I though ye would of comin over later annyway. An why would I tell ye then if tha was the case?

She seemed placated a little, but something still gnawed at her.

—So wha is goin on then? she said.

—Look that's all I can tell ye, an I shouldn't even of told ye tha. There's somethin serious goin down an a couple of fellas need to use the gaff. *For a shower an all.* After.

—Ohhhh, said Elizabeth, pointedly, cottoning on. — Jaysis!

There was a pause as she thought.

—Who are they? she asked, in a softer tone.

—Ye don't know them, replied Shane.

—Is it any of the lads? she said, referring to Shane's mates.

—No. These are serious fellas.

—An it's happenin tomorrow mornin?

He wore a plaintive and hassled expression. This was making him squirm.

—Yeah, but babe, I shouldn't of tellin ye annythin! Serious now, ye can't say annythin to anyone. Not yer mates, not yer workmates, not anyone – an especially not if yer ou an ye have a few jars on ye.

—Ah I'm not like tha! she said scornfully.

It was true. She wasn't one to speak out of turn when drunk. Shane was more likely to do that than her.

—Will I hear abou it when it happens? she asked.

She was curious.

—Yeah, but look, ye have to just pretend I never said annythin. Seriously, I'm under pressure, I don't wanna talk abou it.

—Alrigh, alrigh, she said drawing closer to him. —Is there annythin I can do to relax ye?

Still standing, she kissed and licked him on the neck, tickling him with her tongue teasingly while cupping his testicles in her hand.

—Stop messin, will ye? said Shane, exasperation fading into amusement.

Straight away she felt him stiffen through his jeans though, and she pushed closer, panting softly in his ear as she squeezed his balls. He groaned and went to kiss her, but she moved her face back. She took her hand away and pushed her crotch against his, staring into his eyes while she pressed herself hard against him. Greedily, he grasped at her arse. Over her black work trousers, he groped between her legs as they began to kiss. She arched her back to allow him to feel lower, and he fancied he could feel the heat from her as she opened herself there. Panting still, she kissed him as he slipped his hand down the back of her trousers, between her cheeks. She groaned in anticipation before he pressed his middle finger gently inside her tight bud. She pressed back harder to help him. Her eyes opened and she moaned at the sensation. He stared into her eyes while she stared back, intense. He felt like she was interrogating him with her eyes, reading him. It was exhilerating.

They didn't even make it to the bedroom. She turned around for him and he fucked her where they stood. They didn't even pause to undress, merely pushing their clothes violently either up or down to free the vital parts.

After he'd cum inside her, he held the standing position, not moving, resting his face against her back. Her face was pressed against the wall, and she too stood still, breathing heavily. Leaning on the wall with one hand, his other hand holding Elizabeth's arm, Shane pushed himself up straight. He was nervous about hurting her, or even himself. He had to be delicate taking it out, the way they'd done it. Slowly and gently he pulled out of her. He felt her clench slightly and gasp, tickling him as he withdrew his sloppy cock. He kissed her tenderly on the back of the neck and she relaxed.

—I better have a shower, he said.

—Ye'd have to after tha, she said, giggling softly.

He kissed her again and went through to the bathroom while she pulled up her knickers a bit awkwardly. While he was getting out of the shower she came into the bathroom naked, carrying the towel she always used.

—Leave tha shower on there, she said.

Freshly scrubbed, they chilled out on the couch, cuddled and watched telly.

—Wha time do I've to leave at? she asked.

—Ah wha'ever time, it's not until the mornin.

—Well I can't stay like can I?

Shane thought about this.

—What time are them fellas comin? she asked, making him uncomfortable again.

To be on the safe side, he told her they were coming at half seven.

—Ah well there's no point stayin if I've to leave tha early, said Elizabeth.

Nestled against him on the couch, she went quiet again.

He looked down at her, noticing at the same time his surprisingly protuberant belly. He'd put on weight since he'd been with her. *Must join a gym,* he thought, *before I end up like Chops.*

There was an English soap-opera on the telly. A shrewish cockney harpy was screaming at someone.

—What's her problem? asked Shane.

—Don't know, said Elizabeth.

—Goin ballistic isn't she?

—Mmm, said Elizabeth lazily.

—Is she still ridin yer man?

—Don't know, said Elizabeth.

He knew this wasn't true. She knew everything that went on in the soaps. She even bought the magazines – not just the celebrity gossip ones, the ones dedicated to the entirely fictional worlds of the programmes too.

—What's wrong?

—Nothin, she mumbled.

—Wha?

—Nothin.

—C'mon wha is it?

—It's nothin! she growled.

—Ah for fuck sake Elizabeth, will ye just tell me what it is!

—Aw just leave it Shane, will ye?

She knew very well it couldn't be left now, once down this path she always made her displeasure so pressingly obvious that Shane was forced to enquire until she admitted it.

—Ah look Elizabeth seriously, just tell me will ye?

—It's just ye said to Chops ye were cookin me dinner, but ye never actually cook me dinner! Like, when ye said to him it was a romantic nigh in an ye were makin me breakfast in bed an all I was a bit like, 'Well I wish he'd do tha in real fuckin life!'

—I always have dinner with ye but?

—Yeah, in front of the telly. That's not the same as a romantic meal Shane. Especially when I'm the one who's after fuckin cookin it.

—I cook food . . .

—If I'm really lucky, ye migh put somethin ou of Marks & Spencers in the oven. That's not cookin Shane.

—Look, I'll make ye dinner soon I promise.

—When?

—Well I can't ask Chops to go home for a night *again*. Not for a while.

She looked away grumpily.

—Look, I think he's playin a gig Saturday. I'll make ye dinner then righ?

—Wha're ye makin me? she smiled.

—Wha'ever ye want, he said, trying not to let the exasperation sound in his voice.

She left in an ambiguous mood that night, but gave Shane a lingering French kiss at the door. He left both his phones on when he went to bed, setting the alarm clock for half six on one phone, and seven on the other, just to be extra sure. Sleep came slowly, and it was disturbed and fretful. To calm himself, he had a wank. Sex was fresh in his mind, and he came quickly. The post-orgasm comfort afforded him a half hour or so of real sleep. When he awoke again, he had another and drifted off again for a little while, but when the first alarm sounded, he was awake. He lay in the bed immobile until the second alarm.

Once up, he tidied the house for his visitors, mopping

the floor and cleaning the bath and toilet. This took him around forty minutes. Afterwards, he sat on the couch, time ticking slowly by. Nerves flitted about in his stomach. He looked at his watch. An idea struck him, and he bounced up. Sandwiches. The lads would probably be hungry. He was glad of a task to distract him. Tuna or cheese? They rarely had anything fresher in the apartment. A selection.

Sandwiches made up, he was just about to quarter them into little triangles, the way he liked them, when he stopped himself, knife still pressed into the bread. That wouldn't look right. Too feminine. Roughly he cut them into halves instead. More manly. He put the plate on the coffee table, and got out two mugs and put teabags in them to be ready.

Restless, he watched telly on the couch, the sitting room door propped open to hear the buzzer. He glanced at his watch and phones intermittently, repulsed a little by the insipid early morning television. Time dragged. He checked the bathroom again, making sure there was soap and shower gel. He'd emptied the bag of clothes and towels that Griffo had provided onto the bathroom floor. He folded the stuff neatly, and put the empty bag beside the pile, ready for the clothes they'd be wearing when they arrived. He removed his own towels from the room, uncomfortable at the idea of strange men using them. He put out more toilet roll too, just in case.

Another thought sprang into his mind, and he switched the digital TV box onto the radio stations. The screen displayed a generic still picture, and Shane flicked around for an Irish talk channel. The lads would probably turn up before it made the news though. He looked at his watch. Twenty past.

The tension mounted as he listened to the radio. He could imagine what the broadcast would be like. He would know he'd been involved in it, known about it before it happened. It made it more real. Still time dragged on, and his nerves mounted – he started to worry they wouldn't show up and he'd be left waiting for Griffo to contact him all day. All week even.

Then the harsh noise of the buzzer startled him. He was unused to it echoing through the house like that. There had been no need to prop open the sitting room door – it made it louder, lending the tone an ominous air that scared him. After jumping up, he stood staring into the hall for the briefest of moments before walking out quickly to lift the handset.

—Hello? he said.

—Yeah, said a voice flatly.

Shane pressed the buzzer and heard the door click open over the intercom. Did this mean it had been done? He stood motionless and wondered if he should go down to them and show them the way, or just wait for them to come up. He set out to leave, walking toward the door of the apartment, then dithered in the hall. He heard a soft ding, signalling the lift, then, as he went to open the door, there was a knock.

Shane opened the door to see two men wearing overalls and high-vis vests. They also had gloves and monkey hats on, despite the sun outside. Instantly, the first man pushed forward into the apartment, and the second man followed, both keeping their heads down and neither acknowledging Shane. He recognised the first man. Lynchey, the fella he'd met with Griffo in the earlyhouse that first time.

—Where's the shower? said Lynchey, quietly – sharp and functional.

—In there, Shane half-whispered, pointing to the bathroom door.

—Give him tha, said Lynchey to the other fella.

The man handed Shane a small sports bag, which rustled, and Shane felt a heavy and obvious weight as he took it. Lynchey opened the bathroom door and went in. The other fella followed, and Shane was left in the hall. He didn't know what to do – whether to wait in the hall or go into the sitting room and leave them alone. The sound of hurried disrobing emanated from the jacks. A moment later, he heard the shower come on. He was surprised that they had gone into the room together, but presumed they'd take turns under the water. Compromising, Shane propped the sitting room door open and sat on the couch, leaning forward with his hands clasped. The bag sat beside him. He eyed the bathroom door.

Ten minutes or so later, Lynchey came out of the bathroom, followed by his silent, unidentified accomplice. Now they were wearing normal clothes – jeans and polo shirts. Both of them had caps. Shane suspected that, to look less ropey, they hadn't worn the tracksuits they'd usually wear. The other fella stood behind Lynchey. It felt strange to Shane to share such a heightened moment with a complete stranger when he couldn't even tell his dearest friends about it.

—Let us ou there will ye. He's to give me a few minutes, then he's leavin, Lynchey said, referring to the other fella. — He'll wait in the hall.

—Eh, d'yis want a cup of tea or annythin? asked Shane.

—No.

—There's sandwiches there as well.

—Don't mind tha, just let us ou there quick, he said.

He looked irritated.

Shane complied, holding the door open for Lynchey. The other fella stood in the hall, head down, hiding his face from Shane.

—Eh, I'll be inside, said Shane, feeling awkward.

—Grand yeah, said the fella, without looking up.

The fella knocked on the sitting room door after less than five minutes, and Shane let him out, still with his cap pulled down low, still avoiding Shane's eyes. The door closed, leaving overwhelming quiet. Shane had a look in the bathroom, and saw that they'd left a mess, throwing the dirty overalls on the ground and leaving the towels draped around the place. There was water and suds splashed around. The black monkey hats and gloves had been taken off in a hurry. Balled up, they looked like lumps of coal scattered on the floor of the small bathroom. The lads had even left their underwear and runners.

After bundling all the stuff into the bag, Shane scrubbed the floor even more assiduously than he had that morning, concerned that there could be some sort of forensic trace left. He couldn't hear the radio from the bathroom, but he didn't want to turn it up, paranoid that his neighbours might realise he was listening out for that broadcast and connect the dots. Bag packed and bathroom cleaned, he went back to the sitting room, where he sat and listened to the radio. The chatter irritated him, but he wanted to hear the first mention of what had happened live.

To distract himself from his frantic thoughts, he plucked a book from the top of the bookcase. Not a gangland one, not while he was panicky. *The Mammy* by Brendan O'Carroll. He'd read it loads of times. Rereading the story soothed him.

Just before ten, the buzzer went again. Shane grabbed the conspicuous locked bag from the chair and hurried out to the hall once more.

—Hello?

—Howye. Just here to collect that yoke, said a friendly young voice.

—Sound. D'ye wanna come up?

—Can ye not just drop it down to us there?

—Yeah, no bother, hold on.

Shane grabbed his keys, then bustled down the stairs. Standing at the gate was a small, stocky youngfella about Shane's age. He had a red moped helmet pushed up on his head, furling his blonde hair.

—There ye go, said Shane handing him the bag .

The fella smiled at him. It was a little awkward as the fella had his moped keys in his hand, but he managed to take the bag and swing the strap over one shoulder. It reminded Shane of how he used to carry his school bag – the cool way to carry it, just by the one strap. Sore on your shoulder, but all the boys still did it to look harder.

—No bother, said the fella, still smiling as he slowly shut the steel gate.

—Righ, see ye after, said Shane.

—Take it easy.

The fella fumbled with the gate before glancing around and walking off in the sunlight.

★

Later, Shane went out to the spot Griffo had mentioned. It was an overgrown car park behind an old, empty factory in the area where they'd grown up. Weeds sprouted up through the tarmac outside. Shane emptied the little plastic can of petrol over the bag. He was careful not to get any on himself – Griffo had warned him. The sound of birds twittering in the foliage caused him to look up, startled. He was unused to the noises of the wild.

Standing back, he threw a match at the sodden bag as the thin liquid seeped into it. The first match failed to ignite the bag, as did a second. But the third did the trick. There was no *whoosh* sound from the fire like he had expected, but Shane felt the heat as the flame grew steadily. He watched it only for a second before walking back to his car and driving home.

The second item on the RTÉ News at one o'clock announced, 'A man has been shot dead in a gun attack in Dublin city.' Nauseous, Shane listened. It felt unreal. There wasn't any detail, just that there'd been a shooting at a flat complex and 'one man was left dead'. Then, of course, 'Gardaí are appealing for witnesses, or anyone who knows anything about the crime to contact them.'

Over the next few days, more details emerged, but the item slipped down the billing. Television that night showed the flats. Garda tape flailing in the wind. Girls standing around in pyjamas. Shane hadn't known the fella. Dermot Campbell. Twenty-six years old, the news said. Then that vile euphemism: 'known to Gardaí'. Deserved it, in other words.

Elizabeth had been a little overawed by the whole thing too. The shooting had happened close to where she lived.

Being from the flats, she was used to people being on the wrong side of the law – her da was a bit of a bogey, her uncles had been locked up. But this was more serious than anything she'd experienced before. Cuddling up to Shane in bed that night, she'd asked him to look after himself, warned him not to get caught. Her presence didn't calm his nerves, but Shane enjoyed the reverential way she was treating him.

On Lydia's advice, he cooked sea bass for Elizabeth that Saturday. He drove over to Marino to get the fish. He got the potatoes and veg from Marks & Spencer, but Elizabeth still appreciated the effort. The two of them shared the bottle of wine she'd brought.

On the Sunday, Shane bought the newspapers – the tabloids only. The articles held authoritative theories as to why the man had been killed. Empty catchphrases: 'turf war', 'drug feud', 'gangland slaughter'. Elizabeth peeked over his shoulder, reading the stories with interest. Shane bustled the papers nervously out of the way when Chops arrived home.

Griffo buzzed in on the Tuesday morning. Shane went downstairs to him, explaining that Chops was in the gaff. He handed Griffo two grand in an envelope. Combined with what he'd paid already, and the five hundred Griffo had promised him for his troubles, this cleared the debt from a half bar of coke.

—Nice one kid, said Griffo, as he stowed the envelope in his pocket. —So . . . ye didn't freak ou or ann'thin after ye heard the news?

He was gauging Shane.

—No, no, Shane lied. —Sure I knew the score beforehand ye know.

—Good good . . . Mad shit when it happens though isn't it?

—It's a bit mad alrigh yeah, said Shane unsure of himself.

—An ye didn't say a word to anyone? Not yer bird or anyone?

—No, no, not at all. I'd be worried abou meself too, sure.

—Good man. Righ, well, keep the head down, gimme a shou when ye need annythin again. Here's me new number: 085 . . .

Yet another new phone number. Shane took it down, reflecting on the life he was leading. Despite the paranoia and the nerves, he felt good. Worthwhile. These were the things that made the news, that people made films about. Wrote books about. Drug deals and murders. This was what other people wished *they* could do, and he was in the middle of it now and he wasn't even twenty-one.

Intrigued by the way the men had behaved, how Griffo had organised things, he wanted to do more. For the first time in his life, he was conscious of wanting to learn, to move forward. To move up. To be Griffo one of the days. Griffo would be someone else then – and then he'd be who-ever Griffo had become, and so on and so on. That's how it worked. He'd read it in the papers.

The General, the Penguin, the Coach, the Tosser, the Monk, the Viper, Fatpuss, Fat Freddy. They'd all started somewhere, he'd read their stories. They'd all earned their names. The power – to be feared, to be known by the whole country as someone you couldn't mess with, someone you had to respect – that would mean you'd made it. That was the goal. Then you'd be safe.

Later, he went to meet his mate Dotsy, who owed him a few quid for a bag. Dotsy sold coke as well, but he'd run out one night, and Shane had given him a oner on tick for near cost. Shane had forgotten about the debt until he'd noticed it written down. He always wrote down who owed what in one of the maths copies his ma had bought him in Easons when he'd started the business course in college. Names in blue or black pen on one side, amounts written in red in a straight column on the other. He'd only bothered to go and collect the money off Dotsy at all so that it wouldn't be on his mind that he was owed something.

It was good to see Dotsy. Since moving into town, he didn't often see the lads when he was sober. He missed just relaxing with them on the green, or sitting on a garden wall talking shite for a few hours in the afternoon. Shane always made sure his mates paid their debts as soon as possible. Otherwise they'd have reason to avoid him, and maybe even get it off someone else next time.

—Would ye not get yer stuff off Griffo? Shane asked Dotsy.

—Ah I prefer gettin it off me own fella. Last time I got it off Griffo he was on me back, lookin for the money straigh away an all. Like yourself!

—That's cause I told him wha yer like, Shane slagged.

—Ah I prefer to do things in me own time ye know.

—Griffo's stuff is better than the rest of the stuff around but, said Shane.

—Ah the stuff I get is alrigh . . . I seen Griffo there today actually. Talkin to tha Lynchey fella down the avenue.

—Ye wouldn't know wha them cunts would be up to . . . Some operation Griffo's runnin, I'm tellin ye man. Dogwide so he is, said Shane.

—Ah he's not runnin things. He's oney a front for Lynchey, said Dotsy casually.

—Ah no. Griffo's the top dog there.

—*Are ye jokin me*? said Dotsy. —Lynchey oney has him runnin around to keep the heat off himself. Sure Griffo got into a load of debt for Lynchey an he was shittin it Lynchey was gonna blast him!

—Who told ye this? asked Shane.

—Me oulfella. Lynchey's da is me oulfella's cousin.

—I didn't know tha, said Shane, thinking.

—Don't be sayin annything now, but me oulfella used keep a bit of stuff in the gaff for Lynchey, Dotsy continued. —Shooters, the whole lot. Not anymore like, but it's defo Lynchey who's the boss – he just keeps Griffo out front to do all the runnin around. An so as not to be throwin the eye on himself. I know Griffo acts the hardman an all cause he takes the steroids, but he's a bottlin bastard when it comes down to it. Sure did ye ever hear of yer man Paddy Lawless from town? He got a load of stuff off Griffo years ago – when Griffo *was* doin his own thing – an he never paid Griffo for it at all.

Shane paused in thought, trying to process the information without giving anything away.

—I dunno now, said Shane. —Griffo wouldn't be the type to let someone get away with tha.

—Ah he tried to put it up to Lawless an all, but ended up doin *nothing* over it. Lawless was goin around sayin Griffo ratted him ou, an that's why he wasn't gonna pay him. But he was only usin tha as an excuse cause it turned ou the youngfella he was caugh with was the one who ratted. Tha youngfella only done a few month of his sentence, but Lawless did near the whole lot of his.

—How d'ye know all this?

—Me oulfella was tellin me to stay away from Griffo tha

279

time when Lawless had it goin around tha Griffo was a rat.
Tha was when yer man Lawless and tha youngfella were
only still on remand like, in Cloverhill. But when me
oulfella was in the Joy tha time – remember?

—Yeah I remember tha, said Shane. —Around three year
ago?

—Yeah. He was only in fer a couple of weeks over tha
row in the Merchant . . . He only got sent down at all cause
of all his previous . . . Well anyway, the day me da was gettin
ou, tha youngfella got ou as well. An it was obvious then –
cause his sentence was five fuckin year or somethin like tha,
an he was only after been in there a few month. Now they're
lettin everyone ou mad early cause of the overcrowdin – like
me oulfella got six months and he was out in three weeks –
but not *tha* early like. Before it came out about the
youngfella, it looked like Griffo *was* a rat, cause he never
done any time on annythin.

—Yeah, said Shane.

—Griffo used to be the main man around the area alrigh,
said Dotsy. —Back when yokes first got big – in the '90s an all.
When people were payin a score for a yoke. An tha was punts!
But coke is where the money is these days, sure ye know tha
yourself. Lynchey copped on to tha before the coke even really
took off in Dublin. Griffo wanted to get into it proper, an
Lynchey had it sewn up already so Griffo had to get it off him.
Then he couldn't pay his own debt to Lynchey over Lawless
stingin him. He's been workin for Lynchey ever since.

Shane was struggling to process this double reversal.

—Ah I'm tellin ye man. The serious gangsters don't go
around shapin an throwin the eye on themselves like Griffo.
They're too smart.

A LIST

- Davy King: €100

- Janet: €100. Shane's cousin, for a bag she split between herself and a mate. Shane gave her a good bit extra, though he'd then thrown in a lot of mix to make it weak, wary of his cousin's safety.

- Robbie Boyle: €300. For a oner Shane gave him when he met him out one night and an eighth he rang up to get the next day.

- Aido: €200. Two oner bags on separate occasions.

- Rory: €900. Two weeks in a row he got a quarter off the rock on tick. Shane knew he'd pay.

- Chops: €50. Oner bag at cost.

- Cynthia: €200. Two oner bags she got separately.

- John MacKernan: €100. Oner bag.

- Jenny MacKernan: €100. Probably on behalf of John, who wanted another bag but presumably didn't want to ask because he still owed for the first.

- Farreller: €100. A oner bag a fortnight after Chalkie's funeral. Shane couldn't refuse.

7

The last thing that went through Shane's mind was that he mightn't get to meet Elizabeth that night.

He was out with Griffo, driving him around while he collected money. Friday was the usual collection day. Meeting people the day they got paid was the idea. Before they blew it on the gargle. Half the customers were professionals now, they got paid by the month. And Griffo had been out on the tear Friday, so Shane was driving him around on a Saturday afternoon. Griffo grumbled in the passenger seat beside Shane, supping from a can of Red Bull that was exacerbating the edginess caused by his hangover-cum-comedown.

—Get into the left lane there will ye? he said harshly.

—Yeah hang on will ye, this fella's comin up past me, Shane replied.

I was gonna get into the left lane anyway for fuck sake.

Trying not to let his irritation show, Shane waited for the car to pass them on the inside. To appease Griffo, he changed lanes earlier than he'd intended. Shifting around in his seat, a jittery Griffo checked repeatedly that they weren't being followed.

They were driving north from Shane's apartment, through the inner city to Dublin 13, 17, 5, 9 and 11. And Dublin 7. The areas where Griffo did most of his business. They were still in Dublin 3, not the suburbs though, and both Shane and Griffo felt uncomfortably surrounded by the looming blocks of flats.

—Garda in tha Mondeo, said Griffo.

—Which one? asked Shane.

—The red one there look.

No insurance disc, no hubcaps, two aerials, two culchies. That was more than enough to identify them as Old Bill. Shane and Griffo eyed the car cautiously, even though it was ahead of them. They passed it as it waited to turn right onto the East Wall Road. There was only a little relief. You never could be *sure* that they weren't following you, or hadn't noticed you. One car could come off for another car to come on. Even though they weren't carrying any drugs, they were paranoid the whole time that they were about to get lifted. Not just now, every day. Every minute. Every second.

—Swarmin all over the place they are today, said Shane.

—Yeah, those two youngfellas were shot up the road there yesterday evenin.

—I heard tha all righ. Where was it?

—Up in Aldi car park, Griffo replied absentmindedly. — Life is cheap wha?

Shane laughed before glancing over briefly to see Griffo flicking through the anachronistic little black phone book he carried these days.

—Give us a shot of yer phone there will ye? he said, as he took Shane's mobile from a niche in the dash.

It riled Shane that Griffo was content to dirty up his new phone by conducting business over it. While he was being chauffeured around like a lord's bastard as well. Having finally changed his number – he'd laboriously rung up everyone in his phone book to give them his new number and tell them to delete the old one – he felt Griffo was not only taking advantage, but being reckless by using his new mobile to collect drug money.

The thought of drug debts caused Shane's mind to turn to Dotsy, who'd been locked up for the past few months. Youthful stupidity, drunken carelessness and drugs on credit were a bad combo. Dotsy'd been taking coke to sessions and parties. When he got pissed, he'd end up sharing out more than he sold. He ended up seriously behind on payments. He got more coke on tick off someone else then, to try and recoup some money and repay the original debt. But he was too fond of the gargle, like his oulfella. In the end, he owed more than he could hope to pay back through his own dealing, which had never really been profitable anyway.

He'd agreed to hold 'a box of the bad thing' – a kilo of heroin – for the fella he was in debt to. After holding the gear for a couple of weeks, he'd been told to take a taxi out to Newbridge and deliver it to someone. The taxi had been stopped, and Dotsy arrested – the Old Bill had been well tipped off. Dotsy was still on remand in Cloverhill. Shane hadn't been out to see him. He was worried the Guards were taking note of visitors. The solicitor said Dotsy was looking at ten years.

In exchange for his services today, Griffo had promised to cancel a small portion of Shane's drug debt. Shane would rather have just paid him the cash. Griffo didn't want to use his own car though, because he reckoned there was 'Garda intelligence' on it. He'd been pulled over and questioned by armed detectives a few weeks previously, and the Gards had a database now, the PULSE system. All of them had instant access to it. Shane didn't know if it was over anything specific, but Griffo had been more cautious than ever since the stop. He said he couldn't simply borrow Shane's car and drive it himself because he wouldn't have been insured, but Shane doubted Griffo would have been able to drive in the state he was in.

Driving Griffo around made Shane uncomfortable. He worried about throwing the eye on himself if they were seen together by Garda. If they ran his car reg, then they'd get his name, then his ma's address, then maybe even the detail that he'd been stopped on the street with Robbie Boyle before. Now Griffo was using his phone on top of it. Aside from the security risks, he was too proud these days to see himself as Griffo's dogsbody. Shane didn't want to be subservient to someone he was quickly losing respect for.

—Hello? Yeah howye . . . yeah we're just comin up to Fairview now, so abou ten minutes . . . yeah be ready, I'll just buzz ye again when I'm outside . . . sound . . . righ, go on, bye . . . bye.

They were on their way to Beaumont Hospital for Griffo to meet his first customer. The people he was collecting money off were all drug dealers themselves. Griffo wouldn't get out of bed to collect less than a grand.

When they got to the hospital, he directed Shane to drive past the visitor car park up, to the front entrance. Just collecting money they could be more brazen than usual. Cash wasn't illegal. Yet.

A fella came down and got into the back seat. Shane wasn't driving the two-door Colt anymore, he'd traded it in for a second-hand Passat. It had cost him a few grand too, but it looked less bogey, so it was worth it.

—Alrigh lads, said the wiry fella.

He looked about thirty-five. Rough.

—Alrigh, said Shane.

—What's the story man? said Griffo, not turning to look back.

—There's tha there, said the fella, passing Griffo a roll of notes.

—Give it to him there, said Griffo, still looking ahead studiously.

Shane took the roll of fifties from the fella, and then unfurled and counted the cash. The money flashed through his hands as he rapidly tallied. He'd become practised at this. Griffo kept sketch, eyeing those who stood around the hospital entrance suspiciously, making sure nobody was watching. A dying woman with tattered blonde hair and a grubby dressing gown sucked deeply on a cigarette. Other patients huddled with visitors, chatting between puffs. Thin-cheeked and jaundiced, this woman smoked alone, the drip she was attached to standing silently beside her. Griffo shuddered at the sight. She made his hangover more acute. He even fancied he felt the way she looked.

—Three grand there, said Shane.

—Sound, said Griffo, trying to pull himself together.

Shane folded the money and stuffed it into his sock. If it had been his own cash, he'd have put it in his jocks, but he didn't want to hand it to Griffo from his underpants later.

—Wha're ye, just visitin someone in there? Griffo asked the fella.

—Yeah the oulfella. On the way out so he is.

—Jaysis, sorry to hear tha. Wha is it, cancer?

—Yeah. Lungs.

Griffo tutted.

—Well look after yourself man, give us a shou if ye need an'thin.

—Yeah sound, see ye later Griffo, said the fella, eager to move on.

Give us a shout if ye need anything? What's he gonna do, find a fuckin cure for cancer? No, he just means, 'Gimme a shout if ye wanna buy more coke off me.' He couldn't give a bollix about yer man or his oulfella. All he wants is his few quid.

Shane started the car again.

—Hang on there, said Griffo. —I wanna see where's next.

He took Shane's phone again – without even asking this time – and began to flick through the little black book. As Shane watched the fella recede into the hospital, he thought about Granda Jopa, who had died a few months before. Withering in a hospital ward. Prattling nonsense, stinking in nappies before slipping into open-eyed unconsciousness. A torment to the family that loved him. It was Shane's turn to shudder as he tried to vanquish the thought from his head. And that would be it, that was what the end would be like.

After the funeral, Shane had drunk himself into oblivion, falling asleep in the toilets of the local pub, where tea and sandwiches had been laid on. His da had to drag him out of the jacks and take him back to his ma's gaff, a repeat of that first day in the Pink Pound. Disgusted at his da's touch, Shane hadn't let the incident trigger a reconciliation. He'd mourned this second childishness, mortified by his own behaviour. He had vowed not to get himself into such states anymore. He had joined a gym and started eating healthily. Being fitter made him feel good – not wrecked and depressed all the time like before.

In Shane's car, bleak, tinny Southside accents from the radio forecasted doom for Ireland's economy. Impotently, they repeated the same desolate message: cataclysm was on the way. This had become the sole topic for all talk-radio stations and news programmes. Opposing commentators chattered, disagreeing on the appropriate remedy. No more dissenting voices on the reality of the crisis could be heard.

—Get tha off will ye? said Griffo sharply. —Wreckin me head. Have ye no music there?

Through the mask of Griffo's expensive aftershave, Shane could smell the hangover sweat that glistened on his muscles. Alcohol to cover alcohol. He could also see the trembles Griffo's hand as he tapped a number into the phone. Weakness. Since Shane had started to get his life together, Griffo's flaws had begun to gall him. Petty, childish aggression caused by the steroids. Jitters, stutters and paranoia caused by too much coke. He sensed a gnawing fear in Griffo that shone through the bravado, the tense desperation of a hunted animal made revolting by his efforts to conceal it.

—Howye . . . yeah, where are ye? Yeah I'll make me way over to ye now righ? . . . Be abou fifteen minutes.

Griffo gave Shane directions without revealing a final destination, and then settled down to fiddle with the radio. He tuned through the channels before settling on a pirate station playing rap music. The weak signal from the illegal transmitter waxed and waned as the car moved in and out of coverage. The voice of an RTÉ presenter communicating weak echoes about the forthcoming financial catastrophe intruded intermittently over the hip-hop beats.

This further annoyed Shane as he drove. There were a few customers Shane had been meant to meet that Saturday too, but Griffo had refused to be in the car with drugs. There were also a few customers Shane had wanted to collect money from, but, typically, Griffo had insisted on collecting only his own debts, telling Shane he had other things to do later. Shane understood this to be a lie. Griffo just wanted to get home and sleep it off.

Shane disliked having people owe him money. It made him uneasy. He hated the hassle of chasing them up over the phone or calling around to their gaffs. Robbie Boyle owed him a grand for a heavily mixed ounce of coke. Already into Shane for €300, Boyle had pressurised Shane into giving him the ounce to sell on tick.

—Yeah yeah brother, I know I owe ye tha few quid, just on me bollix at the minute I am, ye know? If ye were able to get us an ounce o decent stuff, I'll get rid of it in no time, and sort ye out then with the full whack.

—Ah Jaysis, Shane had said, feeling coerced. —Ye already owe me tha three ton the past two month man.

—I know, I know, I'm an awful bollix! I've just been all

over the place brother. If ye throw us tha ounce, I've a youngfella there who'll get rid of most of it for me an I'll have yer few quid after the weekend.

—It'll be thirteen hundred then, said Shane.

—Yeah, that's no bother. It's me cousin's thirtieth the weekend. A party ye know. Everyone'll be goin mad for the bag. Be a shame to miss the opportunity brother.

Choosing to believe Robbie was being genuine rather than issue a challenge, Shane gave in. Even though they went through the motions, both of them knew what was going on. Shane handed over the ounce, which was more than a third Creatine. Resentful of Boyle now, he'd danced on the coke, cut it as much as he could get away with. Boyle stuck it nonchalantly in his jacket pocket while smoking a cigarette, drunk outside a city-centre pub. Shane knew he wasn't going to be paid. Boyle had shaken his hand afterwards. Brazen as he was, even he'd seemed a little embarrassed at the blatancy of this manoeuvre. As expected, when Shane rang Boyle after the weekend, his phone was off. He'd changed his number.

Shane had brooded on the disrespect, the insult to his pride, but he'd been too ashamed to tell anyone. He considered selling the debt to one of Griffo's contacts, but then he'd only get half the money back after the heavies were paid. He didn't want to start shit with Boyle either, not on top of everything else. He worried about bumping into him in the street or in a boozer – the shame and fear made him think of Griffo with Paddy Lawless that first day. Then, a month or so later, Boyle had been shot dead in a grotty city-centre pub, confirming once and for all that the debt would go unpaid. Shane had been relieved.

Elizabeth had spooked him though, asking if he thought Lawless's mate 'Andy' – the fella Robbie had battered – had had anything to do with the murder. Shane hadn't thought of that. He had considered his answer, mulling over the scenario. He imagined the clatter of gunshots. Boyle's heavy frame thudding off the short bar stool and onto the pub floor. Blood mingling with sawdust. He said he thought it was too professional. Having experienced Boyle's modus operandi himself, he told Elizabeth that Boyle had probably gotten in debt to someone, and put it up to them when they demanded payment.

This was Shane's train of thought as he followed Griffo's directions. A flutter in his stomach accompanied Elizabeth's image in his mind. Shane had found texts from Lawless on Elizabeth's phone. Her replies had been deleted, but from reading Paddy's terse messages, it was obvious she had carried the conversation on.

Whats the story Paddy new number

Just givin ye me new number

Havent talked to ye in a while thought Id say hello thats all

Not married yet are ye?

No Im not. Well whats the story?

Yeah same.

Shane had puked when he'd read the texts. He was suspicious by nature, but he hadn't expected that Elizabeth would talk to Lawless. Aside from the shit between him and

Paddy, she had always made out she despised him, calling him a scumbag, telling Shane she was glad she was away from him, would never go back to him, wanted nothing to do with him. Without being specific, she still hinted that Paddy had done something really unforgivable to her when she was younger.

Behind me back textin that fuckin scumbag after everything that happened and the shit she used to give me for so much as looking at another bird – the silent treatment every time I went on a session. And she wasn't even that bothered when I went mental at her. That was the worst part. She said there was nothing between her and Lawless still, but she seemed happy enough that I finished it, givin ME shit for goin through her phone. Oh, Jesus I want her back but what the fuck am I supposed to do?

A few weeks before he found the texts, Shane had heard gossip that Lawless had got some youngone pregnant. When he told the story to Elizabeth as further evidence of what a scumbag Lawless was, she had just gone quiet.

—An d'ye know wha he said to her when she told him she was up the pole, Shane recounted. —'Nothin I can do when yer this far gone, it's yer own problem now.'

—No way, said Elizabeth as she stared at the telly.

The way she acted reminded Shane of the way she behaved when she was pissed off with *him*. Surly and silent, she looked ahead, gritting her teeth a little. He repressed the disturbance he felt at her response. The possible cause was too upsetting to contemplate. She'd yielded into his arms on the couch only half-heartedly. Shane did his best to ignore the fact her mind was elsewhere.

When he had discovered the texts, he had been unable

and unwilling to disguise his anger. Smashing Elizabeth's mug of tea against the wall, screaming abuse at her as she stormed out of the apartment. Although rattled at the ferocity of Shane's demeanour, she shouted her own defence as she left. She didn't respond to Shane's abusive texts beyond the requested assurance that she wouldn't tell Paddy Lawless or anyone else any of his businesses or where he lived.

It had now been more than a month since he'd heard from her, but she'd made contact out of the blue during the week, asking if they could meet up and talk. Try to sort things out. Though he maintained a cool facade, Shane had been euphoric when her message had come through. Overwhelming relief swept away the knot of anxiety that had been with him since they parted. She did care.

She was adamant that the only reason she hadn't told Shane about the texts was to spare him worrying. The only reason she had replied to Paddy Lawless was to make it clear she wasn't going to be with him. Shane was torn – he wanted to believe her but the messages were ambiguous. Every time he had tender thoughts of her, they would be interrupted by images of her and Lawless in bed together.

One of his only sources of consolation was the hope that Lawless would soon meet the same fate as Boyle. Shane googled the name of the fella who was killed the day Lynchey and the other fella used the apartment. Dermot Campbell. 'Delboy', the newspaper article said. He read an old article about him getting arrested with Lawless, the time Lawless got sent down for a few years. Shane hoped it meant Lawless was next, but he wasn't sure how to make sense of it all. He'd waited until Griffo brought up the subject before mentioning it. He didn't mention that he knew the fella's background, scared to remind Griffo of the link through Elizabeth. He'd just asked what the shooting was over. He'd hoped they were going after Lawless and his crew. But Griffo had just said, 'Better not to be askin questions kid, that's my policy. Ye know yerself, yeah?'

Shane had been dying to ask him if Lawless was next. He pulsed with excited aggression at the prospect. Given the opportunity, he would have gladly pulled the trigger himself. But he knew that inquiring too enthusiastically was likely to provoke Griffo's suspicion, maybe even get himself excluded from future plans. Elizabeth now provoked some of the same sickness and anger Lawless did, even some of the same fear. But the attraction was still there too. And, underneath all the bitterness, so was the love.

They'd agreed to meet that night. While unsure what he should do in the circumstances, he knew that once they were alone in the apartment he would want to touch her, want physical affection. Want sex. This would press him toward reconciliation. He hoped she'd be able to reassure him, allay his fears and worries. Since he'd stopped sessioning so much, he was lonely. He missed Elizabeth's soft touch – talking to her about her day and the people she worked with, relaxing with her and watching the telly or a film. Holding her and being held. He looked forward to meeting her.

Snapping him out of his daze, Griffo directed Shane into a bland Corpo housing-estate. Shane pulled up at the spot requested, and sat in the car while Griffo disappeared into a neat house with a little glass porch. Two minutes later, Griffo returned with another bundle of cash. As Shane counted it, Griffo made another phone call, again using Shane's phone.

—Hello? . . . What's the story. I've to get a bit of paper off ye . . . Yeah that's righ . . . Where are ye now? . . . Eh, I'm in Artane . . . How long will ye be? . . . Can ye not make it any sooner? . . . Yeah I know it yeah, but can ye not make it any sooner, I've a youngfella here drivin me an he has to be somewhere ye know . . .

Shane noted the ease with which Griffo lied.

—Alrigh then . . . Righ then . . . Yeah the gym, I know it there yeah, yeah, yeah. Eh, wha time is it now? . . . Righ an hour, alrigh go on.

Griffo sighed as he hung up the phone. He handed it back to Shane.

—This fella's messin. Changin the arrangements. It's not even my money, I'm oney collectin it for someone else.

In his frustration, the mask was slipping. Griffo was revealing his own subservience. Shane guessed Lynchey had told Griffo to collect the money. So far as he understood, it was all Lynchey's coke anyway. Unless Lynchey was a front for someone else as well. At this stage that wouldn't have surprised Shane either.

—Fuckin told him I'd be down around here at this time, now he says he can't meet me for an hour.

—Where are we goin? asked Shane, exasperated.

—Ye know the Northside Gym just off the main road down there? There's no point goin down there now but. D'ye wanna get some grub or somethin?

Griffo turned to Shane, all pally again now that there was time to kill.

—Yeah whatever, said Shane starting the car. —Where d'ye wanna go?

—Just head down to the McDonald's there will we? That's the handiest.

The thought of greasy food repulsed him, but Shane didn't voice his objection.

His drug phone rang as they pulled into the McDonald's car park. Though her number wasn't saved in it, Shane recognised Elizabeth's sequence of digits. He'd left his personal mobile at home, but Elizabeth had the other number as well.

—Go on ahead there, said Shane to Griffo. —I'll oney be a minute.

Griffo obeyed, glancing around instinctively, surveying the car park before he got out of the car. Shane pressed the green button to answer the call.

—Hello?

—Howye, said Elizabeth.

—What's the story, said Shane guardedly.

—C'mere the water's after goin in the salon so they let us off early, they had to close up fer the day.

Griffo's radio station was still playing, and Shane had to struggle to hear her voice over Tupac's staccato: 'Now let me welcome everybody to the wild, wild West/A state that's untouchable like Elliot Ness/The track hits ya eardrum like a slug to ya chest . . . '

Shane turned it down, irritated.

—Yis've no water in the hairdressers?

—No, it's fuckin broke or somethin, not even a drop ou a the taps. Can't do anything we can't. Where are ye? she asked.

—I'm just ou at the McDonald's in Artane.

—Well could ye not come back over to the apartment now? I don't wanna hang around town for hours like? said Elizabeth.

—I've to meet a fella in abou an hour so there's no point in me comin back now, I'd only have to head off again.

Elizabeth could hear the music faintly as the rapper crooned 'Weeeest Coast' at the end of the song.

—Where are ye meetin him?

—Eh, Westside Gym, said Shane, distracted.

There was silence as Elizabeth thought. Each was still unsure of the other's mood and intent. They were both holding onto their anger, and it rested under the surface of their conversation, each waiting for the other person to allay or ignite it.

—Righ, well, I'll just go home now then an come over to ye later. Wha time will ye be back? said Elizabeth.

—I'd say there'll be a few more to meet after tha. We'll just leave it till when I said to be on the safe side. Bou half six? Shane replied.

—Righ, well I'll ring ye before I leave the house anyway to check righ?

—Righ go on, I'll talk to ye later.

—Righ, byeee.

He took the keys from the ignition, silencing the radio completely. He allowed himself to savour the calm for a moment, realising how much the noise had been irritating him. Letting out a deep sigh, he recounted the conversation with Elizabeth in his head a few times before he got out of the car.

There was a little grass slope up to the McDonald's entrance. As he was going in he watched another unmarked Garda vehicle leave the car park. Probably after getting their lunch out of the drive-through, he thought. Don't even pay for it, the Gards. Cunts.

Inside was busy, but Griffo signalled for Shane to join him and skip the queue.

Parents waited tensely in line. Kids in stripes milled around, firing bits of paper at each other from straws.

—You're dead! a little girl roared at a boy, after shooting him with a wet paper ball.

—No I amn't!

They reminded Shane of pygmies with darts and blow-guns. Hyperactive pygmies.

Flinching at the children's antics, Griffo perused the illuminated menu over the counter as he queued. Once inside, Shane found himself surprisingly hungry. He ordered plenty of food, struggling to choose healthier options. While waiting, he felt someone stand too close behind him – and then a sudden pointed pressure on the back of his head.

—Don't move, a voice said.

Shane recoiled from the unwanted touch, whirling to see who was there. Relief mingled with mild annoyance as Rory, standing with an outstretched finger pointed to mimic a pistol, laughed at his skittishness.

—What's the story man, he chuckled in his broad D4 accent. Bit jumpy there?

—Stop man will ye – yer after givin me the frigh of me life! said Shane, his shocked expression settling into a reluctant smile.

Taking up a tray as his food arrived, Griffo eyed Rory inquiringly.

—I'll be over there righ, he nodded to Shane.

—Sound yeah, said Shane before turning to Rory. — Wha has ye ou this side of the city?

—Aw man, was on an absolute mad one last night.

Stayed in some bird's gaff, just getting a bitta nosh before I make my way home ya know.

—Yeah? She nice? asked Shane

—No man, she was a total skanger, Rory said unselfconsciously. —I was com-*pletely* out of it. When I woke up this morning I was like, 'Get me out of here!' Seriously man.

—Ah every hole's a goal! said Shane cheerfully.

—Not this one man. More like her hole was on the dole! What about you, what're you up to yourself?

—Just grabbin a bit of grub, headin over to a mate's.

—Where are you guys sitting? I'll come join you, said Rory.

Shane didn't want to offend a good customer, but he didn't think Griffo would be impressed with Rory joining them. After an awkward pause, Shane nodded toward where Griffo was sitting. Still a little drunk, Rory didn't notice Shane's discomfort. He plonked himself down beside Griffo and started nattering away.

As it worked out, Griffo got along grand with Rory. Shane had forgotten Griffo had his own wealthy customers, and that he was exceptionally good at masking his selfishness when ingratiating himself with new people. For his part, Rory sensed Griffo was a rung above Shane and his interest flattered Griffo's vanity. When the conversation turned sociably to drugs, Rory focused his attention on Griffo, making it clear he knew the score. Sensing Rory would like to skip him – and buy direct off Griffo – Shane was keen for the conversation to end. Rory was *the* major source of income for Shane, and he was jealously protective in case his Golden Goose waddled off to lay those precious eggs for someone else.

Even though Rory was clocking Griffo for future refer-ence, Shane knew such a move wouldn't be made while he was in their company. *Dublin's too fucking small though,* he thought. Griffo and Rory were sure to run into each other again at some stage. Annoyed by this prospect, in the end it was Shane rather than Griffo who made Rory feel uncom-fortable. Even through the haze of a drug-and-drink hangover, Rory sensed the resentment. After he finished his food, he bid the pair goodbye and left to catch a taxi.

The conversation became stilted after Rory left, but Griffo and Shane knew each other well enough to be com-fortable in silence. There was still some time to kill, and Griffo sat back in his chair, sated. Shane glanced around the McDonald's as the place settled a little. He looked out the window at the bit of greenery in heart of the Northside.

The upside down 'V' of a modern church reached out of the shrubs into the sky, reminding Shane of an Egyptian pyramid. He glanced at its steeple, remembering a school retreat to the parish centre next door. As schoolboys, it was there that they'd been lectured about sin – and then had received some cursory sex education from a priest.

His speech had centred on an elaborate description of a metal speculum that would supposedly be inserted into the penis of anyone who caught an STD. He reluctantly – but painstakingly – related how the steel instrument would be inserted and then opened, umbrella-like, and slowly dragged out, scraping the interior of the urethra clean of infection. As they listened, the boys winced, their hands moving involuntarily to cover their shriveling willies.

And the lads writing anonymous questions on bits of paper and putting them into a hat and the priest pulling them out and reading them aloud, answering them all real serious. One fella asking what to do if only one of your balls dropped and another asking the priest if he had ever abused anyone in the Artane Boys' Band.

Then the priest at Jopa's funeral. Me oulfella giving him a wad of notes after the service. Do they not get paid by the church? What do ye have to pay them again for? Is it not their job? Funerals and weddings and christenins, sure what else do they do?

Nearly felt sorry for me oulfella that day, but still don't wanna be talkin to him after what he done though. Poor oul granda stinking in the bed like that, lying there with his eyes open. Was he gone already at that stage? Couldn't be anything of him left could there? Maybe somewhere in there. Was he in pain lying there or maybe it was just the drugs they gave him that made him like that? Maybe it's not so bad when you're just out of it.

Wonder which would be worse, that way or the way Chalkie went? But did he go in his sleep or was he awake? Like sometimes after a session when you get that panicky feeling when your heart won't stop beating and you're too hot, lying there you can't move but ye think you're gonna die in the bed. Or did he just drift off, never know. I suppose he can't come back.

And Robbie Boyle . . . what was that like? I wonder did he see it coming? Elizabeth freaking me out, asking me if I thought it had anything to do with that youngfella. I wish I had just left it that time in the Mercury. He didn't clock me when he came into the jacks. I should have just said nothing. Jaysis the fella blasting Robbie twice with a shotgun at close range. Now he's gone though I've no connection to get a shooter if I ever need it – other than through Griffo. But I wouldn't even want him to fuckin know. Boyle must have seen it coming. Still, it had to be quick. I wonder, was there any pain?

Even if there was, there was defo more pain with Jopa. Sure, before he went into that sleep, he was sitting around wasting away for weeks. No privacy, never even got a chance to talk about things or say ye loved him or whatever. Always other people around: patients or people visiting or Da sitting there and it being awkward, not wanting to talk to him but having to answer him when he spoke to ye in front of Jopa because ye didn't want to upset him. And Lydia and Ma in bits at the funeral as well.

Then I go and make a fool of myself. I'm a fucking dope. Disrespectful as well, cause Jopa didn't approve of getting drunk like that. Just wasn't thinking. Didn't bring any coke and forgot how locked ye do get on just the gargle. Then the oulfella having to drag me out. Sometimes wish I could just give up drink altogether.

—How did ye meet tha fella anyway – what's his name, Rory? asked Griffo.

—Ah me ex put him on to me, Shane replied.

—That's where the money is. Yer better off stickin with the poshos man. Less hassle, said Griffo.

This rung a bell with Shane. A jaded memory came to mind of Griffo telling him the exact opposite the first morning they'd met. Griffo was shameless in self-contradiction.

—Not like this other eejit I've to meet now, he said looking at his watch again. —Fuckin probly won't even show up.

—Who is he? Shane asked.

—Don't even know the chap, he's Lynchey's fella, Griffo said indiscreetly.

Shane wondered what exactly the story was between the pair. It wasn't just like himself and Griffo, it was more formal. Shane did a few things for Griffo, but only to get a few quid knocked off what he owed. Lynchey had real sway over Griffo. Must have been a very big debt Griffo was into him for.

—Would ye not tell Lynchey just to do it himself? Shane ventured.

Normally, he'd never ask Griffo about business beyond looking for general advice, but Griffo seemed in a complaining mood, so Shane felt safe risking the question. Griffo sighed.

—There's no use talkin to him kid. Lynchey knows how to get his own way, said Griffo. —We go back years. I wouldn't have a word said again' him. He can just be an awkward cunt sometimes ye know.

—Yeah . . .

As expected, Griffo was still trying to make out like it was an equal partnership. There were nerves behind the bluster though.

—Aggro as well. Better off just humourin him, he said, looking depressed. —C'mon we go for a spin.

If what Dotsy had said was true, and Lawless owed Griffo money, it must have been a real kick in the teeth to Griffo being in thrall to Lynchey over that debt. Having to take shit off someone for owing them money when the people that owed *you* couldn't give a shite. It seemed to Shane like Lynchey was making a bit of a thick out of Griffo.

As they walked out to the car, an Indian-looking woman carrying a child accosted Shane.

—Can you help please? she said pointing to her car, uncomfortable in English.

—C'mon, said Griffo impatiently, nodding at Shane to follow.

Griffo had ignorantly mistaken the woman for a gypsy beggar.

—What's the matter? said Shane, a little suspiciously.

She beckoned Shane to follow her the short distance to her car. Two more small children sat in the backseat. Griffo strolled away and stood by Shane's car, pointedly. The Indian lady pointed to a jump-starter pack that was on the tarmac beside her car.

—Do you know how to work? she asked Shane.

—Eh yeah, yeah, he said. —Can ye open the bonnet?

—I try it already. It cannot work, she said, putting the small child in the back of the car with the others and pulling the latch to open the bonnet.

Shane gave the pack a go, but it seemed to be out of juice.

—Do you have . . . leads? she asked him.

—Jump leads? Eh no, I don't, said Shane, glancing around.

A likely looking oulfella came out of McDonald's and Shane asked him if he had a set of leads. Then another two youngfellas, but none of them had any. One of the Indian woman's kids started crying, prompting Shane to go further afield to try and help.

He spotted a fella in a tracksuit and cap opening the passenger side of a blue van, messing with the glovebox.

—Sorry mate – have ye a set of jump leads by any chance?

The fella flinched in fright, jumping back before hurriedly tidying something away. Shane could hear a deep exhalation of relief before the fella spoke.

—No, I haven't any, he said shakily, his voice betraying annoyance.

—No bother mate, said Shane.

The fella's reaction amused Shane. It was obvious he'd been stowing coke, or something else illegal in the car. Probably thought it was the cops coming up behind him. Or maybe he thought he was going to get shot. *It's fucking everywhere*, thought Shane, smiling to himself.

Eventually he found an oulfella with leads. Luckily, the oulfella was also eager to take over the job, so Shane was rid of the nuisance. Just as the woman thanked him, it started to hail.

—Ah for Jaysis sake!

He could see Griffo over at the locked car, grimacing – they were both only wearing T-shirts. Legging it over, Shane pondered how the day could turn so quickly from sun to hail. The little bullets of ice hurt. Wind accompanied them as they pattered down in violent waves. It was a relief to get into the car, but Griffo was tetchy after his wait in the cold.

—For fuck sake, wha were ye doin over there, gettin yer one's number or somethin?

Shane ignored him and turned the ignition.

—Where are we going?

—It's too early to head over to this cunt. Hold on till I see is there anyone else we can meet in the meantime? said Griffo.

He perused the address book before ringing a youngfella from Finglas. The youngfella only had five hundred quid of what he owed, but they went to collect it anyway, just to kill more time. On the way, they noticed another cop car. Silver Mondeo this time.

Fucking shitebags. Look at them sitting there, thinking

they're deadly. It's easy to be a hardman when you have radios, bulletproof vests, backup guns and the whole State behind ye. Then they sit there acting aggro and getting smart with youngfellas. If ye asked one of them for a straightener, they'd probably shit themselves, the fuckin bullies. Why don't they go after the politicians and posh cunts for the scams they do be pulling? You never see any Southsiders getting locked up in the Joy – nobody from Dalkey or Blackrock – and sure it's not like they're not doin coke over there too.

The South Inner City heads get locked up, but they aren't Southsiders, not the way we mean it. The real divide in Dublin is between the East and the West. Southsiders just means rich cunts. They could be from the Northside, technically, like Howth or Clontarf, the same way people from Crumlin or Drimnagh are proper Dubs, not Southsiders even though they're from the Southside.

Who do the Garda stop and search? Only the proper Dubs, and then they do be letting the rats away with it for the info. The touts practically have the Gards on their side. Fellas getting set up left, right and centre, so the ones that get locked up are the ones with a bit of morals or the weak and stupid – the easy targets. But the most devious and dirty cunts are left to keep going, cause they're the ones that give the Gards the info.

The sly ones get some youngfella who owes them money to mind a few ounces or a couple of thousand yokes and then set them up for the Garda. That's probably what happened to poor Dotsy. Too much of a coincidence, him getting stopped. Probably the fella he was movin it for keepin the Gards off his own back by throwing them a little fish every now and again so he can still be the big fish.

Or people just getting rid of their enemies by ratting on

them so the Gards or the newspapers do be just doing the gangsters' dirty work for them.

I'd be better off getting away from Griffo, maybe buying it off one of the other lads. Dotsy was right, Griffo's only a waster and that Lynchey fella is dangerous. And then worryin about the Old Bill on top of it. Sometimes I wanna just get away from it all, buy a little gaff down the country, a little cottage with a hammock and flowers out the front – get me up out of all this fucking shite. Maybe save up and buy it. Maybe me and Elizabeth could move down and she could set up her own salon or something.

No, I could never get that sort of money together now. Buying a gaff is mad money. I've no way of getting a mortgage unless I set up a way of cleaning it all, paying a bit of tax. Maybe I could do it. They're giving worse cunts mortgages now. Cheaper down the country too.

But then she's wrapped up in all this shit as well. Dunno if I can even trust her, especially with this shit texting Paddy Lawless. Jesus fucking Christ, I wish to fuck she was never with him. I don't want to be angry with her, but I fucking hate her sometimes. I shouldn't feel like this. Maybe there's something wrong with me. How can I hate a beautiful girl, someone I'm supposed to love? But when I think about it, I want to fucking go through her sometimes, it hurts me so much. And that's just what I know's gone on. Why would she lie to me face like that and just betray me?

Man it's all too much. Every time I go out now, I'm panicky afterwards. No wonder Chalkie had a heart attack. The pressure would be enough to kill ye, let alone the drugs.

The Valiums I take after a session aren't even working these days. Feels like something terrible is going to happen at any moment, but that it's my fault, that I've brought it all on meself, that I'm going to be punished. And it lasts the whole week now – used to just be for a day.

Griffo must feel the same. He's shaking here beside me, barely holding it together. He has something terrible on his mind as well, scared of his shadow. Mind you, this fucking hail is freaking me out too. It's like a plague. Where the fuck did that come out of I wonder? Will they dent the car? The fucking noise of them, I never seen anything like it.

The bleak housing estates were never pretty to look at, but under the hail cloud, the whole world seemed washed out and devoid of colour. They arrived at the fella's gaff. Only a youngfella, he ran out from the door in the hail with his tracksuit hood up. His ma was probably inside. Unhealthy looking, he shelled out his wad to Griffo, who looked unimpressed with the bundle of notes, which he then passed on to Shane. The youngfella had a drawn-out wanness, a sort of pallor that unsettled Shane further.

—Righ, lets go an meet this other eejit, said Griffo, tapping away on Shane's phone again.

Shane could hear the phone ringing as he drove toward the gym.

—No answer. Fuckin prick, Griffo tutted. —I haven't got the head for this today.

—Wha'll I do? asked Shane.

—We just make our way over there. Give him a few minutes, Lynchey can fuckin do it himself if yer man doesn't show.

—Sound.

The fella rang back straight away though, Griffo showing his annoyance in his tone as he answered the call.

—Yeah? . . . Yeah we're just on our way over there now –

are ye there? . . . Will ye be long? . . . Righ go on, we'll be in the car park. Give us a bell when ye arrive yeah . . . go on.

—What's the story?

—He's on his way, just got held up. Spoofer if ye ask me. Aw man, I just wanna get home, this hangover's gettin fuckin worse instead of goin away!

—It's tha Red Bull man, I'm tellin ye! said Shane.

—Tha helps sure.

—Ye just think tha! It actually makes it worse. Ye get a rush for a few minutes with the caffeine and the sugar and then ye crash. Then ye crave more of the stuff even though it's makin ye feel like fuckin shite!

—Ah I dunno, said Griffo looking out the window.

Shane dropped it. Griffo didn't want to know what was bad for him. While on their way through Cabra toward the Navan Road, they copped yet another Garda car, Shane spotting it this time. A Passat. Spending so much time driving around, you'd expect to see a few Garda cars – especially in this part of Dublin 7. Still though, every time they saw one, they wondered.

The hail had slowed, only faintly falling. Shane didn't turn in to the gym when they got there. He drove down the slip road to a roundabout, then took a turn off that was a dead end. The planned apartment blocks had never been built and the exit was incomplete, surrounded by the wasteland of an empty building site. The road had been almost finished, but now it didn't lead anywhere. Perfect for Shane to turn back on himself and see if they were being followed. No other cars made the same manoeuvre, so he pulled in to the gym car park.

The hangar-like structure of the gym displayed a garish

neon sign that flashed 'Northside'. The cardio area on the first floor was visible from the car park. Lithe women bobbed on treadmills, focussing intensely on going nowhere. Big young Dublin men in fresh tracksuits strolled amidst Mercs and BMWs in the car park.

—Gangster central, laughed Shane, spotting a muscle-bound Griffo lookalike getting into a Beemer.

—Ye should see it durin the week pal, it's even worse. Every single cunt in the place is a bogey. Nine to five all your Joe Soaps are workin, but the gyms do still be busy. We're their bread and butter!

Griffo and Shane laughed together.

He's fuckin righ as well. Down me own place, Monday to Friday it's nothing but gangsters and youngfellas that sell drugs that keep them gyms in business, so we do. We should try and organise a group discount for fuck sake.

Come to think of it, if it wasn't for us, the drug squad wouldn't have jobs or CAB or half the fucking reporters and writers in the country. They all make their share out of it, selling papers, writing books and making films – but it's us who pay the real price.

Looking forward to seeing Elizabeth tonight. Haven't touched another person in ages, not even a hug or a cuddle. Even been a while since I got me hole. That Laura one again. Good to have her offside, but I feel more comfortable with Elizabeth. I do be happy just sitting there with her. It's not the same on me own or with anyone else.

So good to have someone beside you to share the time with. Why does it make it so much easier when you have somebody there? It's not like she can do anything to protect me, but just being there she makes me happy, like when I was a little kid

*and me ma used to pick me up after school. You need some-
one else. I suppose it calms you down, two of yis in it together.*

*Griffo's getting restless again. I know the feeling. That
comedown where you can't stay awake and you can't sleep. I
hope this fella turns up soon. I've a few of me own debts to
collect and a few customers of me own to get to. I want to get
it done before Elizabeth comes over, but I'll have to go back to
the gaff first. Griffo wouldn't get in the car with drugs in it,
sketchy bastard. He looks after number one.*

*Maybe that's the best way to be in this game. Still though,
wouldn't want to rat on anyone else. Fuck that shit. I hate the
Old Bill. Don't want to end up in the pocket of cunts like that.
But you can't trust anyone. Lynchy and Griffo have some
balls. You'd think they'd be worried someone would rat them
out or even go witness against them over the other thing.*

*I thought Griffo was me mate at first, but ye cop it then he's
like that with everyone – the only thing you mean to him is
money. Still though, he's just a selfish cunt, not a psycho. I
suppose when ye get a bit older, maybe ye cop that's the best
way to be. Maybe in life as well, like with your bird, you can
never really trust her one hundred percent. Even family, you
can't trust. Look what me own fucking oulfella did on me.
Yeah, maybe that's the best way to be: just look out for yourself, fuck everyone else.*

*Maybe I could get a youngfella selling for me, take the heat
off me, give him a small cut. They're my customers after all. It
was me who found them and set it up. Maybe don't touch it
at all meself anymore. That's the way even Griffo's gone now
with the coke. Gets someone else to drop it off – that little
blondie fella with the moped most of the time. Seems like a
nice chap so he does. It was mad that shit, that fella getting*

shot. Mad buzz thinking about it, knowing it was going to happen beforehand, then hearing it on the news.

Lynchey must be dogwide all the same, having youngfellas under ye like that. But they'd start snorting a load themselves and owing ye money, so ye'd have to be feared for it to work. Make enemies that way too though. Lynchey must be well connected. You wouldn't know what he'd be up to. I don't have the nature for that. Maybe simpler just selling it direct.

I wonder will Elizabeth stay tonight. I'd say she will. She probably misses it too. Still though, they can get it whenever they want. A girl like her, off whoever she wants. Imagine that. Fucking hell. Walking into a nightclub and knowing you could have any girl there. I'd give anything for that and that's what it's like for her all the time. Still though, it makes it more of a compliment that she's even bothered with me. But she has to pick someone, I suppose, and I'm as good as any of the youngfellas – better than half the wasters around this town.

I'd miss Dublin if I moved down the sticks. Just heading into town, not knowing which boozer you're gonna end up in, who you're going to meet or what's going to happen – that's the beauty of living in a city. The only downside is the aggro and all the stress.

Dublin's small enough. Everyone knows your business. Can't walk through town without bumping into someone ye know. Ye couldn't hide from anyone here for long, but there's nothing like the banter and the craic with the lads. Might head out tomorrow night. Maybe with Elizabeth if she stays over – maybe celebrate if we get back together.

—Where's this cunt? said Griffo, staring at his watch again.

He looked more disheartened than annoyed now,

resigned to suffer the effects of the night before, as if it were his just punishment.

—D'ye wanna bell him again there?

Looking out the window, Griffo thought for a moment.

—Nah, we give him another few minutes kid, he said distractedly.

—Is tha him? asked Shane.

Why does he have his hood up? No, it's not hailing anymore, no. Is it him no? He's walking over this way. No, I recognise that red . . . oh no no

A BROADCAST

A double murder investigation is underway after two men were shot dead in Dublin this afternoon. It's understood that the shooting happened in the car park of a gym on the Northside at approximately three o'clock. The gunman escaped in a silver Opel Astra driven by an accomplice. The car was later found burnt-out nearby. The state pathologist arrived at the scene earlier today, and the bodies have been removed to Beaumont Hospital, where full post-mortems will be carried out. Gardaí have appealed for witnesses, and to anyone who may have seen anything suspicious in the area between midday and three o'clock to come forward. The area remains sealed, pending a technical investigation. Both men received several bullet wounds and died at the scene. The victims were from Dublin. One was in his thirties, the other in his early twenties. Both men were known to Gardaí.